BRIDES OF REVENGE

BETHANY AMBER

Printed and bound in Great Britain by
Cox & Wyman Ltd, Reading

CHIMERA

Bride of the Revolution published by
Chimera Publishing Ltd
PO Box 152
Waterlooville
Hants
PO8 9FS

Printed and bound in Great Britain by
Cox & Wyman, Reading.

BRIDE OF THE REVOLUTION

Bethany Amber

She took a fearful glance over her shoulder. They were gaining on her. The slap of their feet on the muddy ground made Grace sob; a sound that caught in her tortured throat. Grace's chest hurt. She could scarcely draw breath. They were gaining on her, would catch her.

A huge hand fastened like a vice about her tiny wrist. With a breath she felt must surely be her last she managed a scream of fear. Her flimsy rags, sodden with rain, clung and caressed the length of her creamy body as the man whirled her round.

Chapter One

'Philipe, *mon cheri*?'

Madame de Genlis lay on the tumbled linen of her love bed, her breasts thrust high, stomach sucked in and her shapely legs thrust asunder, the rounded treasure of her sex mound thrust high. In an attitude of complete abandon her hands were clasped firmly behind her shining and abundant black locks while her violet eyes, misty with unknown dreams, were focused upon the silk draped canopy above the lovers.

A murmur came from her lover, Philipe, Duc d'Orleans, who lay between her statuesque thighs. His long, graceful fingers grasped the smooth flesh of madame's buttocks, the better to raise the altar of his desire. His lips were otherwise engaged than in conversation.

'Philipe!' Madame de Genlis tangled her ringed fingers into the tumbled hair of her patron. She admired the sparkle of the jewels bestowed upon her by her master as the flickering candlelight caught the shimmer of their well-cut facets. '*Ecoute moi, s'il vous plais!*'

Madame, in truth, was not in the first flush of youth, but her expertise in matters of pleasure more than made up for this. She was richly voluptuous with breasts and belly in which a man could bury himself and sex pot which was ever willing to take a cock or tongue, be it man or maid.

The object of her anger opened dark and heavily lidded eyes. Reluctantly, he lifted his head from the bountiful nest. His head reeled from the sensuality he found between his mistress's thighs. He licked his lips, savouring the droplets of her musk which ran so copiously from the flushed and open lips of her swollen cunt. '*Oui, ma petite*?'

'I have a most wonderful idea!'

Madame de Genlis did not close her thighs, nor lower her dimpled knees. The position was lewd, wanton, but oh, so inviting!

With his aristocratic fingers he caressed the generous and pouting outer labia which framed the scarlet bud of her clitoris. He watched her shiver pleasurably as he stroked the pads of his fore and second finger along the flanking valleys to collect the pearls of sex dew. With warm and tender lips he kissed the lower swells of her breasts and watched them shudder at his caress. He saw the thud of her heart within her chest; the beat of excitement. Her wide violet eyes were luminous in the soft flicker of the candles and her parted lips shone as she allowed her tongue tip to flicker lightly about them.

'Tell me later, *ma petite*!' he begged. His needs were urgent. They were always urgent these days. One never knew how long the old order could continue, how long the court would survive. The murmurings one heard were frightening and Philipe, once more, buried his head between his lover's thighs, closing his ears, shutting out the discontented mutterings of the populace, the frightening cries which grew in volume on the streets of Paris. Some said that the Bastille, that impregnable fortress, had been stormed; that many of his friends had lost their heads in public on the guillotine. He shuddered and probed his tongue deep into the liquid warmth of his lover's cunt.

Madame de Genlis rapped her closed fan on Philipe's slender shoulder. 'I insist, *mon cheri*!'

'Oh, *mon amour*!' he grumbled. 'I wish to love you as you deserve to be loved.' His words were somewhat muffled, spoken as they were from the dark depths of his lover's flesh. However, he knew that he would not receive any peace until he listened to what she had to say. He sighed and fumbled between his own thighs to feel the comforting throb of his engorged penis, the silky globe

6

which was slippery with spunk, and to caress the heaviness of his balls. Perhaps his own body would give him the comfort he sought.

Again the fan rapped his shoulder. 'Philipe, *mon cheri. Ecoute moi*! Listen to me.'

With a heartfelt sigh he eased himself up her body, feeling the warmth, the liquidity between her thighs moisten his skin with silky offerings. His slim chest lay upon the cushion of her belly and he nuzzled his musky lips into the hollow of her navel.

'Come, come, Philipe! I wish you to lie beside me, *ecoute moi*!'

Philipe did not wish to talk, neither did he wish to listen. He wished to play with his mistress; he wished to sip the offering of her musk, feel her delicious release and finally drive his penis into the willing softness of her body. That was what a mistress was for, after all, he grumbled to himself. If he wished to talk, to discuss, to listen, he could do so with his tutors or the court officials. No, a mistress was not for talking.

The violet eyes beckoned him as did an index finger, drawing him up the length of her voluptuous body.

'I promise you, Philipe,' she said in her sultry voice, 'you will enjoy my idea.' She paused and her nostrils flared, she allowed the very tip of her tongue to trace the perfection of her parted lips. 'We shall both enjoy my idea.'

There was a something in madame's words that hinted at delightful decadence, and Philipe dragged himself a little more willingly up her body. Not that decadence was anything new in the court of Louis XVI. It was redolent with it. The richly decked passages, the halls, the reception rooms reeked of the pungent perfume, the musk of every kind of degeneracy, depravity and wantonness. Could madame truly have found something new?

Holding up her shapely arms, so pale, the colour of finest alabaster even in the rosy glow of the firelight and

7

the flickering flames of the candles, Madame de Genlis welcomed her lover. She held his head to the comforting cushion of her breasts, persuaded his lips to take each erect nipple in turn as she related her idea.

'We shall find a girl, Philipe!' The sultry voice became softer, more caressing, but this did not lessen Philipe's sense of vague disappointment. However, his lips sucked diligently upon each nipple in turn and he massaged the flesh with his long fingers as if he wished to encourage the milk to flow. He missed that comfort which he was given by his wet nurse until he was seven. Eyes closed, he lapped his tongue about the hardened bud, sucking with all his might, hoping even yet to feel the warm, sweet trickle of milk on his tongue.

A girl! What was new about yet another little whore in the court? He gave a grunt of disappointment into the yielding flesh. He quickly became tired of the little harlots who were brought regularly to Versailles. They were so coarse; spreading their thighs for all to see and pinching their sex lips open to display their jutting little clitties. He gave another grunt, this time of disgust.

'She will be innocent, Philipe, so innocent!' Madame de Genlis gave a sigh of longing which was husky with lust. 'A virgin!'

Nuzzling into the pliant flesh, smelling the delicious scent of mature woman, Philipe could not think of anything he desired less than an innocent girl. How boring, how utterly boring! A virgin, no less. One could not play naughty games with innocents, tease every orifice, prod and please for hours on end. Oh, *mais non*, thought Philipe, allowing his delicately long fingers to slide down madame's belly and to rest in the dark, luxuriant forest which sprouted so lushly on her pouting mons.

'We shall train her,' continued madame, arching her buttocks and circling the plump nest against Philipe's questing fingers. 'It must be the right girl, of course,

Philipe. She must look the part, act the part, no matter what is done to her.'

Now, thought Philipe, driving a slender digit into the liquid softness of the woman's flesh, this sounded a little more interesting. With his thumb he, again, prised the swollen petals of madame's sex open, sliding it down to tantalise the upthrust nub of her clitoris. He could feel it hot and hard, probing out of the fine flesh, searching and flushed, ready for excitement. Philipe lifted his head from the delights of the breast. 'And will you allow me to do anything I like to this innocent?' he said.

'Do not stop, *mon cheri*!' begged madame, arching her body, her splayed legs stiff with desire, her splendid body arched and her heels driving into the tumbled bed linen, trembling, yearning.

'Yes, I shall allow you to play with this girl!' she said, her voice trembling as much as her urgent flesh. The perfect skin, the satin smooth alabaster skin, glowed with the sheen of exertion. He saw the flushes of her orgasm darken her body for the merest instant and he felt the fluttering of madame's sex flesh about his intruding finger. He thrust the digit hard into her womanhood, felt the barrier of the lower limits of her womb, felt the flood of her satisfaction flow about his finger and found it almost as satisfying as the taste of a wet nurse's milk.

'You may do anything,' she purred, easing him over her and looking into his tortoiseshell eyes, 'when she is fully trained in my ways.'

Philipe gasped with disappointed dismay, but Madame de Genlis had him firmly inserted into her clutching cunt and his penis was painfully turgid. He could do nothing but thrust into the willing flesh, pump and butt until he at last gave up his come. But he could hardly credit the bitch was going to make him wait while she, the wanton harridan, played with the young innocent maid, whoever she might be. It made Philipe angry and he probed his organ cruelly into the pulsing wetness. He drove his

9

fingers into the yielding flesh of madame's softly rounded shoulders, cutting the pale skin with his sharp fingernails, kept specially long for this very purpose.

'Ah, *oui*!' sighed la de Genlis. 'Pain, sweet pain!' She arched her body higher, supporting his slight frame with her splendid and voluptuous one.

He knew he had broken the skin, that her blood was beading in slow scarlet rivulets to spill upon the linen of their love nest, and this very knowledge made him thrust harder into her wanton body.

'We shall teach this innocent girl all the wonders of pain,' she murmured, 'how it can bring her to the peak of ecstasy.' Her sultry voice rose a pitch and her breathing became harsh, quick. He could feel her heart beating faster and faster, could see the pulse beneath the voluptuous flesh.

Philipe groaned, arched back his slender neck as his passion grew. His slim, boyish body became tense, putting his whole effort into the thrust of his stiff organ into madame's silky funnel. Why could not this pleasure last forever? Why did it have to end? It grew, he reached his peak. His seed spilled copiously into her. What a magnificent receptacle this woman was, even if she was not as young as she might be.

Hardly, had he sunk from the summit of his passion than Madame de Genlis was talking again. *Merde*! Beautiful as the woman was, he wished that she would use her lovely pouting lips to better purpose than to spill such nonsense.

'Philipe, *mon cher*,' she murmured, and she pushed him from the comfort of her enveloping breasts and belly, 'bring the water to bathe my wounds.' She lay on her side, her breasts not flopping as many would with such mountainous flesh, but staying firm and pert. For all she was a chattering parrot, he was truly a most fortunate fellow.

Jumping from the high and ornate four-poster, not

stopping to cover himself with his satin robe, Philipe ran naked to the gilt and marble washstand to pick up the china ewer. He was well-endowed. His prick, although flaccid from the spend of his passion, was still thick, heavy, against his thigh. Warm. It comforted him in this strange frightening world. Only the previous night a courtier was found dead and mutilated in the palace forecourt. He turned his attention once more to his cock. It throbbed, almost ready to spear upwards yet again to taunt him and madame and this new little whore which she promised him. Perhaps he could have fun while madame was elsewhere. The thought made him smile as he poured water into a bowl and picked up a square of soft linen before returning to madame.

'Oh, Philipe, *mon cher*!' she murmured. 'Stay as you are. Allow me to admire your young beauty.'

He held the bowl in front of him, partially hiding his still thick but lowered staff.

'*Non, non*!' chided madame. 'Put the bowl to the side, rest it on your hip. Do not hide your beauty from me. Let me see it all!'

Philipe did as she asked. He, happily, did not suffer from false modesty and, as an extra bonus, delighted in posing his boyish body. He had modeled for a statue of Achilles, the god with wings on his heels, and the marble edifice stood in the palace grounds, in the beautiful gardens at Versailles.

'Do you know what I shall enjoy most, Philipe?'

Legs astride, his slender hips thrust forward, the bowl resting lightly upon one, he shook his head. The movement caused his manhood to swing back and forth against his spread thighs. Narcissistic above all things, Philipe enjoyed the feeling of his flesh swinging from side to side.

'I shall enjoy seeing the two of you, my chosen girl and you, doing naughty things on this very bed!'

This was more like it, thought Philipe! What a delicious

11

thought. He watched madame throw her body face down, wriggle the gloriously full buttocks upwards and burrow her mons into the tangle of linen which was their tumbled bed, spread her thighs, being careful to pose her sex so that it was tilted to display the dark curls, the flushed folds and the seepage of his own fluids to best advantage. 'You hurt me tonight,' said madame, lifting her shapely arm to tap the weeping little cuts with a fingertip. 'You wicked young man! You passionate, wicked young man!'

Philipe, soaking the linen in the warm water brought by a servant when the two lovers were at their most passionate, chuckled, revelling in his own wickedness. 'Will you allow me to do the same to the girl?' Madame sighed as he smoothed the cloth very gently over the tiny cuts. He watched the blood spread like scarlet inkblots across the soft cloth. The sigh was of pleasure, not of pain; the pleasure of the afterglow of wounding.

'After a while,' she said in her sulky, sultry, husky voice, 'but you must promise never to mar the girl in any permanent way.'

Philipe gave a wail of distress and smacked the voluptuous mound of one of madame's buttocks. 'You promise things and then say horrid words, marring my pleasures!'

'You are a spoilt brat!'

Big though she was, Madame de Genlis was as lithe as a Greek athlete and, her shoulders bathed to her satisfaction, she twisted round, grasping Philipe's shoulders, throwing him onto his back. In the same graceful movement she straddled him, her thighs trapping him, making him helpless. She could feel his cock, first soft, but quickly hardening, becoming a warm ridge of iron rubbing into the soft wetness of her sex lips, the tip butting the burning bud of her nubbin.

'I must punish you!' she said, licking her lustrous lips and smiling her special smile, showing her white teeth, sharp and even, as if they had been filed that way. She put a fingertip to her chin, tapping it and pursing her wide lips, pretending deep thought. '*Comment*? How, I wonder, shall I do such a thing?'

Philipe played his part, pretending to quail in abject fear, his cock throbbing in her wet flesh pot. 'Oh, no, mistress! I beg of you!' His long fingers were clasped together as if in prayer in church. The folded palms shook back and forth as he pleaded. 'Not that!' But for all his protestations he could not hide his eager smile, the shine in his dark eyes, his newly risen cock, the trembling of his excited body.

'Ah!' Madame grabbed his thickened flesh with one hand and Philipe saw her smile as she felt it twitch and throb hungrily. 'I know the worst punishment of all!' Her fingers slipped down to gently grasp his balls, cup them, heft them, roll them back and forth. 'I shall eat you!'

'Oh, no mistress!' Philipe shuddered, not in fear, but in sheer delight. He loved it when madame took his manhood into her mouth, swallowed it, took its magnificent length deep into her throat.

The talk at the court had it that other mistresses, although they agreed to perform this act, could not do so without gagging. His own la de Genlis did so as if she was taking the smoothest of gruel into her gullet. It took Philipe to heaven and back. Her tongue and lips could perform the most wonderful tricks about his cockstem.

With palms flat along the length of his wavering shaft, madame pretended to mould the flesh as if it was clay. She paid attention to detail, slithering the tightness of the foreskin over the bulb and holding it fast beneath the swollen globe. She groomed the silky curls, the golden wisps of hair, which were scattered over the full sac. She sat back on her heels, her thighs splayed, allowing him to see the glory of her own genitals; glossy with creamy beads of dew, swollen and flushed with need. She smiled, licked her lips, snarled deep in her throat at which Philipe must pretend that he was paralysed with fear. Only then did she bend, crouching like a beast of prey over her quarry, her open mouth slavering over the particular part of her choice. Philipe could not help but thrust up, eager to feel his naked tip brush against her palate, but she placed her strong hands on his thighs, holding him down. This, too, was part of the game. 'Behave!' It was a command which must be obeyed. He must lie perfectly still while she dived under the pillows where she had earlier hidden silken ropes.

'Mistress...' he begged. He panted, his tongue lolling from his mouth like a trained dog, his hands limp like a puppy's paws.

'Be quiet!' She gave him a light slap across the belly, which far from giving him pain brought him pleasure, shown by the sudden jerk of his turgid cock. 'I shall make you be quiet with this!' Another instrument assuring good behaviour was brought from a small cupboard at the side of the bed.

'The scold's bridle...' Philipe said the words slowly, savouring each syllable. His eyes widened with pleasure. He held his hands high, his arms spread wide. His legs straddled eagerly across the bed, his toes pointed.

'I shall bind you first, *mon cheri*!'

Philipe shivered as the magnificent woman slid from the bed and busied herself with the silken cords. He allowed his eyes to feast on her heavy breasts, so perfect in their roundness. In particular he found the lower swell, the pale smooth voluptuousness sweeping up to the wine-dark nipples enticing. He shifted his gaze to the swell of her belly sweeping down to the lush darkness of her nest, dewed with her love honey and his own copious flow. Delicious!

The feel of the soft silk against his wrists and ankles was a sensuous delight. It caressed his skin, petted the inner sides of his wrists and ankles, but that was only the beginning! The bed was huge, wide and long, while Philipe was slight and quite short. This meant, of course, that his bonds must stretch him to the fullest. His arms and legs must be fully spread. There had been times that he felt that he was on the torturer's rack with his belly sucked in and his ribs placed under almost unbearable tension. His skin puckered in a shiver of apprehension. But madame was an expert with the cords. She knew just how tight to pull them to prevent dislocation of his shoulders and hips, and, naturally, this stretching had the most wonderful effect on his cockstem. It reared up, the veins full and clambering around the rigid organ. His balls were heavy with their renewed contents. His whole being was focussed upon that excited part of him between his straddled thighs. Just one thing was needed to make his enjoyment complete.

'The bridle!' he moaned.

Madame tutted. 'Such impatience. I must kiss this little fellow before I apply the bridle, for I wish to hear your moan without any impediment from the beastly thing.'

Much as he tried, Philipe was quite unable to move. He wished, with all his might, to writhe under madame's expert lips and tongue, but he was held fast. Oh, those lips! They were so soft. Her mouth was so wet and slippery. How it petted his length. How her long, agile tongue dipped into his pulsing eye. Only when she had sipped the dribble of pre-issue did she stop. Yes, she stopped for many long moments! This was the worst torture of all.

'Only now the bridle, *mon cher* Philipe,' she purred.

He aided her, of course, by lifting his head from the pillow. The bridle was a difficult implement to fit. There was only one correct way to fit the leather gag upon the tongue, holding it fast, down deep into the reach of his mouth. The bridle was fitted to an iron band about the head, and a nosepiece just barely allowed breathing.

'Oh, Philipe, you look so pretty!' said madame sitting back on her heels, her thighs spread, showing her open love lips, so swollen and shining with their coating of female honey. Philipe could see the erect bud of her clitoris throbbing with her own need, arching out of its drawn back hood.

'I cannot wait to find a little companion for you; sweet and obedient in all things,' madame continued huskily. 'We shall all have such fun, my darling. I am going to train your little playmate according to the teachings of Rousseau. Do you know what that means, Philipe?'

He shook his head, his eyes fixed upon madame's open flesh pot, unable to think beyond its beauty and the bonds which held him fast. The bridle about his head and tongue made him feel gloriously vulnerable. Unless the teachings of Rousseau included bondage and discipline he was not at all interested. What did he care if, as madame said, the girl would not be taught language or literature? What good were those things in bed anyway?

Madame pouted her glorious lips and circled them about his cock, her rich brown hair floating in shimmering cascade over Philipe's tautly bound body.

It was torture! It was ecstasy!

Her tongue caressed his globe, expertly pressing the foreskin back below the ridge, making it all the more sensitive. In a moment she would begin another of her favourite tortures. He wanted to scream with joy in anticipation of this, but he could make no sound. None whatsoever.

'I shall teach her to be graceful,' said madame dreamily, bobbing up and drifting her fingers over the iron struts of the bridle, tracing the dreadful implement's features. 'Teach her about beautiful attitudes, but above all,' she concluded, 'I shall teach her sensuality! Can you imagine how beautiful she will look; splayed just as you are splayed, her head imprisoned in the bridle just as yours is now? Helpless, Philipe, quite helpless. Her sex lips spread and moist, her pert little clitty pouting upwards, but still a virgin as pure as an angel.'

Again Philipe tried to groan, but his tongue was held

down by the strut of metal which reached deep into his mouth. All he managed was to writhe, and even this was nigh on impossible. The silken bonds were so skilfully tied that any movement was prohibited. His upright cock swayed and a drop of clear pre-issue oozed from the pore.

'Oh, you naughty fellow! What wicked thoughts must be in your mind!' Madame brought a short length of silken cord from the hiding place beneath the pillow and swayed it before Philipe's eyes. 'And you know what I do to naughty fellows!'

Philipe again tried to writhe but all he managed was a slight lift of his hips which made his cock spear high into the air.

'How very obliging,' murmured madame. 'You always know exactly what I require.' She allowed the cord to tickle the very tip of his cock, and he silently cursed the gag which he loved.

Madame sat back and allowed her fingers to drift lazily up and down her love lips. Teasingly, she pressed them together, pulled them down, made them swell. Only then did she again spread them open, allowing Philipe to feast his hungry eyes on the contents of her pouch.

'*Et maintenant...* and now...' she murmured. So swiftly and expertly did her fingers twist the cord about the base of his cock that Philipe scarcely had time to draw breath. Her lips closed about his globe, sucking very gently with her soft lips and then, with a smile, sat back and began to work at one of her nipples until it was hardened to a sharp point. Philipe's eyes widened as she bent over him once more. She worked his globe very quickly with finger and thumb and pressed her teat into the pulsing pore. He felt her whip the silk cord from the base of his cock and remove her teat at the same moment. The desire to scream with joy was strong as a silvery thread of his come followed the dark teat.

As he calmed his tethered fingers itched to press into madame's beckoning wetness. He longed to hear the sound of two of his fingers driving into her depths, and then three, perhaps even four, filling her up until she cried out for mercy. These lewd thoughts and the predicament in which Philipe delighted were too much for any man to take for any length of time. He watched her slip one finger into the flushed and slippery flesh between her open thighs. A second followed and he heard the sucking sounds he so desired. He watched the ball of her thumb press the hardened tip of her nubbin, and such was his pleasure in the sight that his cock began to rise.

'Must I again punish you?' she said, wagging a warning finger that quickly joined the others in the open depths of her flesh pot. She bent over his cock, taking it fully into her gullet which squeezed his length just as her sex passage had done such a short time ago. Philipe was light-headed with pleasure and attempted to arch upwards from the bed. Madame gave him a warning slap on the belly and released his cock from her lips. Another pearly fountain jetted from the tip, splashing warmly on his taut belly and chest, while madame shook her head in pretended distaste and disgust. But this did not stop her bending over the young man's body to sip and savour every last drop of her patron's offering.

The minor court of Philipe, Duc d'Orleans, was as decadent as that of his brother, Louis XVI. The aristocracy at the palace of Versailles knew only a hint of the dreadful poverty, the hunger of the populace in the mean streets of Paris in the turbulent days of 1792.

Grace was one of the people. Poor, thin and insubstantial as a wraith, her ragged clothes hung about her willowy frame in tatters, but yet, despite her slenderness there was an eye-catching voluptuousness that spoke of a secret sensuality. Beneath the flimsy rags which scarcely clothed her, her tiny waist flared out to shapely hips and pouting buttocks. Often, when the winter winds blew, the pale swell of her breasts were

18

bared to the biting cold and the piercing chill made the buds of her wine-dark nipples spring out sharply, jutting against the worn rags, fine and transparent as gossamer. Never, in all her young life, had Grace known a winter such as this in 1792. Winds of change, the winds of a changing world, blew through the dark, filthy alleys, fluttering Grace's rags, moulding them to her tiny frame.

Had there been water to spare to wash her hair, soap to rinse away the grime, the tangled tresses would have been revealed as a raven black cascade, shot with blue lights. Her oval face was perfectly formed although its beauty was hidden beneath the grime. Her skin was unblemished beneath the filth; pale and smooth as moonstone. Round eyes were startling in her dirty face, and although dull from lack of nourishment, were a dark verdant green sometimes warming to hazel, flecked with shimmering gold. Despite the hardships she suffered her soft lips often curved in a beckoning smile or pouted deliciously in a perfectly round and inviting O.

The girl sat upon a low stool by her mother's bed, cooling the older woman's fevered brow with a scrap of rag dipped in a cup of rainwater.

'Promise me!' The woman's cracked voice was barely audible above the sound of the rain on the roof of the makeshift hut which served them as their home.

'Oh, mother,' sighed Grace. 'The aristos will not listen to one such as me.' She smoothed a wisp of hair, white from suffering, not from age, from her mother's forehead.

'They will, *ma cherie*!' cried the older woman, her claw-like hands clutching her daughter's arm. 'I heard a rumour before I became…' A cough, debilitating, rattling in her throat cut off the words and left her breathless and weaker than ever. 'A rumour that a girl, such as you, beautiful and young, was required at the palace,' she went on, long moments later. Grace smiled, but the expression on the lovely face was disbelief despite the upward curve of the soft, tempting lips. The gentle eyes

19

with thick lashes fringing them, glossy as ebony, looked sadly down at her mother. The sweet features were drawn momentarily tight with bitterness.

'There are always rumours, *maman*! Rumours that the palace is giving away food, that there is wine by the barrel, a gift from the king!' She shook her head and dipped the rag into the small bowl of rainwater and used it, once again, to try and cool her mother's brow.

Unable to believe that any aristo, any blue blood, would look at her, Grace was entirely innocent of her own beauty. On the very brink of maturity she occasionally felt strange stirrings between her thighs; a swelling warmth between the silky raven fronds which protected the still closed gateway to her body.

An unbearable irritation began between the plump folds hidden betwixt her thighs. Intrigued by this, oft times when her mother slept, Grace opened her legs and, with trembling fingers, touched the quivering swell of her little belly and would allow her hands to drift down to the heated soft, silky pleats. These she parted, searching for the source of the irritation.

What she found was a bud of flesh, hard as a little nut, inflamed to a dark flush and jerking eagerly from a tiny veil of fine skin, smooth as silk and bathed in warm creamy fluid which seemed to come from nowhere. When her tentative fingertips touched this, Grace heard herself gasp with wonder. A feeling too glorious to describe surged through her body. Again she rubbed, harder this time and the feeling came again; a wave of glorious sensation which spread like ripples upon a pond, drifting over Grace until she felt that she would go mad if it was not appeased. The bud of flesh burned under her fingertips and she noticed the satin-smooth skin become slicker with the creamy exudation. Her whole body glowed, trembled, shuddered with an indescribable joy. Wave after wave of this pleasure surged through her, until she sank back, exhausted, on the thin pallet upon which she slept.

'Always there are rumours,' Grace repeated, her pleasant daydream fading.

With a sudden reserve of strength the claw-like hand grasped Grace's wrist and dragged the girl closer. 'Promise me!' The wizened, sick face glared at the girl in the rainy gloom, the eyes suddenly bright, fervent. 'You are exactly right for the aristos.'

Grace flung herself to her knees on the dirt floor, hugging her mother's thin shoulders. 'Do not excite yourself, *maman*! Please! You are very ill and you must save your strength.'

'Pah!' the older woman scoffed. 'We both know this is the end for me... You have a...' The light was fading in her mother's eyes, Grace noticed, and she was struck with a dreadful feeling of panic. She would be all alone. No one to whom she could turn.

'Mother...'

'Promise me!'

'I promise, *maman*!'

Her mother gave a sigh, a long sigh of satisfaction, and darkness veiled her eyes. It was as if a light had gone out, and Grace bowed her head over the shrunken body.

Two neighbours helped Grace to bury her mother. The priest said a few words over an unmarked grave and it was all over. Lost and terribly alone, the dark green eyes lustrous with tears, Grace turned to leave.

'*Ma petite*!' One of the neighbours ran after her, his eyes shining, his hand at his groin adjusting a heavy bulge in his filthy breeches.

Grace turned, her hair hanging in gleaming wet ebony tendrils over her shapely shoulders, cleaned and wetted by the still teeming rain. Her cheeks burned as she watched him rub something between his thighs. '*Oui, monsieur*?' Her voice, sad though it was, clear and sweet. '*Aidez-vous*?'

'It is I who can help you,' said the man.

His companion joined him, his head bowed, shy but looking suspicious in Grace's eyes. Bare feet shuffling backwards, huge eyes staring, frightened, framed by lashes dewed with rain, Grace began to stumble away and then to run, looking this way and that for the priest, but he was gone. She was alone, without help, in the rain-drenched cemetery. She was unsure why she was afraid. It was something, she was sure, to do with those strange feelings that came over her when she touched that place between her thighs in the darkness of the night.

'Do not go!' said the first man. His feet began to move quickly over the muddy ground, gaining on Grace. He was big, large framed, heavy, far taller than she was.

'Do not be afraid!' said the second man, his shy demeanour gone.

She could hear the slosh of their feet, bare like hers, as they ran after her. She could hear the urgency in their voices, the rasp of their breath above the steady sound of the rain.

'We only want to offer you a home!' cried the first man. 'In return for...'

Grace closed her ears. Despite her innocence it was not difficult to imagine what she must do in return, and she could not. She had promised her mother, although the Lord only knew how she was to fulfil that promise.

She took a fearful glance over her shoulder. They were gaining on her. The slap of their feet on the muddy ground made Grace sob; a sound that caught in her tortured throat. Grace's chest hurt. She could scarcely draw breath. They were gaining on her, would catch her.

A huge hand fastened like a vice about her tiny wrist. With a breath she felt must surely be her last she managed a scream of fear. Her flimsy rags, sodden with rain, clung and caressed the length of her creamy body as the man whirled her round.

She could smell them; the odour of garlic and sour wine. Her captor laughed and used his free hand to cup the pouting mound of one of her breasts. His thumb and finger pulled upon the sensitive skin of her nipple and she felt it harden, become painful. Cold rain splattered the upper swell as he tugged down her gown. She felt his hand graze the tiny swell of her belly and felt an all too familiar warmth suffuse her body.

Again she tried to scream, to tug away, fearing her own eager desires. 'Shut up, *putain*!' he growled, transferring his caresses to muffle her cries.

She was pulled closer and she felt his male flesh lengthening beneath his breeches, stiff and swaying against his belly. It frightened her. Never in her life had she seen a man's body. Her father died before she was born. Neither had she felt this strange thing in the man's breeches.

Her thighs were forced open by the other man and a rough hand cupped the soft fullness between them. She felt her little pouch swell, the inner folds become hot and slick with moisture. The forbidden delight, that which she felt in the lonely darkness of her mother's hovel, became unbearable. Sensual by nature, she bore down upon the cupping fingers, felt a growing heaviness, a filling of her labia which his fingers tugged down and open, a seepage of her hot fluid bathing her churning cunt.

The other man remained behind her, his hands locked about her tiny waist, his fingers tracing the swell of her hips. Grace could feel his male flesh, hard, bare, wetted by the relentless rain, probing the tight ravine between the rounded hillocks of her bottom.

It would have been so easy to allow them their lust. Something told her, some animal need within her, how she could fulfil herself and them. Her breasts were swollen with her own desire; painful with her needs. The buds of her nipples burned as they sprang tightly against the flimsy cloth of her wet and tattered gown.

But she had made a promise.

Flinging back her head, her eyes huge with both desire

and fear, she came to her senses and screamed. '*Maman*!'

The bigger man, the one who stood before her, gave a rough growl and again thrust his filthy, stinking hand over her mouth.

'*Merde*! Shut up, you little fool!' His lust fevered eyes shone into hers. He tore at the tatters which served her poorly as clothing. The never-ending rain struck her bare skin. The chill was such that it turned the porcelain paleness to a delicate transparent blue. Pain, cold, fear filled her world and she became pliant, accepting the inevitable. The smaller man bared her taut buttocks. He sank to his knees behind her, caring nothing for the muddy ground. Grace shuddered, but not entirely with loathing as his thin, bony fingers drove into her bottom flesh, parting the firm hillocks.

'She does not scream,' he murmured.

Grace quivered with shame. He could see her most private parts; her tight bottom hole, the lush black curls of her cunny lips, perhaps even that strange little bud of flesh which gave her so much pleasure when she rubbed it back and forth.

'A whore, like all women,' grunted his companion, his voice muffled in Grace's shivering breasts.

The rough tip of a thick thumb stroked across the tight pleats of her anus. Grace felt a renewed unbidden surge of pleasure bring a warmth to her belly. It took all her strength not to bear back upon the caress. The naked softness of her sex folds seemed to swell unbearably and pout between her thighs. A flood of heated honey trickled, joining the chill slick of rain, down the inner sides of her thighs.

'Lift your hands,' growled the bigger man, raising his head from her flushed and swollen breasts. 'Place them behind your head.'

Mind spinning with the sensations that were growing within her, Grace hesitated for the smallest instant.

'Your hands!' he hissed again.

Fingers trembling, Grace did as she was bid and linked her hands behind the sodden raven mane of her hair. The position rendered her more vulnerable; at their mercy. A flutter rippled through the pouting and heated folds of her sex. She felt the burning bud of her clitoris jut hard from its silky bed, thrusting from its tiny hood. Unprotected and grossly engorged.

He grinned through the rain as if he knew what she felt, and, in a swift and vicious movement, he tore the rags of her gown from neck to hem.

Grace gasped, but whether this was from fear or her deep, sensual need, she scarcely knew.

The tip of a wet tongue flicked over the clutching little pleats of her rear entrance and she knew that her breathing was quick, harsh; a certain clue of her feelings.

'Are you a virgin?' grunted the bigger man.

His own breathing was ragged and his spearing thickness, dark male flesh, probed out of his ragged breeches. His thick fingers grazed up and down the rain-wetted flesh, pausing only for a moment to smooth the slick of his pre-issue over the engorged and swollen tip.

Grace, her head lowered demurely, her hands clasped obediently behind the sleek raven fall of hair, said nothing. Naked, humiliated, her plump bottom abused and all but invaded by the smaller of the two men, her mind was a confused whirl of emotions. Her need for satisfaction was becoming unbearable.

'What does it matter?' she murmured at last, her voice low and without hope. 'Do you spare virgins?'

The big man laughed. Allowing one hand to remain upon his turgid flesh, he reached out with the other to cup the heaviness of one of her breasts and thumbed the tender hardness of a nipple.

'We spare no whore, virgin or not,' he rasped, and his fingers closed like a vice upon the pliant paleness of the bared breast.

The pain of his grip brought tears to Grace's eyes. Her

legs buckled and she felt the sharpness of broken teeth biting into the soft cushion of her sex lips, pulling them open, and a tongue lapped at the very tip of her nubbin.

'I submit,' she sighed weakly, as she sank to the muddy ground. 'Use me in whatever way you wish.'

Beyond the pain, beyond the surging of pleasure, beyond the biting cold and the sough of the wind, Grace heard the urgent gallop of several horses and the clatter of carriage wheels on the cobbled road beyond the cemetery. Voices reached her ears, angry voices, and she felt herself clasped by many hands. She heard the crack of a whip on flesh, cries of pain, and yet she felt nothing. Could she, she wondered, be on the threshold of death? She sank into darkness and knew no more.

Chapter Two

A terrible lethargy stole over her. A warmth centred upon the pit of her soft belly and beneath it in the delicate folds nestling between her thighs, a seeping wetness.

She heard voices, not harsh like the men who tried so hard to violate her, but soft, caressing tones which came and went, whispering over her like gentle waves upon the banks of the Seine. They did not threaten her, these voices, but Grace kept her eyes closed, fearing what she might see, and allowed the ebony lashes to remain closed, although fluttering upon the pale moonstone cheeks. But, obedient in all things, Grace kept her slender fingers fast behind her head, just as the man had ordered her to do on the muddy ground of the cemetery.

'The poppet!' said a woman's voice admiringly.

'A poppet? She is filthy,' said a man's voice. He was young, Grace knew that and, perhaps, his youth made him a little afraid. 'And heaven only knows what those disgusting fellows did to her.' Beyond the jolting of the carriage Grace felt him shudder against her. '*Mon Dieu*! She is probably riddled with disease. Don't touch her, madame, I beg of you!'

'Oh, don't be silly, Philipe!' The woman sounded older, impatient. 'I am sure we found her before they...' She paused and gave a soft laugh, and Grace felt her slender thighs prised apart. 'Watch, I shall prove to you...'

Grace gasped. A soft palm was cupped about her pouting mound, the skin as soft as silk, cool and clean as spring water. She bore down, only slightly, just brushing the damp raven curls of her pussy upon the caress. No matter how hard she tried she could not prevent her sex lips from swelling upon the woman's palm.

'She is not a virgin. She is a whore, did I not tell you? Not an innocent at all.' The carriage yawed from side to side as the young man flung himself into the corner, as far away from Grace as the space would allow.

'Nonsense. She is sensual, just as I required. Naturally sensual by nature. We shall have such fun with her.' Behind closed lashes Grace watched the hooded eyes become heavier, the smouldering smile become broader, and tried not to shudder in apprehension. A gentle finger and thumb parted her plump sex lips, baring the inner folds. 'Do you see the delicate pinkness, Philipe? A virgin if ever I saw one!' The woman pinched her nubbin, held it in soft fingers, rubbed the sides of its little shaft, drew back the tiny hood.

Grace could not help but let out a sigh of pleasure. The seat upon which she lay was padded in velvet, cool and plush beneath her buttocks. She felt her breasts swell and her belly quiver under the woman's touch. She could not help the growing heat within her. It was as if her innards were melting.

'Virgins do not know how to be sensual,' grumbled the young man, who Grace now knew was called Philipe.

'Some women are born with that gift,' retorted

madame, and Grace felt the butterfly brush of a fingertip upon the bud between her pouting love lips. She moved under the touch. She could not help herself. She wanted more; so much more. 'Just as I was,' whispered madame.

'Open your eyes, my darling,' Grace heard, the words as caressing as the fingers.

For a moment she hesitated. The raven lashes remained tightly closed and she felt the warmth of a fat tear trickle down her pale cheek.

'Oh, how sweet,' purred Madame. 'Isn't it delicious to see tears in a young girl's eyes? Doesn't it show her innocence? She is innocent as I said, Philipe. Didn't I tell you she was the one for whom we have searched all these weeks? Come now, sweet one, open those lovely eyes.'

Grace, at last, managed to allow her eyes, round and glittering with tears, to flutter open. With the very tip of her pink tongue she moistened her parted lips and gazed up at the woman who held her across her broad lap.

As madame let her hands flutter away from Grace's body she found herself falling, quite naturally, into a sensuous pose. Her slender legs, marred by streaks of grime and the drying dew of rain, fell gracefully apart. Her breasts, firm and tip-tilted, were peaked by hard and dark little buds. The tatters of her rags, draped beneath her breasts across the slight swell of her belly, parted above her mons, enhanced rather than spoilt the beauty of her body.

Her gaze flew nervously from one to the other of her two captors. A young man, handsome as a Greek god, looked at her across the narrow space between the luxurious carriage seats where they sat. He frowned, but touched the sudden bulge in his breeches, stroking its length hungrily.

Grace averted her eyes, focussing them, once more, upon the woman, pleading for gentleness and mercy.

'Are we going to bind her?' asked Philipe. 'Truss her wrists and ankles, make her helpless as a kitten?' Grace heard him groan and, from the corner of her huge hazel eyes, saw him release his cock from his straining breeches. It was so clean and darkly pink, the fine skin stretched by its fullness, its bulb bursting out at the broad tip. It was not at all like those of the men in the cemetery. It made a hunger grow, a strange hunger in the very pit of her belly. Her lips parted at the sight of it. Her tongue tip trembled as her mouth formed a perfect O and a sound, soft as a kitten's mew, sighed from her lips.

'She wants my cock,' said Philipe thickly.

Madame frowned at him and wagged a warning finger.

'Is it not beautiful?' she asked of Grace, her voice husky with lust as she looked at the spearing cock.

Grace said nothing. She felt the flesh of her thighs flinch, her plump mound pout higher and the warmth of seepage between her love lips.

'Yes, it is beautiful,' said madame, answering her own question. 'And, one day, when I have trained you to perfection, I shall allow you to take it in your mouth.'

Grace could not help but gasp at such a suggestion. Her dear mama, poor though she was, had been very strict in her upbringing and a lewd suggestion such as this shocked the sheltered girl.

'To feel the delicate smoothness of the skin, taste the purity of its fountain, the warm creaminess... to delve that lovely little tongue tip into its depths.'

Again Grace heard the young man groan and she ventured a look at his cock. It looked so thick and long, almost angry, with its head moist and the pinkness darkening to purple.

At this point madame bent her elegantly coiffured and powdered head and brushed her lips across Grace's sex. The moist tip of the older woman's tongue probed the trembling lips apart and the feeling which quivered through her body was wrong, she knew, but she could not help but delight in her own shame. The girl shuddered, but her natural feelings could not prevent a new spread of heat across her lower belly. Madame stiffened her tongue, curled it into a silky cylinder.

Again Philipe groaned. Eyes open to their fullest, Grace glanced towards him over madame's shoulder. His graceful hands slicked up and down the spear of flesh at his groin. His eyes were closed and his lips were parted as he panted his pleasure.

Madame, her eyes gleaming, raised her head. 'Pout your lips, my precious, cosset my tongue,' she said in a low and seductive voice.

Bewildered, Grace creased her smooth brow. Her narrow shoulders lifted in a scarcely perceptible shrug. 'I do not understand,' she whispered.

'Ah, so deliciously prim,' sighed madame, and stuck out her tongue, a smooth and dripping scarlet rod of tissue looking, Grace realised, like Philipe's cock.

'*Comme ma bouche*?' she said softly, tracing the perfection of her soft lips with the tip of a slender, but grubby, finger.

'*Oui*,' sighed madame. '*La bouche*.'

The thought of her task caused Grace's breasts to swell, become tender and the brown tips become hard as little stones. The place between her legs became hotter and more liquid. Her hand parted the tatters of her gown and eased down over the swell of her belly. Her fingers trembled and her dark eyes darted to madame, asking a nervous and silent permission to ease the delicious tension as she did in the darkness of the night in her mother's hovel.

A smile wreathed madame's plump cheeks but, Grace noticed, the smile did not reach her eyes. A chill struck deep into the girl's heart and, fearful, she replaced her hands on her head.

'Splendid!' The word was like a whiplash. '*Maintenant*... now... *la bouche*!' The long pink tongue, stiff and gleaming with spittle, protruded from the lips once more.

Grace formed her lips into that soft and perfect O and raised herself until her face was exactly opposite madame's painted and powdered visage. She felt warm arms encircle her slender, almost naked, body. An exotic perfume enveloped her, making her head reel. Slowly, she engulfed the tube and began to suck.

More than aware that Philipe was watching the scene with feverish eyes, Grace felt her face and breasts suffuse with heat. The kiss was so intimate with her lips sliding rhythmically back and forth along the silky, throbbing length that she could almost imagine that she was indeed petting Philipe's cock. She closed her eyes and gave herself up to her task and the woman who held her and caressed the throbbing swell of her breasts, the vulnerable pouch of her sex and the firm mounds of her buttocks until Grace was lost in a mist of delightful desire.

Her eyes were heavy as she gave the woman a look which pleaded for more; much more. She turned the look to Philipe and the cock he still petted with aristocratic fingers. It looked so much more inviting than those of the horrible men who attacked her in the cemetery. Yes! She should caress that cock with her mouth; could worship it with her body.

The carriage came to a halt and the girl heard subdued voices. 'Later, *ma petite*,' whispered madame, gently pushing her away. 'We shall play more games later.'

Grace felt her face suffuse with heat. The woman knew what she was thinking.

The door opened and she saw liveried servants waiting to attend them. She shrank into the corner of the carriage, aware that her breasts were exposed between the tatters of her gown, but worse, they were flushed and swollen, the burgundy nipples erect. Huddling her knees close to her chest she tried to hide their heavy fullness.

A laugh, mocking and cruel, preceded their descent from the carriage. 'She tries to hide her titties,' chuckled Philipe, 'but exposes this!'

31

Grace felt the smooth tip of a finger probe softly between the moist plumpness of her love lips. It slicked up and down the deep ravines between her inner sex lips and the flushed bed where her nubbin stood hard and erect. Her eyes darted to madame, pleading for her to end this new intimacy. Her inner self admitted that she wanted it, but she feared it.

'Does he not touch you gently?' murmured the woman, leaning forward eagerly to look at Grace's unwitting exposure. 'Do your silky fluids not flow? Does your bud not arch sweetly from its hiding place?'

All these things were true, Grace realised, but her body burned with humiliation that the several servants waiting to attend them were watching every detail of this newest degradation.

Madame de Genlis sighed. 'Perhaps it is time that we got her settled in her quarters.' Grace saw Philipe pout and, very reluctantly, remove his fingers from the warm slipperiness of her cunt.

'Where are you taking me?' she managed, her voice hoarse with fear and apprehension.

'To a life of luxury, my precious,' murmured madame, 'such as you have never known.'

'If you behave yourself and do as you're told,' added Philipe, as he adjusted his breeches.

A warning look was passed from madame to Philipe and that look, somehow, struck a chill in Grace's heart. She was swung easily into the arms of a footman who was dressed in the finest blue satin.

'What is this place?' she murmured as he strode easily across the cobbled courtyard, carrying his burden as if he carried a sack full of feathers.

The satin felt deliciously luxurious and silky against Grace's near nakedness.

'The palace of Versailles,' he whispered. The strong arms which cradled her rounded buttocks and her slim upper back, caressed the slender curves. His voice was soft and his eyes kindly.

'Why am I here?' Grace fought back the tears. It had already been a long and trying day, and who knew what was before her.

The footman shrugged and she felt his hand brush the side swell of her breast. 'Some whim of her ladyship's, no doubt.' He brushed her cheek with his lips and his sorrowful eyes sought hers. 'She will tire of you, and when she does...' He shrugged again.

Grace let out a small scream as she and the man were sent flying across the wet and muddied cobbles by a hefty shove from another servant. Philipe stood behind their attacker, his face thunderous.

'How dare you talk to my new toy?' he grunted.

'And do not think we did not see you touch her so intimately!' screamed madame.

'We shall have you both flogged!'

'Oh, yes.' Madame clapped her ringed fingers. 'What fun – naked and flogged!'

Grace gave way to the threatened tears and lay her raven mane upon her hands, uncaring of the wet and mud in the royal courtyard.

'Doesn't she look fetching?' asked Madame de Genlis, who lay naked upon freshly laundered feather pillows trimmed with lace and satin ribbons. The plump cushions not only supported her elaborately coiffured head, but a further mound was slipped beneath her buttocks, having the effect of arching her sex and spreading her statuesque lower limbs.

Philipe lay beside her, his cock spearing from his groin, purple and angry in its turgidity. One hand stroked his organ lovingly while the other delved between the juicy folds of his lover's sex lips. 'You have broken your promise again,' he complained.

Grace could scarcely concentrate on the words being bandied back and forth. Her full breasts pained her, so widely were they stretched across her slender ribs and so tightly erect were her nipples.

'Not at all,' disagreed madame. 'We shall flog them as soon as we tire of just admiring the gorgeous creature with her raven pussy so pert and open.'

'Let me touch her,' begged Philipe.

Grace tugged vainly at her bound wrists, but this only put more strain upon the full flesh of her breasts. Her ankles, too, were placed in such a position that her slender thighs were spread and her plump little cunny was open to its limit.

'Does she not make a perfect base board for our love bed?' asked madame, petting her own mountainous breasts.

'She certainly looks better now she is clean,' agreed Philipe. '*S'il vous plais*, madame,' he craved, 'allow me to feel the tautness of her stretched limbs, her inner thighs, the moistness of her cunny, the arching readiness of her love bud...'

The young man begged and pleaded but the words faded in Grace's consciousness. What was to happen to her? Was not this torture enough, being spread-eagled at the base of the bed to be ogled by these two? What more could they do to her?

When she was first brought into the palace she was barely conscious after being dragged by her hair over the cold wet cobbles. When she finally came to her senses she could not believe the luxury of her surroundings. The chamber into which she was delivered was small but cosy with rose damask lined walls and velvet sofas standing on tiny gilt legs. By a crackling fire, wonderfully warm and glowing red, a porcelain bath was set and wraiths of steam rose from its scented surface.

She was attended by a maid, a pretty girl, fair as Grace was dark. 'I must bathe you,' she said shyly, approaching the shivering girl.

Grace wrapped her slender arms about her waist,

shrinking away from the maid, embarrassed at the suggestion even though the tatters of her clothes revealed more than they hid. No matter how tightly she hugged herself the pert mounds of her breasts with their taut nipples were bared between the shreds of filthy clothing. The delicate swell of her belly and the fullness of her mound with the fluff of raven curls refused to be hidden by the torn strips of her gown.

The maid, in her plain but pretty dress, stepped forward, her rosebud lips curved in a gentle smile. 'I shall not hurt you, mistress.' She looked so clean, thought Grace, with the pale swell of her breasts lifted so enticingly by her tight basque.

'I am not a mistress,' whispered Grace.

The girl, her fair curls shimmering in the warm light of the flickering candles and the glow of the fire, bobbed a curtsy. 'But you must be,' she insisted. 'If I am your maid, you must be my mistress.' She laughed, a pretty tinkling sound, and darted forward, catching Grace by her tiny waist, pulling her shivering form close.

The two girls stood close, their pert young breasts heaving, brushing one against the other. Dark hazel eyes gazed into twinkling, mischievous blue eyes. Grace made a sound, a whisper, a mew of pleasure.

'Yes,' said the maid, 'I knew when you arrived in the carriage that you were sensual.'

Grace felt dainty fingers caress the plumpness of her sex pouch, and she could not help but bear down upon the invading fingers, encourage the fingertips to delve deeper into her moist flesh.

'No...' The murmur of denial was scarcely audible.

Lips, soft and warm, brushed Grace's own and she felt a hand cup the growing heaviness of her breast. She did not resist when the girl gently slipped the tatters of her gown from her shoulders. She stood, shy and trembling, her cheeks on fire with embarrassment, while her nakedness was inspected.

'I see why master Philipe and madame desired you,' whispered the girl. 'No doubt his blood boiled when he looked upon you.'

Only then did Grace bow her head, letting the heavy raven tresses fall forward to hide her burning face, sway back and forth across each swollen mound of her breasts.

The girl eased her into the scented warm water and Grace felt that she would swoon with the sensations the girl drew from her. Her gentle hands, creamed with the most luxurious of soaps, massaged her breasts, her belly, between her open thighs, her buttocks. Grace felt the wild jerk of her clitoris as dainty fingers slipped up and down in the soap-slicked valley where it lay hidden. She felt the girl open her flesh lips and bare the hardened bud. Grace craved that the invading fingers would probe her virginal entrance, but as she reached each peak the digits drew back, leaving her trembling with frustration.

The maid patted her dry with a towel as soft as velvet. Grace had never felt so clean. Looking down at her body she could not believe that this pale, porcelain skin was hers.

'Try to be brave,' whispered the maid.

Grace creased the smooth skin of her forehead, puzzled. 'I... I... don't understand,' she mumbled, her words hesitant.

'They will be cruel,' whispered the maid. 'They will humiliate you. Shame you. I have heard them talking.'

'Cruel? Humiliate?' Grace shivered despite the glowing warmth of the fire before which she stood.

'Be brave,' said the maid again, and she slipped a plain muslin gown over Grace's head. It hid nothing. The darkness of her freshly washed pussy bush could be clearly seen through the gossamer cloth, and the flushed darkness of her nipples brushed against the floating material, especially when the maid tied her wrists behind her with silken cord.

Grace was led to a larger chamber through passages

brightly lit with glittering chandeliers and peopled with richly dressed courtiers who did not hesitate to caress her heavy breasts through the fine material as she was pushed through the throngs. One bold young man lifted her fluttering skirt and openly fondled her plump love lips. Helpless because of her bonds she could only stand passively until he pushed her away. Another fondled her buttocks, parted them and peered at the tiny pore that lay hidden there.

Tears were hot under her lids as she was led to madame's chamber, and she could not stop her lips from trembling.

'At last!' was madame's greeting.

Oh, they were gentle enough at first. Their hands stroked and teased when the flimsy gown was removed. Madame greeted her with a kiss on each breast while Philipe cosseted her plump flesh pot. Grace became hot with shame, so intimate was their touch.

But there was much worse to come when they bound her to the frame at the foot of the bed. Hours seemed to pass, or perhaps it was only minutes. Grace's body was displayed like a living and naked statue.

'Speak to me!' The words were rapped out by Philipe who knelt at the foot of the bed, stroking her widely splayed legs, feeling their painful tautness, especially on the inner sides where the flesh was most tender.

Suddenly fully conscious and with eyes which flashed open with shock, Grace gazed down at him. 'Yes, sire? What must I say to please you?'

Madame chuckled. 'You see how quickly she learns, and I have scarcely taught her anything? What a perfect little dear she is, to be sure.'

'Is it painful?' asked Philipe, ignoring his mistress.

Grace wished fervently that she could shudder at the touch of the aristocratic fingers upon her already tortured flesh, but her bonds were too tight to allow the luxury of this slightest of movement. She did not answer, and cast

37

her eyes downwards. Like a midnight curtain her heavy cascade of blue-black hair caressed her pale cheeks, her milky smooth shoulders and the upper swells of her breasts.

'Answer me!' Philipe's voice sounded petulant and, at the next moment, Grace cried out as searing pain shuddered through her tautly stretched buttocks. The shimmering torrent of freshly washed hair drifted from side to side of her pale face, caressed her breasts, swung with the force of the blow.

'You must answer, *cherie*.' Madame's plump hand was raised to render another blow upon Grace's burning bottom.

'A little painful, madame,' managed Grace, with a scarcely concealed sob in her throat. She felt a kiss, no more than the brush of swansdown upon her heated bottom.

'An angel,' Grace heard madame whisper, and her buttocks shook with the force of another blow. Tears, round and hot, spilled down Grace's cheeks. Other moisture, also warm and beaded into creamy pearls oozed from silken flesh in the folds of her sex pouch. She could feel the wetness at her still-closed and virginal entrance, and the heated hardness of her love bud probing from the trembling folds of her sex purse.

Philipe's fingers caressed the inner flesh of Grace's thighs, trying to force them further apart. 'Do you know the term, orgasm?' he murmured.

Heat suffused Grace's pale cheeks. 'No,' she whispered.

'Liar!' snapped Philipe. 'I can see the gloss of love juice on your thighs.'

Please, begged Grace silently, don't let him cup my sex purse, nor open the leaves, nor feel my bud. The stretching of her body, the tautness of her breasts, the fluttering of her belly had all served to excite that part of her between her thighs, dewing it with love pearls.

'Sire,' she whispered. 'I promise you that I have never known a man. This…' she bowed her head and gestured between her splayed thighs. 'The dew is for you, should you require me.'

Madame de Genlis chuckled and threw herself upon the bed, her hands busy between her own thighs. 'Not yet, my precious,' she said, 'but it is sweet that you are so willing. I think I might have a treat for you.'

Looking over his smooth shoulder, Philipe frowned at madame.

'And for you, too,' she said. 'Take her and suspend her upside down.'

'Upside down?' Philipe pouted his lips and petted the silky length of his cock with trembling fingers. 'What good will that do?'

'Do it, you stupid boy,' rasped Madame. 'And when you have done it you will discover a new joy.'

The strips of leather, knotted painfully and twisted around Grace's wrists to the upper strut of the four-poster bed were slowly unfastened. The sudden release of the bindings caused a rush of blood along her arms, held so long in the upright position. A pain that was almost sweet in its severity replaced the numbness. Grace gave a soft mew as the pain hit her and she crumpled, face forward, upon the bed.

A slender finger stroked her naked and vulnerable sex. 'She looks so helpless, madame,' murmured Philipe, 'still bound at the ankles and spread upon our bed, so open and vulnerable. So ready for a cock. So open. Could I not…?'

'*Non*!' Madame was firm. 'Do as I say and unfasten her other bonds and position her upside down.'

Philipe sighed, but did as he was bid, releasing the leather strips that cut into the delicate skin at Grace's ankles. Again she felt the exquisite pain as blood flooded the limbs bound so tightly and for so long. She could not quell the little sound, a blending of pain and relief, which sighed from her soft lips.

Flipping her over Philipe grinned down at her. She tried to move her cramped arms to cover her shuddering breasts. Painfully, she attempted to curl her slender legs to hide her splayed sex.

With the flat of his hand Philipe slapped her arms outwards, smacked her belly and flicked his fingertips at her inner thighs.

'Open,' he grunted. 'Always open for us to gaze upon, to touch.' Nervously, he looked to madame, but the woman only smiled her agreement.

Grace, her wide eyes closed, felt fingertips spreading the plumpness of her outer sex folds. A smooth thumb grazed over the pouting erection of her clitoris and Grace felt her body flush with humiliation as she heard herself sigh, a whisper of sheer pleasure, as that sensitive place was touched.

'Enough of that!' snapped madame. 'Put her up as I suggested; her wrists bound to the lower strut and ankles to the upper.'

Philipe frowned, sitting back upon his haunches, his hands straying to the still stiff and throbbing length of his cock. 'But she will then have to support herself upon her hands, her wrists, the length of her arms,' he complained.

A soft whimper of apprehension came from Grace's soft and open lips. The thought of renewed and even greater pain was almost more than she could bear.

'Oh, come now, my darling,' whispered madame. 'Think how graceful, how pliable, how sensual my training will make you.' She smiled a secret smile. 'And I am sure that little sex pouch is already feeling delicious benefits. Feel her again, Philipe. Tell me how it feels.'

The smooth fingers opened her and Grace knew that her sex skin was scarlet, livid with desire. The folds were swollen, open, beaded with love pearls and, in the centre, jutting proudly, was her clitty; jerking with excitement, throbbing in and out of its little hood.

'Splendid,' murmured madame. 'Bind her as I

instructed and we shall all have even greater fun.'

Deftly, Philipe bound her. Within seconds Grace's slender arms were tormented with a dreadful ache caused by the strain of supporting her body weight. The only relief was the suspension from her slender ankles, her legs splayed to their limit. The young man could not resist a caress of her open, moist and very vulnerable sex, and Grace could not stop the answering flutter of her sensitive part.

'*Et maintenant*?' he queried of madame. 'And now?' He was impatient. Grace could tell by his crisp words.

Madame laughed coarsely. 'Well, what have you been wishing for these several hours?'

'Relief!' grunted Philipe.

'*Exactement*!' Madame lay back, her eyes heavily lidded with lust, her lips parted, her legs thrust asunder, her knees allowed to fall outwards to display her sex pouch fully.

'But you said…'

'You could not fuck her, *oui*!' Madame chuckled. 'But does she not have other delightful orifices which I have made available to you?'

Grace's eyes, wide and gleaming with pain, peered between the tumbled raven blackness of her hair, were drawn to the bloated veins of Philipe's rigidity pulsing with eagerness.

'Her rear?' he queried, not trying to hide his fervent desire.

The wrinkled bud nestling between the plump mounds of her buttocks twitched involuntarily and Grace, using all her strength, tried to move in her bonds.

'*Mais non*,' murmured Madame de Genlis, but her voice was husky with wanting. 'That must come very much further in her training.'

Grace could see the pearly dew drop glistening upon the bloated globe of Philipe's penis. It shimmered in the guttering light of the candles scattered about the chamber and the glow from the dying coals in the ornate fireplace. Madame tapped her parted lips and raised an eyebrow at Philipe.

The young man smiled and his pale eyes glittered with delight. Grace saw him look down at his grossly thickened and throbbing length.

'Do you think she could?' he asked, smoothing his delicate fingers along the silky and juice-slicked skin. He smoothed a fingertip along the soft margins of Grace's mouth and she could taste the creamy saltiness of his dew. Unable to help herself she lapped at the taste as eagerly as she could in the face of her torture.

'Do you see, *mon cher* Philipe? How she loves your taste!' Madame was ecstatic in her enthusiasm while Grace felt her face burn with humiliation at her own actions. Despite this fact she felt a warm trickle of her own cream ooze between the taut cleft of her buttocks, and a throb she could not ignore in the depths of her sex pouch. 'Come, Philipe,' urged madame, 'position yourself. Place your cock in her deliciously soft mouth. Let her lips massage its length until it gives up its contents.'

'If she gags,' said Philipe, a pout never far from his handsome but spoilt mouth, 'may I deal with her as I think fit?'

Grace's head ached abominably from her tortured position, but she saw Madame de Genlis wave one of her ringed hands, her mouth pursed with anger, her powdered forehead creased with fury. 'I wish to enjoy the sweet sight of her mouth filled with your cock! Do it and stop arguing!'

'Open your lips fully,' ordered Philipe, turning his back on his mistress. 'No! Not like that, you stupid girl! Moisten them nicely first.'

Tongue tip trembling, Grace did as she was bid. Philipe shuffled his naked legs through the lower strut of the oak bed until his bloated and purplish globe was level with

42

her open lips. He sighed blissfully as her mouth gently sucked the pearly driblets that oozed from the pulsing eye.

'More,' he ordered hoarsely. 'Suck harder. Take my whole length into your mouth.'

The feel of the sword of flesh sliding into her throat did not perturb Grace in the slightest. Far from it. It was a pleasurable sensation and took her mind from her other pain and discomfort; the ache in her head, her tortured joints, the leather bindings at her wrists and ankles.

'She can do it!' gasped Philipe. 'She enjoys my whole length in her throat!'

His thickness was such that it stretched her mouth to the full and Grace, being a very caring girl, made sure that her teeth did not graze the tender skin. She managed a gentle, sucking rhythm which was in tune with the powerful throb she could feel in his cockstem.

'I can feel my tip at her gullet,' murmured Philipe, overcome with joy. 'Oh, Madame! It is delightful. I do not think I can hold back.'

He thrust and Grace could feel a powerful pulsing in the length trapped between her lips; could taste the salty cream jetting at the back of her tongue.

Philipe juddered with pleasure and the soft curls of his pubis tickled Grace's face as he moved against her. She wished she could hold him close, caress his slender body with her hands, but she was helpless. She could only receive his offering, drink the warm creamy juices. Jet after jet spilled into her mouth, coating it, smearing her throat.

The ache and heat between her own thighs, if it was unbearable in its intensity before, was greater now. The spillage from her folds was a constant stream and she was sure that her bud was clearly visible, scarlet and hugely erect, peeping from the raven curls which fluffed so prettily on the plump outer lips of her sex pouch.

'Oh, Philipe!' murmured madame wistfully, her voice

husky with need, her breasts vastly swollen and flushed, the nipples like ripe plums, rounded and richly purple. 'I wish you to come and lie in my arms.'

A groan, part exhaustion and part satiation, reached Grace's ears. The young man lay, his cock still between her lips, unable to move for the delicious trembling of his slender body.

'She is so delightful, madame,' he groaned. 'Her mouth is like oiled silk and it sucks like quicksand, draining me dry.'

Grace felt her cheeks suffuse with heat at his praise and felt a flutter in her sex folds, the needful jerk of her clitty and the slow trickle of her juices.

'Come here, Philipe!' The command was rapped out.

Green eyes darkened by both the pain of the tight bindings about her wrists and ankles, the strain of supporting herself on her hands, and the unrelenting sensual sensations which racked her tortured body, Grace turned her gaze to madame.

The voluptuous woman lay upon the satin ribboned linen, her shapely legs spread to their utmost. Immediately the innocent captive closed her eyes, not because what she saw disgusted her or was abhorrent, but because it heightened her own feelings.

'Come here, Philipe.' The command was softer, throatier.

'Must I unfasten the girl?' came the petulant reply.

'You may look upon me, my precious girl.' Madame's eyes were hooded with lust and her voice was husky. Philipe's query was ignored. 'Look upon my beautiful mound with its silky lush curls. Look between my love lips, at my clitty, which is burning for stimulation; to be kissed by loving lips.'

Grace felt compelled to obey and saw the lustrous forest on the plump mons with its curls tickling the tops of the spread and statuesque thighs.

'I know how it stimulates you,' continued madame.

'And see here...' The ringed fingers peeled back swollen outer folds baring the slick inner leaves. 'No, don't you dare close your eyes! Look at my clitty, isn't it a fine nubbin with its hood drawn back? There are some men at court who would give their right hands to have a cock so fine, I can tell you!'

A fingertip grazed the scarlet glossy tip in question and Grace longed to touch herself in the same manner. If only her hands were free.

The skin surrounding madame's clitty was slick with her juices. It was pearled with creamy droplets on each fine leaf, and the droplets merged to drool slowly down the plump hillocks which were the path to the woman's bottom.

'Well?' snapped Philipe.

Madame continued to caress her splayed sex, petting her clitty with slow, circular strokes and dipping the same finger into her pulsing entrance. 'Hm?' she managed at last.

'Shall I release her?' he snapped. 'The girl?'

Slowly, madame came to her senses. '*Non, non*! I wish to gaze at her in her delicious torment before I sleep.' She beckoned her lover. 'With you in my arms, my sweet.'

His slender limbs trembling with both weariness and satiation, Philipe crawled over the tumbled linen to lie in the crook of his mistress's arms, his head pillowed upon her bounteous breast. In a moment he turned his head to take the swollen and purple nipple between his lips.

Grace, her face smeared with Philipe's copious issue, tried to console herself that she had pleased her royal captors and, although racked with the most terrible pain, she would be warm and well fed for a little while at least.

Chapter Three

In the depths of sleep Grace felt a gentle tug at her sex lips until they were splayed open. A chill drifted across the heated and moist flesh within. She shifted sleepily into a ball, her rounded buttocks pouting outwards and her sex pouch tucked away at the apex of her thighs. She mewed soft words. She licked her lips and felt her cheeks flush at the salty taste. Her raven black hair, shimmering with blue lights in the ill-lit room, coiled over her breasts and tumbled like a midnight cascade in the valley between them.

'So submissive, so sweet and pliant. The perfect girl.'

The words caressed Grace's ears, but she did not know whether she was truly awake or asleep. Was she dreaming?

Tentatively, she allowed her lashes to flutter open, but almost immediately she closed them again. She was no longer in the comfort of madame's chamber. Her new surroundings were dark, cavernous, unwelcoming.

She was shocked fully awake; fearful, terrified of the rusty iron bars at the edge of her vision, the walls slicked with trickles of water and streaked green with lichen.

'Where am I?' she murmured, shuffling on her bare buttocks across a floor which was cold and uneven, strewn with filthy straw and the rotting remains spilled from discarded bowls of food.

Lighted sconces were fixed into rusty iron brackets in the rough hewn wall, shedding flickering light and petrifying shadows which danced like ghosts around her. A rustling noise made her look down into the straw strewn about the stone floor. She screamed as she saw the long, grey and sinuous shape of a rat scurrying there.

'Don't be afraid.' Strong arms gathered her to a broad chest, but Grace fought this new captor, hurting her small fists as she pummelled muscles as hard as the iron bars that held them prisoner.

'Where am I?' she asked again, straining against the almost naked man who held her. 'And who are you?'

'We're in the dungeons below the palace,' he said. His voice was deep, soft, like spoken velvet. He wore only a scrap of filthy cloth held about his waist by rough string. The cloth was lifted, Grace noticed, by the massive thickness, his cockstem, beneath it. 'And you don't remember me. I am being punished for holding you too close.'

'The servant in satin,' she murmured, remembering.

He laughed mirthlessly, touching the scrap of rag. 'Satin no more.'

Grace felt his fingers stray to the swell of a breast, the deep dip of her waist and the splendid rise of her buttocks. She lowered her head, allowing her midnight hair to fall forward, curtaining her full breasts and hiding the flush that came unbidden once more to her pale face. The fingers trembled as they petted the swell of her belly and strayed downwards to the darkness of her bush.

'No,' cried Grace, managing to push him away. Despite her sleep, her sex pouch was still swollen, still creamily wet and hot as fire. If the servant touched her she would be lost, she knew.

'You're a virgin,' he murmured in awe.

'And must remain so,' she said, 'or be punished severely by Madame de Genlis.' She paused, her eyes raised to his, round and fearful. 'Perhaps even executed.

A sound rang out in the dank and sprawling cave-like rooms. A crack that could have been a pistol shot echoed over and over again. Grace screamed.

'No talking!' A huge shadow emerged, solid and fearsome, from all the other shadows which flickered against the ancient walls. It held a whip, long and snakelike, darkened by years of body fluids. It flicked between the bars, its tip touching the wine-dark nipples of Grace's breasts. A gasp of pain was drawn from her.

'No talking,' repeated the rough voice.

The green eyes widened at the sight of their gaoler. Tall and broad, dressed only in a scrap of worn leather drawn roughly into a pouch about his heavy genitals, he grinned at Grace through the bars before fading back into the shadows.

Her companion drew his finger across his lips indicating that they must be silent and mouth their words. Grace, fighting back tears, nodded, doubting that she could speak for the painful lump in her throat. Perhaps she would have been better to take the offer given to her by the men at the cemetery than suffer the tortures offered, one after the other, by her new captors.

The palace seemed nothing more than a torture chamber. Wearily, she lay her head upon her companion's shoulder.

'Listen,' he whispered and grasped her arms, shaking her, forcing her to watch his lips. 'You have been in their chambers all night and it is well known that they are the most rabid sensualists in the palace.'

His breathing was rapid and harsh, Grace noticed, and the square of rag was pushed to the side displaying a cock that speared straight up and was fully turgid.

Grace shrugged, her wrists were inflamed where the leather bindings scored them and every muscle in her slender body felt strained. Strained or not, the feel of her companion's arms about her, the warmth of his muscular body and his excitement, increased the yearning between her thighs.

'They did not try to despoil you?'

She shook her head, her warm eyes seeking his, which were onyx and glittering with need. He was a handsome man, with sharply honed features. How easy it would be to allow him her body, allow him to break the precious barrier that made her so valuable. Perhaps then madame and her master would leave her alone.

But she shook her head, thinking more carefully. 'It

would be more than my life was worth,' she said.

'We are to be lashed, you and I,' he told her.

Grace did not resist this time when the man cupped her sex pouch, his rough fingers caressing the deep valleys where her pouting sex lips met her thighs, held it gently, not trying to invade it further. She felt a warmth there, a pleasure she could not resist and, involuntarily, she bore down upon the touch. But then the full import of the servant's statement made her shiver.

'By that... that... creature?' she murmured. 'The gaoler?' She shuddered, seeing in her mind's eye the leather pouch that scarcely covered his huge cock. And seeing the whip he wielded so enthusiastically. What did it matter, in that case? What did anything matter?

She felt him place the flat of his palm against the heat of her sex, spreading her silky moisture across the fine raven curls. The caress made her feel pleasantly lethargic, heavy in her limbs, and a heat swirled about her belly. A further bubble of her juices oozed from her cunt and she lifted her head, her lips parted, moist, ready to be kissed.

'Do you want me to fuck you?' he breathed.

The coarse words shocked Grace but excited her at the same time. She felt her clitty jerk under the protective outer folds and a slow trickle of juices wet her curls. Her sex felt hugely swollen, open and more than ready. She glanced warily into the shadows of their prison, looking for the gaoler, and nodded.

'Oh, my darling girl,' the man groaned. 'What an honour you bestow on me. I shall not care if I am executed if my cock has known the beauty of your silken funnel.'

The man, whose name she did not know, slipped the square of rag to the side and Grace felt the smooth heat of his cock tip nudge between her thighs. She held his broad shoulders, arching back to give his full access to her sex. She parted her shapely thighs yet further and allowed him to saw his thickness back and forth against the silky

49

blackness of her moistened bush. It throbbed against the wet heat of her swollen sex lips. It touched the very tip of her clitty, petting it as it jerked up his length.

Grace, becoming bolder, insinuated her slender fingers between their embracing bodies. She cupped the heaviness of his sperm sac, feeling the firmness of his balls beneath the skin. He groaned, and Grace thought the gaoler would appear at any moment, stopping their forbidden pleasure. Although fearful and terrified of the pain she might feel she urged the man to penetrate her. At last she felt it! The dewy moistness of his grossly swollen tip stroked against her entrance.

'Now,' she whispered, and she felt a slick of her own juices bathe him in readiness.

His lips sought hers, hard and punishing, full of passion and, so engrossed were they in the joy of their bodies that they did not hear the sound of footsteps upon the mossy stone steps.

'Stop that!' It was madame's voice, shrill with fury. 'Philipe! You must stop them, this instant!'

The sound flung the lovers apart like a shot from a cannon. Grace threw herself to the rough wall, shrinking to the floor, hugging her trembling breasts with fear. She felt the heat and moisture of her sex purse cooled by the dank stone of the floor and felt the stilling of her need within her belly.

'Gaoler!' Madame, the silk of her gown rustling as she bustled across the dungeon, her face a mask of fury, peered into the shadows of the gaoler's cubby-hole. 'I shall have you beheaded! How dare you sleep when I have given you such a valuable prisoner? How dare you risk her virginity by placing her with this servant?'

It was such a temptation to Grace to reach out to the footman. She longed to feel his hard nakedness against her own; the promise of his cock within her moist and willing, but still shuttered, depths. Shuddering, she remembered how it nudged gently between her love lips and against the very tip of her clitoris, drawing juices from her depths.

Philipe strode angrily up and down, swiping the rusty bars of her prison with a wooden rod. Grace, her heels tucked tightly into the cushion of her sex, crouched, her glossy black hair sweeping across her breasts, titillating the hardened teats.

'I cannot wait to punish you,' Philipe hissed, his pale eyes glaring at her, glistening with pent up cruelty. But although his lips said these words he meant something else entirely. Grace knew! Oh yes, she knew that the very moment he had the opportunity and had her alone he would do far worse than punish her. Grace could not still the quiver which ran through her naked body. The very thought of what the Duc d'Orleans planned sent a forbidden quiver of excitement through her. His words and what they might mean thrilled her with wantonness.

His eyes sought hers, his lips pursed and curved in a wicked smile. She remembered the silky feel of his cock in her mouth, the wetness of his come slipping down her throat.

The gaoler appeared, scratching the leather pouch that scarcely held is genitals. 'Madame,' he said with an obsequious bow, 'sire. I had scarcely dozed when...' He paused, seeing the black fury in Philipe's eyes as they turned upon him. 'I am sure they had no chance to fuck.' He shook his long greasy locks. His filthy hand strayed to the pouch and his fingers stroked the growing bulge as he looked down at Grace. She saw his tongue lap lasciviously about his parted lips and he stroked the dewy tip of his cock as it peeped upwards beyond the pouch.

'Never mind that.' Madame joined Philipe and stared with narrowed eyes into the filthy cage. 'Put her on the rack!' The order was hissed with some glee.

'But I thought you did not wish her to be harmed,' objected Philipe, giving his mistress a sideways glance. But the thought of Grace's lovely form splayed helpless

51

upon the rack made the discomfort about his groin all too plain.

Grace bowed her head, hiding the tears, clutching to herself the misery of what her life had become. The only light on the very distant horizon was the pleasure she was promised when her virginity was, at last, spent.

'The rack!' repeated madame.

Between the dark fronds of her long hair Grace could see the gaoler, could see how he rhythmically thrust out his massive bulge and put strain upon the leather pouch. She saw how the holding strands cut into his hips as the thin leather truss became fuller.

'She will not be harmed,' consoled madame. 'Her delicate frame, her limbs, her breasts, will just be a little stretched. All part of her training for sensuality. I am sure Rousseau would have approved of my methods.' Her eyes gazed lustfully at Grace's huddled figure. 'It will, after all, make her more graceful, more supple, more mysterious, I am sure. We shall have every man in the palace lusting after her.'

'No!' The rusty bars were rattled by angry hands. 'You cannot! You cannot treat this lovely creature so cruelly.'

Grace raised her head, her eyes dark with misery, and looked at the imprisoned footman. She tossed the fall of black hair from her pale face and beseeched him with a whisper, her hands raised. 'Please,' she begged, 'don't put yourself in danger. I am not worth it.'

Her fellow prisoner crouched down and Grace found her eyes drawn to the heaviness of his cockstem, still thick from his desire of her. 'Your beauty is such that I would gladly die for you...'

He was dragged to his feet by the huge gaoler and the dank rooms of the dungeons rang with the sound of cruel laughter. 'Aye, young fellow,' he growled between his coarse chuckles. 'Your wish will no doubt be granted.'

'Indeed,' added madame. 'Bind him to the whipping post and choose a lash which will flay him alive.'

Grace bowed her head and tried to hide the tears that fell so heavily down her cheeks, but the tears were not for herself. Her throat was full for the young footman, who came so close to being her first lover. Behind her moist lids she saw the beauty, the splendour, the thickness of his cock with the foreskin drawn back to bare the glossy globe.

'Lift your head, my darling. Look at me.' Madame spoke softly as she ordered Grace to gaze upon her.

Still crouched like a whipped puppy, hugging her slim arms about her breasts, Grace slowly raised her head and dried her tears with trembling fingers. She choked back her sobs, threw back the mane of jet-black hair and looked defiantly at her captor.

Madame smiled. 'That's how I wish you to look, my darling. Brave, courageous...'

'Oh, stop wasting time.' Philipe was by Grace's side, his fingers closing like a vice about her upper arm, dragging her to her feet. 'I want to see her splayed upon the rack.'

Eyes wide with fear, Grace was dragged from the cage-like cell. She stumbled, fell to her knees, and Philipe screamed with impatience.

'It won't help you, falling,' he said, his voice harsh with anger, and his hand grasped a handful of the midnight hair, wrapping it around his fist to drag her over the uneven flagstones.

'Don't damage her, you fool,' pleaded madame.

'I am frustrated!' Philipe's voice sounded crazed. In her mind Grace felt again the thickness of his cock sliding down her throat, but glanced away, her flesh pot swollen with need and her head aching with pity for the man who could have been her lover given just a few moments longer.

Through pain glazed eyes Grace saw the footman, his hands manacled high on a tall post, his feet scarcely touching the floor, his cock semi-turgid and arching from the base of his flat and muscular belly. Did fear do that to a man; fear and pain? Did it bring his cock to readiness for a woman?

'Be brave,' he mouthed silently to Grace.

Before she could reply Philipe dragged her to a shadowy corner of the chamber. The roots of her hair darted pain to her scalp as she was heaved upon the crude bench, but this eased as Philipe released the black tresses and transferred his grip to her breasts. He worked the heavy flesh as if it was dough and tweaked her nipples until they were hard little points. His lips enclosed hers in a cruel and punishing kiss but Grace resisted. She held her body tense and when he attempted to splay her legs she clenched them hard together. He grabbed her wrists in a vice-like grip.

'Gaoler! Come here! I need your help in fastening these manacles,' he said crossly. He leaned over her, pressing her arms wide apart, flat upon the bench. Grace could feel her full breasts flatten upon her ribs as he made her arch backwards, her belly become concave and her mound proud and full between her thighs.

'With pleasure, sire.' The gaoler scurried across the shadowy chamber. 'We simply click these manacles to her wrists and...'

Grace felt the chill of the iron as it was fastened. Hard and resilient.

'And we spread her thighs wide to fasten the anklets,' continued the gaoler. It would have been foolish to resist such a strong man.

'*Oui, oui,*' chuckled Philipe excitedly, hopping around the cruel device.

Grace lay helpless upon the rack, her arms stretched to the limit, her wrists inflamed from the earlier binding. She saw the gaoler stroke his leather pouch as he looked down at her, and she turned her head away from the vulgar creature.

'So open and vulnerable,' whispered madame. 'So

54

perfect and submissive – the perfect woman.' She stood by Grace's side, her ringed fingers hovering over the tautened breasts, seeming to wish, above all things, to twist the wine-dark nipples. 'Tell me, Philipe,' she said, and her voice trembled with excitement, 'how does her cunt look?'

Philipe groaned and Grace, despite the dimly lit and shadowy chamber, was sure that his legs buckled with desire as he walked to the end of the bench.

Grace, unable to bear more humiliation, tried to close her eyes, but was stopped by a shrill order from madame. 'You must watch, my darling. Watch how Philipe adores your little cunny with his eyes, feasts upon its juicy flesh.' The woman's eyes flickered to the gaoler, who stood over Grace, watching eagerly. 'And the gaoler, too,' she added with a chuckle.

It was as if Grace could feel the intensity of the two pairs of eyes on her most private place in a physical manner. Within her belly she felt warmth and a swirling sensation as if the men touched her, very gently, within. Much as she tried, she could not stop the feeling of fullness in her sex pouch, the drool of silky liquid upon heated skin. She tried to twist her supple body to hide the object of their interest.

'Stop that,' ordered madame, rapping her arm with her fan. 'Gaoler, turn the handle. Make her tauter upon the rack... just a little. Only a little, to take up the slack. Prevent her trying to hide that lovely part of her body.'

A drool of spittle oozed from the gaoler's grinning mouth and Grace saw him adjust the straining bulge between his thighs as his big hands grasped the handle which would stretch her even further open.

A loud and threatening click echoed through the cavernous chamber and Grace gave a tiny mew, not of pain, but of discomfort as her limbs became tauter. She looked up at the gaoler, who stood at the end of the bench. His gaze was fixed on her fully open sex lips. She knew they were dreadfully inflamed with her wanting – her need. She knew her jet-black curls were moist with her juices and were spread outwards, making the full folds of her sex open and the finer, inner leaves part to bare the arch of her nubbin, making the whole more available, more visible. She felt her inner sex lips flutter and saw the gaoler's fingers stray into the bulging leather pouch to rub up and down the thick stem which strained there.

Philipe spoke, startling Grace. 'Oh, madame... such a delightful sight!' The aristocrat crouched at the end of the bench. 'Her mound is thrust higher by the tension of the rack and the plump folds swell deliciously. It makes me want her more than ever.'

Grace could not stop her lashes fluttering closed as she tried to shut out her shame. She knew she was disobeying orders and punishment would follow.

'One more notch,' said madame, instructing the gaoler. 'Or perhaps she can stand two? She is such a supple and graceful creature.' She smiled into Grace's eyes.

It was almost as if madame was bestowing a gift rather than a punishment, thought Grace.

The slow tension made the tortured girl feel more vulnerable. It seemed to lift the fullness of her sex closer to Philipe's eager eyes. Helpless, she could not move a muscle under the restrictions placed upon her ankles and wrists. Her breasts were stretched across her ribs and her nipples were tight buds, their darkness begging to be taken between caressing lips.

'Tell me,' breathed madame huskily, 'how open is her cunny? How moist and dewy?'

'The full lips are stretched wide open,' sighed Philipe, 'and the fine inner lips are flushed with desire. Creamy dew beads the scarlet folds...' His voice was hoarse and his breath came in short, sharp gasps.

'And her clitty?' Madame bent over Grace's breasts, one after the other, and took the urgent nipples between her lips. 'How is that? Leave nothing out, I pray you.'

'Proud,' answered Philipe. 'The hood is drawn back and the tip is bared.' His voice was barely audible. 'May I kiss it, madame?'

Grace knew that her helplessness and the tension on her limbs had excited her, but to hear it described so boldly was doubly humiliating. Her shame knew no bounds.

'I wish the gaoler to have that privilege,' whispered madame. 'As I am sure my girl does too, is that not true, my darling?'

A violent shudder rippled through Grace's body at the thought of the unshaven lips and broken teeth gnawing at her intimate flesh. The shiver caused her pain, but this seemed only to enhance the feelings in her belly, the flutter of longing.

A sulky pout and a frown spoiled Philipe's handsome features, but he fumbled about his breeches, easing his cock from the flap. 'I suppose you won't object to me pleasuring myself as I watch?' he snapped sarcastically.

'Indeed not,' the woman granted. 'I intend to do the same.' She lifted the yards of silk to expose her belly and the dark triangle beneath it. There was nowhere the girl could look and not see swollen, moist and inflamed genitals.

Rough thumbs pressed open her outer lips, baring the flushed inner skin. She could feel the damp heat of his breath upon her and knew that her clitty, rearing up from its soft and silky bed, gave an anticipatory jerk. She mewed as a ripple of glorious feeling shot through her. For all that the gaoler was an ugly distasteful creature the sensation he created within the open folds if her sex were delicious. Looking down her body she could see her mound, sweetly decorated with blue-black curls. She could see the gaoler's head busy between her splayed legs, his unkempt hair brushing the tender inner skin of her open thighs. Warm and wet, his tongue tip caressed the inner folds and his spittle merged with her creamy juices to bathe her pert clitty in a cascade of moisture.

The cell was redolent with the scent of excitement; her own sweet musk, the heavier perfume of madame, the stale heat of the gaoler, and Philipe's youthful masculine aroma.

Grace was powerless to prevent the whirlpool of pleasurable sensations within her. She reached that peak of pleasure from which there is no return. A whimper of ecstasy began deep in her throat and ended as wave after wave of soft moans.

'Oh, mistress,' groaned the gaoler, bobbing up from between her thighs. 'She pumps her fluids upon my tongue and I gladly drink them.'

'Spurt your come upon her belly, her breasts, her mound!' ordered madame huskily. Her fingers were busy working at her pleasure within her own sex flesh, flashing up and down, her pelvis thrust forward and her thighs open.

Both Philipe and the gaoler had their cocks between flashing fingers and Grace, her eyes heavy lidded from her own sensual experience, watched the lengths bulge as they came closer and closer to their climaxes. The pulsing was strong in both men, as though they had stored their pleasure for a length of time. Grace felt the spurt of the warm and creamy juices splash upon her belly. More trickled down her breasts, droplets falling from her tautened nipples. Her shame was such that she could not hold back the tears and they streamed down her pale cheeks to slide like liquid crystal to her breasts, merging with the pearly spills of come.

'Such a graceful and willing girl,' murmured madame, her own orgasm ending with a pleasurable whisper.

With a luxurious rustle of silk she put her gown to rights.

A scarcely audible echo of pleasure whispered across the shadowy dungeons, and Grace turned her head in its direction and gasped. The naked footman, despite his pain and discomfort, writhed against the chain that suspended him. His body arched as his feet tried to gain purchase against the post that held him. With her womb still pulsing from the rigours of her orgasm Grace could almost imagine that he had impaled her. A stream arched from his cock, long creamy arcs that splashed the mossy flagstones.

'Oh, let him go,' murmured Grace, her voice choked by sobs and full of compassion. Her own discomfort was forgotten; the mounds of her breasts flattened by tension, her nipples gathered into painful buds, her belly so taut that it was almost concave, but this concavity enhancing the proud pad of female flesh.

'Let him go?' rasped Philipe. 'Let him go? He must be punished, whipped until he learns...' His eyes darted to the gaoler who was selecting whips from the array hung above the rack. 'Until he learns not to make free with our property.'

At last Grace felt her own limbs released. Her aching body was sponged with a square of clean flannel to wipe away the male spillage. Madame took great care to carry out the cleansing process in the most sensual way possible. Grace shuddered as the warm flannel was wiped about her breasts, over her belly and in and around her pussy. Only then was she gathered into madame's arms as if she was a long lost and dear friend, or a daughter lost and finally found.

'If I might suggest,' said the gaoler, 'the girl needs further disciplining.'

Madame, her ringed hand cupped against the fullness of Grace's breast, raised a quizzical eyebrow. 'We were thinking of a light whipping,' she said, 'Philipe and I. Have you any other suggestions?'

The gaoler shook his long greasy and tangled locks. 'Whipping, no matter how light, can damage a property,' he said. 'I have some fine chains here which might suit your purpose better.'

59

Grace heard the sound of fine metal upon metal.

'Perhaps you might wish to suspend her as I lash the other prisoner.' The gaoler had his eyes upon Grace's body as he spoke, but he handed a tangle of fine chains to madame. 'These hold the legs fully apart, while these stretch the wrists to a hook in the roof of the chamber.'

Grace felt, in her mind, the renewed tension upon her thighs and wrists and shuddered as she imagined her breasts again pulled so taut that the skin might burst.

Madame considered the matter, tapping her forefinger on her lower lip and eyeing Grace, who now stood, head bowed, awaiting madame's decision.

'Very well then,' said madame. 'Let us see how she looks in the chains. I am sure we shall not be disappointed.' She lifted Grace's chin and kissed the soft lips with her own full ones. 'It is for your own good.' Madame smiled. 'It is to make these...' she cupped the weight of Grace's breasts, 'firm and pert, and these...' she thumbed the hardening nipples, '*very* sensitive.' Grace felt her belly quiver. 'And this flat and taut,' added madame. With a sigh she handed her to the gaoler and indicated that the chains be wrapped about Grace's limbs.

The smooth-linked chains were wrapped about her wrists. They felt cool, almost soothing against her skin. A long loop dangled loosely over her belly and between her legs, brushing her mound like gentle fingers.

'Stop,' commanded madame.

'Something wrong?' asked Philipe, his eyes darting from Grace, whose head was bowed meekly, to madame. He was enjoying the sight of her full breasts pressed together by her bonds, and he could not keep the annoyance from his voice. 'What is it?'

'Bring the chain between her flesh lips,' said madame, lifting the loose end herself and allowing it to sway between Graces slightly parted thighs.

'Of course, madame,' agreed the gaoler. '*Naturellement*! Tight to part those pretty petals and stimulate the female bud.'

Grace tried to ignore the coarse face of the gaoler close to hers as he slung the chain between her thighs, and to ignore the rough fingers as he spun her round. The links of the chain were chill against her sex flesh. They made her shudder and she winced as they were pulled tighter, abrading her nubbin and driving into the soft moistness of the folds.

'*Très jolie*!' murmured madame, testing the tightness of the chain at Grace's belly and buttocks. 'Very pretty. Don't you think so, Philipe?'

'Indeed,' agreed the young man, his eyes shining with lust. '*Absolument*!'

The gaoler knelt at her feet to coil more chains about her ankles and a bar to keep her legs stretched wide apart. Grace felt the heat of his breath against her bound pussy. She felt her face burn with shame as he nuzzled his nose into the chained valley of her flesh pot.

'Up, up now,' ordered madame. 'Pull her up just a little from the floor, and let us see just how submissive we can make her.'

The chains made frightening clanking noises and Grace felt her body stretched once more, her limbs pulled unnaturally and the smooth links pressed deeply into her moist heat.

Bound once more, Grace found herself staring wistfully into the eyes of the footman. He seemed resigned to what was to come, even happy. His wide lips were curved in a smile, parted as if ready for a kiss. She could see the tension in the muscles of his arms, the heave of his broad chest. Her eyes were drawn to the arch of his cock, still turgid despite its release moments earlier. A pearl of semen still hovered at the swollen bulb, glinting in the flickering light of the sconces.

'Turn him round, gaoler,' ordered Philipe. 'His grinning face is insolent.'

Grace, in the fine but strong chains, her legs thrust

wide apart and her arms shackled to the ceiling of the cave-like dungeon, felt bereft of the man's companionship when she could no longer see his face. His broad shoulders, narrow waist, and muscular buttocks, were small compensation.

'Get on with it,' Philipe, as always, was impatient.

'Yes, sire. I think you'll find the lash I've chosen more than adequate for the task.' The gaoler, sweating with his considerable duties that evening, held up a long and rigid leather handle, attached to which were several fine chains into which were slotted sharp pieces of metal.

Grace could not help but let out a gasp of horror. She tugged on the chains that held her to the ceiling, making her bonds tinkle angrily and the links drive into her flesh. She felt her breasts move against her upper arms, brushing the nipples to hardness.

'Be still!' ordered madame. 'Or the gaoler will be forced to use the implement upon you.'

'Don't hurt her,' begged the footman, his voice muffled by the post to which he was tied. 'Flay my flesh from my bones, but don't hurt her.'

Madame chuckled. 'It shall be as you say.'

The dank air whistled as the awful implement was brought down upon the footman's vulnerable back.

Chapter Four

'I think,' said madame, stroking Grace's naked body which lay, very still and languid, at the foot of her bed, 'it is time to allow the rest of the court to view you.'

The green eyes widened questioningly.

'You are so very pretty and your training is coming along nicely.'

Madame trailed her fingers across the dip of her charge's waist and up to the underswell of each breast.

Grace felt the need to part her legs.

'Exceedingly nicely,' added madame.

Grace could not help the flush that came to her cheeks.

'After all, you do not wish to spend the rest of your life cloistered in my chamber or... in the dungeons.' The slight pause before the mention of the last drew a shudder from Grace and brought back a recollection of the smell of blood, the lacerated body of the young footman.

'You are not ready, of course, to dance,' added madame, 'at the assemblies, but I think it only fair that we should allow them to see your beauty.'

The fingers drifted down to the curls upon Grace's mound and rested there, very lightly. 'Open your legs more,' madame whispered, 'and allow me to see the glories between your thighs.'

'Madame,' Grace began hesitantly.

'Oh, my darling,' madame interrupted huskily. 'Your skin is so delightfully pale and yet there is a ripeness about it which tempts one.' The woman tapped her lips with a thoughtful fingertip and frowned, her brow creased in thought. The frown was swiftly replaced with a smile. 'It is like a peach, ready to be plucked, sucked with lips and tickled with the very tips of a lash!' She shuddered at the delicious thought. Madame trailed her fingertips along the inner sides of Grace's thighs, merely brushing the midnight curls that were such a contrast to the moonstone skin of her legs.

Such was the increase in her sensuality brought about by the training of the last few weeks that Grace could not help but straddle her legs to their full extent, giving her mistress full access. She yearned to feel a man's cock, but still madame would not allow her maidenhead to be broken.

'You are so wet, my darling,' groaned her mistress, 'and your clitty is throbbing, darting from its hood in its eagerness, and such a colour! It darkens from pale peach to ruby and, finally, the deepest wine.'

Grace could not but help rock from side to side upon the tumbled bed, nestling her plump and rounded buttocks into the luxury of the fresh linen.

'Beautiful, my darling,' murmured madame, who was now crouched between Grace's straddled thighs.

The girl felt the caress of the woman's lips, brushing across the sap-moistened curls, and felt the warmth of breath upon the open fullness of her sex. The kisses were planted in the very centre of the slick and heated folds. Grace groaned and urged up, swaying the peak of her body back and forth upon madame's tongue and lips.

'I wish...' murmured Grace. The tongue lapped back and forth upon the tip of her pulsing clitty. 'I wish...' Such was her passion that Grace could scarcely speak.

Madame's face was flushed with desire, her mouth slick with virgin juices. She panted as she rose from the arch of Grace's buttocks. 'What is it, my darling?' She caressed the firm hillocks, playfully prising them apart. 'What else can I do to increase your pleasure?'

'Oh, madame...' Grace, too, was breathless. 'I wish I might know a man!'

Face thunderous, madame rose up, her ponderous breasts shaking with fury. With an open palm she slapped Grace's belly, making the pale skin flush with the force of the blow. She slapped the inner side of the thighs until they glowed scarlet.

'You lustful minx!'

Tears burned under Grace's eyelids, but still the warm feeling remained in her sex. The itch refused to go away from her pert clitty. Creamy juices beaded those same folds and gathered into a stream, which trickled down her bottom valley.

'Is this how you repay me for my hospitality – my training?' Madame slapped Grace's belly with her other hand. 'Is this how you repay me for training you in the manner of Rousseau... to be graceful, sensitive and sensual?'

'Perhaps, madame,' Grace began hesitantly, 'you have trained me too well.' The tears fell, hot and plump, down the pale cheeks. 'Perhaps my sensuality has gone beyond the bounds of reason.'

At the sight of Grace's tears, the soft and trembling lips, the passively open thighs between which nestled the open nest, madame's anger dissipated and her tongue flicked eagerly back and forth along the fleshy margins of her mouth.

'Do you really think so, my precious?' murmured madame huskily, and she trailed a finger down the full margin of one of Grace's breasts. The movement was slow, tender, caressing, leaving the lovely hillock ill-prepared for the spiteful finger smacking which followed.

'Well, I do not!' Madame's tone became swiftly harsh as the smacking became harder. Grace's buttocks were still raised from the tumbled linen and madame administered another sharp slap on the creamy bottom. 'I think you were a sensual little thing before ever Philipe and I picked you out of the filth of the Paris streets.'

Her lips trembled at the accusation and her eyes widened, but in the softness of her belly there was a melting which confirmed her sensuality. It was there always and becoming worse as each day passed. Grace shook her head in mute denial, whipping the midnight hair across her breasts.

'Oh, don't deny it!' Madame administered another slap to the raised buttocks, harder this time, making the flesh ripple and the skin become rosy with heat. 'I know it! Do you think my memory is so short that I have forgotten how we caught you in the footman's arms on the very verge of allowing him to *fuck* you?!' Madame bawled the crude word at Grace's face, making her shudder and quail. She tried to draw back from her tormentor but she was held fast with hands like vices upon the smooth slopes of her shoulders.

'To penetrate you,' continued madame, grating out the

words through gritted teeth, 'with his turgid cock, breaking the tight and beautiful gateway of your maidenhead?'

'I did not mean...' attempted Grace, not daring to wriggle in the cruel grip.

'No excuses! Turn over!'

At that moment there was a frantic knocking at the door. 'Oh, madame. Come quickly. It is *le duc*. He needs you urgently!'

Madame's hands froze on Grace's body. Her eyes became wide with fear. 'What? What has happened to Philipe?' she shouted through the closed chamber door. 'Has the palace been stormed by *les paysans*?' She jumped from the bed and dragged on her peignoir, a gossamer fine garment which revealed her heavy breasts and the inviting swell of her belly as much as it hid them.

Grace huddled on the bed on her knees, her breasts heavy and hanging loose, smarting from the finger smacks.

'Wait there,' ordered madame, not bothering to close her gown. 'Do not move.' Her eyes burned fiercely as she looked at Grace over her shoulder.

'*Oui*, madame,' said Grace meekly. Her arms ached as she supported her upper body by them, and she shuddered as the heavy door banged shut behind madame. She wondered what could have happened to Philipe, not that he had ever endeared himself to her.

Almost immediately the door opened very quietly on oiled hinges and she heard the click of the lock as the key was turned. Grace lifted her head, thinking madame had returned. 'Philipe?' she murmured in surprise. 'Madame thought...'

The handsome features twisted in a cruel smile. 'I sent the message,' he said, his voice thick with lust. 'I wanted you alone. She never lets me play with you, and she promised.'

He sounded like a petulant child rather than the

handsome grown man he was. In his hands he carried a coarse rope, some fine silk scarves and something which made Grace shudder, although she scarcely knew why.

He laughed. 'You wonder what I have for you, eh?' He shook his treasures as he approached the bed where she knelt. He laughed again. 'You will find out soon enough, my pretty, and you will enjoy it just as I do. But first I just want to play with you, touch you, kiss you in all those inviting places she keeps from me.' He threw the rope and silk scarves on the bed, but knelt in front of Grace, pushing the strange implement into her face. 'Isn't it beautiful?'

Grace felt the cold of the tempered iron struts on her hot cheeks.

'The scold's bridle,' he said huskily. 'Do you know what it's for?'

She shook her head, not daring to even think what Philipe had in mind. His free hand cupped one of her breasts, which still hung, soft and loose. He tossed the bridle on the bed and sniggered. 'Well, you'll find out soon enough.'

'Madame was worried about you,' said Grace. 'You should not have frightened her so.'

Rage suffused Philipe's face. 'You dare to tell me what I can and cannot do? You? A *putain* dragged from the streets?'

The insult made tears fill Grace's dark eyes, but this did not make Philipe any more tender. He threw her on her back, pushing her thighs open with his knees. He wore a flamboyant satin suit much decorated with lace and ribbons, and the tight breeches bulged lewdly at his crotch.

He leaned over her to reach for the rope and she felt his thickness, covered only by the fine satin, rub against her open sex pouch. Grace experienced that need again in her belly; the skin fluttered against him, a heat she was sure he could also feel, and she felt her sap flow.

'You will enjoy this rope, I know,' he said huskily, and she felt him slip its scratchy thickness about her waist. He looked into her eyes as he slung the rope around her belly and tugged it tight, knotting it in such a way that it made her flesh swell over the knot which pressed into her just above the neat triangle of blue-black hair.

She heard his strained breathing and saw his hands release the panel of his breeches. The knot was placed at the very point beneath which the first excitement comes to a woman. The tickling coarseness of the rope prickled her skin, and Philipe slid down to nestle his ball sac in the soft wetness of her open sex, and his cock speared up from her parted sex lips. He brushed her nipples roughly with his fingers, which increased the feeling within her belly. Her eyes were drawn to his cock, its thickness, the veins throbbing and the globe bulging from the skin stretched in folds beneath it.

'Touch it,' he said hoarsely. 'Gently. Slide your fingers up and down. Slowly.' The words were spoken haltingly, as though he could barely summon breath to speak them.

Fearing punishment, Grace reached out with both hands, her fingers trembling so that their tips palpated his cockstem. She heard him sigh, saw him throw his head back in ecstasy, and she wondered when he would use her. With madame gone from the room and the door locked, her thighs pushed wide and aching, the rope pressing into her belly, she stood little chance against Philipe's invasion.

'You are rubbing too hard,' he said suddenly, his eyes blazing. He smacked her breasts, first one and then the other, and Grace could not help but whimper.

He bent and kissed each quivering breast, sucking as if he hoped to draw sweet milk from their heaviness. 'I did not mean to hurt you,' he said tenderly. 'It's just that I want our pleasure to be long.' He pressed the knot of the rope into her belly and swayed his ball sac into her wetness. 'But I doubt my patience,' he said, his voice hardening once more. 'I want to see you in the scold's bridle, tied with my silken bonds.' He closed his eyes and his fingers played with his throbbing thickness. He said nothing for some moments, and Grace wondered if he had drifted into a doze or a dream.

'Quickly now!' he said suddenly. His hands released his cock and he fumbled with the tight knot at her belly, becoming impatient when it did not release immediately. At last it was free and he tugged it roughly from her. It burned her skin, leaving a raised red weal as, unknotted, it was slid from beneath her and she gave a little squeal, not so much of pain, but of surprise.

'Be quiet, you little fool,' he said sharply, giving her breasts a light slap and watching pleasurably as the flesh quivered. 'Do you want madame to find us? Don't you want to feel my cock breaking your maidenhead?'

The question made her draw breath quickly. It was as if he had listened to the conversation that took place earlier with madame. Her belly rippled and she looked with longing at Philipe's cock.

He laughed and edged further up her belly until he sat at the deep dip of her waist. The tip of his cock gleamed with pre-issue and he squirmed on the smoothness of her flesh, thrusting his cockstem further towards her mouth. 'I know you do,' he said, answering his own question. 'Do you think I don't know how you loved it filling your mouth?' He nodded as he looked into the honeyed darkness of her eyes. 'Yes, and you will love it within your flesh pot all the more. But first...' He reached behind her and, as she raised her eyes, Grace saw the silk ties rippling in his hands. 'Throw your arms above your head... spread them wide. Wider... higher.' He leaned over her and the tip of his cock brushed her lips. She could taste its salt, the intriguing bitterness as she meekly lapped it with the very tip of her tongue.

The silk was wrapped around each wrist; smooth, cool, but cruelly tight, pulling at her arms, stretching them just as she was stretched on the rack. She sucked in her belly, as if this would ease the tension.

'There,' he said, pride in his eyes. 'Doesn't that feel delicious? I love it when madame does it to me. Love it!'

He slid down between her thighs, taking a moment to gaze at her open flesh pot and drift the silk over her mound, causing a tickle amid the jet-black curls and making Grace squirm her buttocks from side to side. He chuckled and slowly pushed the silk ties between her sex lips, bunching the soft cloth about her nubbin. Satisfied, he closed the love lips over the ball of silk. Grace felt her cheeks flush with shame as her nubbin twitched pleasurably against the intrusion. He chuckled again and spread her sex lips, pulling the lengths of silk from the wet cup of her pouch.

'Soaking,' he remarked. 'Saturated,' and he waved the wet silk under Grace's nose. 'Do you see, you naughty little thing, how easily I excite you? You are on the very verge of your pleasure. Can you not smell your musk?'

Grace said nothing. Yes, indeed. She knew her musk was strong. It excited her beyond bearing. It caused the sensation of melting at the very point where the knot of rope had pressed.

'I know you can.' He forced open her mouth with finger and thumb and laid a short length of silk upon her tongue. 'Taste,' he purred. 'Taste your naughty, shameful juices. Is that any way for a virgin to behave?' He drew the length of silk from between her lips, drawing it across his nostrils, giving a sigh as if he sniffed the sweetest of perfume.

'Madame taught me...' began Grace.

'Indeed she did!' chuckled Philipe, and knelt with his back to her, spreading her legs to their fullest extent across the wide bed. She felt the damp silk lengths wrapped about her ankles and tied tightly to the carved oak bedposts. 'And now I shall teach you the most glorious pleasure created for man,' he added, shuffling round on his knees to face her.

'Helpless, my precious,' he murmured, looking at her with a proud expression on his features. 'How does it feel?'

It felt no worse than all the other times she had been bound. Perhaps, if anything, more comfortable lying on the feather-filled mattress rather than splayed at the bed end.

Philipe was hurriedly tearing off his clothes and Grace found her belly shivering with need of his body.

'Tell me!' he rapped. He leapt back onto the bed and settled himself between her thighs, his cock swaying, thick and upright, before her eyes.

'It is good,' said Grace meekly as he held the scold's bridle above her head, like a religious icon to which he paid homage. She licked her lips, dry with apprehension, and her eyes ached from staring at the strange contraption.

'Lift your head,' he ordered, his voice husky and low. He leaned over her, his cock brushing between her breasts, and she felt the hardness of the iron struts against her head and already felt the helplessness caused by the bridle. She tried to resist as her tongue was pressed down by a backward extension of the iron struts.

He sat back on his heels, smiling at her and his handiwork. 'You are so very beautiful, and now you will be mine. You can do nothing as I suckle these...' His lips closed about her nipples, taking each in turn into the warm wetness of his mouth. Grace could do nothing as delight swirled in her belly. 'And this...' He slid down between her legs, his hair tickling her sex lips. He placed his palms flat against the taut skin of her inner thighs as if he desired to push them ever further apart. 'This salted little bud between your sex lips...'

Grace would have done anything to murmur her pleasure, but her tongue was held fast as his flickered rapidly over her nubbin, making it arch up and become

71

bone hard. It jumped like a tiny cock and she wanted to hide her head in shame at the luscious beauty, the lewd feelings within her belly created by Philipe's tongue. But how could she hide her head when it was caged in iron and her hands were spread and tied high above her head?

He lifted his head, just a little, and peeped at her over the silken jet of her pussy curls. She noticed his face was smeared with her shimmering sap, and he lapped at the spillage with his tongue tip.

'Hm, you taste delicious,' he murmured, 'and you are so wet, so ready for me. Do you know that, my darling?'

Grace tried to shake her head, but the iron bridle held her neck still. It was not that she did not know of her wetness, for she could feel her sap seeping warmly down her thighs. She tried to shake her head in fear that, at any moment, madame would return and then they would both be punished. The palace seemed ominously quiet, like the gardens before a storm.

'Are you ready, my darling?' asked Philipe. 'Ready for me?'

She could feel his body, slender and muscular, between her thighs, lithe and supple, sliding upwards. She could smell her own musk on his lips and taste it as he probed her tongue through the struts of the bridle, pushing it into her imprisoned mouth. Her flesh quavered as she felt his thickness between her sex lips, the globe resting in the cup of her pouch. If her limbs had been free to do so she would have trembled with the forbidden excitement. She was on the very brink of fulfilling the need she voiced to madame.

'It is now, my darling,' he murmured, and she felt him draw back for the thrust.

At that very moment the heavy door was burst open and several attendants stood with their arms wrapped about a tree trunk, which they used as a battering ram.

'You wicked fellow!' Madame's voice was shrill with anger.

Philipe, his cock pumping his issue, rolled from Grace and she felt a splash of it upon her breasts.

'You!' Madame turned upon the servants. 'Get out!'

Grace closed her eyes with shame as she saw them craning their necks to peer between her outspread thighs and at the bonds which held them open.

'And how am I to deal with you both?' Madame's voice was sorrowful. She marched to the bed and smacked Grace's breasts and belly before pinching her flesh leaves and patting the very tip of her nubbin. 'Did you?' she asked, turning to Philipe, and she slapped his cock. 'With this wicked thing?'

'You didn't give me chance.' Philipe began to shrug into his clothes. 'You promised me that I could play with her and—'

'Play, of course,' said madame, turning again to Grace and peering suspiciously between her sex lips, at the creamy meltings which lay like pearls on the flushed skin and at the hardened nubbin. 'But I warned you...' She rounded on him. 'Get out until I decide what to do with you.'

Philipe, wearing only his breeches and white silk hose gave her a thin-lipped, leering smile. 'I need punishment, madame,' he said, his voice husky and thick.

Her back to him, madame caressed the swell of Grace's breasts, pushing them inwards until they formed a creamy valley. She kissed the place, running her tongue tip up and down the vale as if she caressed smooth, hairless sex lips. The feeling was sensual to Grace, especially in her helpless state.

'I need it, madame,' repeated Philipe. 'Severe punishment.' His feverish eyes turned to Grace and, between the struts of the fiendish contraption on her head, she saw him looking at her bonds and the bridle with outright envy.

Her eyes still averted from Philipe, madame slipped off her peignoir and stood, magnificent in her nudity, wearing only a silken cord about her waist which hung in a heavy tassel to her sex mound. At every movement Grace noticed this swayed inward to tickle her flesh lips.

'And you shall have it, Philipe,' said madame with a thin smile. 'Do you remember how we hung Grace upon the frame to admire her as we made love?'

Philipe's face paled to grey, but Grace noticed how the satin of his breeches bulged.

'And to increase the punishment,' said madame, her words cooing softly, 'we shall remove the bridle from Grace and place it on...'

'Me!' interrupted Philipe, his face glowing with pleasure.

'*Oui*!' snapped madame. 'But as an additional punishment you must wait for this. I must continue Grace's training which you interrupted so rudely.'

'But...' Philipe rubbed the lewdly bulging satin and looked at Grace with fury in his pale eyes.

'No buts!' snapped madame. 'Go until I send for you and don't ever dare play such a trick upon me again!' The tassel swung violently back and forth between her thighs as she pushed the young duke from the chamber.

'At last,' she sighed, slipping the silk cord from her waist and using it to fasten the broken door. 'We must not be disturbed.'

Grace wanted to ask what punishment was in store for her, but with the bridle still in place, this was impossible. Her belly quaked at the thought, but madame was surprisingly gentle as she unfastened the silk bindings.

Chapter Five

'Did he smack you?' asked madame, as she eased the iron bridle from Grace's head.

Tongue dry and swollen by its long confinement, it was

74

some moments before Grace could speak.

'I believe he did,' continued madame. 'Here, and here.' She touched Grace's breasts and the delicate rise of her belly with her fingertips. 'But this is what I am really concerned about.' With fingers and thumb she spread the flesh leaves and stroked the silky inner skin, paying special attention to the pert nubbin, pinching it until Grace made a little murmur. 'And this...' With the pad of her middle finger she circled the still closed opening, making Grace shiver with a delight which was tinged with fear. Madame shook her head and tapped the swollen flesh leaves from side to side. 'There is still much training to be done before you are ready to be plunged by all and sundry. There are many pleasures I must teach you.'

This was said in such a way that Grace could not help the shiver which made her belly ripple.

'Turn over, my precious,' said madame, tapping the side-swells of Grace's buttocks. 'Bottom nicely raised, knees tucked beneath your breasts, but thighs open.' Madame's voice was soft as she gave these new instructions.

The contortion would have been difficult had Grace been anything but supple. Her soft breasts were moulded like clay by the hardness of her knees and the butting made the nipples become painfully erect, but she scarcely had time to be aware of these discomforts before strong fingers grasped each flushed bottom cheek.

'It is time, my darling,' whispered madame, bending low over Grace so that her ponderous breasts brushed the girl's smooth back, 'for you to become aware of another pleasurable orifice rather than that which Philipe tried to enter.'

Grace said nothing, not daring to move in case the vice-like fingers tore the trim buttocks from her neat bones. She felt the hillocks being spread wide and knew her mistress could see the tight pleats of her bottom hole. The

75

thought made her blush to the roots of her tumbled hair. She also knew, because her buttocks were lifted high, that madame could see every detail of her sex purse; could see the parted plumpness of her sex leaves, the erect hardness of her clitty, and the creamy gateway of her female opening, and these thoughts made her shiver with renewed humiliation.

'And knowing you as I have come to do,' madame whispered joyfully, 'you will enjoy every moment of this new knowledge.'

Face buried in the bed linen, Grace trembled at the thought of what this new torture could possibly be. No, she told herself, it was not torture. She had to admit that she enjoyed the wonderful feelings of sensuality madame gave her with her probing and stroking.

'But first I must make your bottom wonderfully ready for what is to come.' Madame eased her grip upon her bottom cheeks. Grace allowed herself a tiny sigh of relief, but the relief was short-lived. The room, large and opulent, suddenly echoed with the sound of slaps, delivered so rapidly that Grace did not have a chance to object or cry out. Her buttocks quickly began to feel as if they were on fire, and she knew the pale skin was no longer pale, but scarlet and swollen, raised from its original smooth line. What was worse, far worse, was the swift reaction of her sex folds, which swiftly became newly bathed in her juices and pouting open to reveal her swollen clitty.

The slapping slowed and Grace could hear madame's harsh and rapid breathing. She heard the rustle of linen as her mistress relaxed and sat back to rest from her exertions.

'Don't move, my darling,' ordered madame, 'or I shall be forced to continue where I left off.'

Crouching very still, Grace wished for a poultice of ice to be placed upon her raised and burning bottom, but yet again the pleasurable surging within her belly and between the puffy folds of her sex were something she hugged to her, like a lover.

'And now, my precious,' purred madame, as her breathing eased, 'the next stage of your training.'

Tense, waiting, Grace tried to prepare herself. There was nothing she could do. It was as if some invisible silken ropes bound her. She dared not move, or perhaps, did not wish to.

A wet warmth touched the tightness of Grace's bottom hole, caressed it, touched it so lightly that it was as soft as swansdown.

'You see,' crowed madame, 'I knew you would delight in it, you darling sensualist!'

The touch came again, harder this time, and wetter, and Grace realised it was madame's tongue. It was such a contrast to the hard slaps administered moments earlier, that Grace found her body becoming deliciously heavy, melting into the linen and the feather mattress beneath her.

'Can you feel your bottom becoming open and ready?' murmured madame, between the laps of her tongue.

A ripple of pleasure tore through Grace. She felt the sensation begin in the pit of her stomach. It ripped through the swollen bud of her clitoris and surged in a great whirlpool of pleasure through her whole body.

'Oh, my darling girl.' Madame breathed her ecstasy over Grace's beaten, hot buttocks. 'Such an orgasm and I scarcely titillated your little bottom hole. Just a lap of the tongue, and certainly no penetration. Delicious! I knew you were a naturally sensual girl. I knew it! You delight in everything I do to you. Perfection! Sheer perfection!'

Grace continued to hide her face in shame, her cheeks burning as hotly as her bottom. But despite her shame she could not help but be proud of the achievement described by madame.

'Now I wonder what will happen when...' Grace's mistress paused and the girl felt her buttocks being stroked in a wonderfully loving manner, but she could not push away the apprehension, the thought of what might happen next. Her flesh pot and bottom hole were still pulsing from the last orgasm, and trickles of creamy issue spilled from her.

The long wet tongue snaked out and lapped at Grace, sipping the spillage and smearing it liberally about the sucking bottom hole. Only seconds later Grace began to feel an even more erotic sensation. The tiny opening was caressed by the stiffened tongue tip until it slipped inside the tight, dark tunnel. She gasped but did not try to pull away. It was a gentle, pleasant sensation and she bore back upon it, urging the tongue to penetrate deep inside her.

'And still there is more pleasure to come, my lovely,' whispered madame, relinquishing the pulsing little opening just for a moment.

Unable to help herself, Grace butted back and forth into the linen, arching her buttocks into the air and spreading her thighs to their fullest extent.

Fingers stroked the soft wet folds of her sex purse and pulled them first wide apart and then close together while the tongue tip probed open the tightly wrinkled orifice. Grace felt the fingers rub back and forth across the creamy peak of her raw and exposed nubbin. She felt the first ripple of pleasure she had come to know was called an orgasm. It was far more intense than any she felt at her own hands in the dark lonely hours of night in her mother's hovel.

The pleasure swirled in her belly and she was not sure whether its source was her bottom hole, so fully and deeply penetrated by the tongue that slipped back and forth, or the fingers that danced over the sensitive tip of her nubbin. She knew her sex folds were creamily lubricated, and there was a need within them that she desperately needed to be fulfilled.

Grace raised her head, gasping for breath, a light film

of perspiration giving her pale body a glowing sheen. Lips parted, she mewed with delight, and the mew grew to a long drawn out moan as each wave of pleasure hit her more strongly.

'My lovely, sensual beauty!' Madame wrapped her arms about Grace's shuddering body, caressing the delicious breasts that seemed to pulse in the woman's kneading hands with a rhythm similar to the pulse of orgasm.

'I have never known a girl who is so passive and so pliant,' whispered madame, 'and yet so sensual.'

Sleep claimed Grace, the languid doze of restitution. The long jet lashes fluttered to brush the pale cheeks and she lay against the cushion of madame's naked breasts.

She did not know how long she slept. Perhaps only moments, or maybe hours, but Grace woke refreshed.

'Ah, Sleeping Beauty returns to me,' cried madame, who was dressed in her translucent peignoir which drifted like gossamer about the opulent curves of her naked body as she hurried over to the bed where Grace lay.

A sleepy smile raised the corners of Grace's parted lips, and she stretched her arms high and pushed her slender legs apart.

'Ever the sensualist,' said madame, her eyes darting to the open slit of Grace's sex.

Grace, suddenly awake, curved her back and huddled her knees to the softness of her breasts.

'No, don't you dare hide your pouch from me.' A frown made the mistress's features dark and angry as Grace tensed and opened her limbs, but cupped her hands about her mound, again trying to hide the cream-slicked folds. 'Don't you dare.'

The pleasant languid feeling with which Grace awoke was dispelled and was replaced by a flush of embarrassment, a renewed sense of humiliation. Obediently, she spread her thighs, lifting them a little to make her sex yet more vulnerable, shutting out the feeling of shame.

Madame gave a sigh of pleasure and bent her head over Grace's belly. 'That's how I like to see my girl; open and ready, gloriously moist and pert.'

Warm breath whispered over Grace's puffy slit and she arched up, offering her moist sex and erect nubbin to her mistress. She heard madame whisper sounds of appreciation and felt the ripple of pleasure that preceded her climax. Her lips pursed, forming a perfect O, a mew of need.

'*Oui*, ma cherie,' murmured madame against her fluttering sex, 'come for me. Come again and again. Let you little fountain bubble upon my eager tongue.'

Arching her belly, Grace pressed her open folds against madame's mouth. She felt a tongue smear silky fluids from the still-closed gateway of her sex, to the jerking hardness of her clitty. She felt the tongue fold back the little hood to bare the most sensitive tip, which it then flicked back and forth until Grace could not help but emit a tiny scream. The pleasure was so intense it was almost unbearable...

The magic of that moment between the two women was shattered by the angry crash of the chamber door, already damaged by the battering ram, being smashed open violently.

'You promised you would punish me and I find you playing with our little toy again!' shrilled Philipe. 'I want to be punished. I did wrong to try and take her. Punish me!' He threw himself towards madame.

Grace cried out with fear and huddled at the top of the bed, a bundle of linen held close to her trembling breasts. Philipe's angry and pleading eyes darted between madame's voluptuousness and the juices that beaded her smiling lips.

'Only after I have trained her,' madame reminded him, 'and there are still many stages before she is ready to be turned over to you.' She pursed her lips in anger. 'And it seems to me that I have much to do in training you!' She shook her head in frustration. 'Even when she is ready you do not deserve her maidenhead.'

Ignoring Philipe, madame rubbed the heel of her hand very slowly into Grace's sex flesh. The folds slipped open, separating and baring the swelling bud, which popped from its little sheath, shining with fluids. Again the girl moaned; her breathing changed, quick and shallow.

Philipe's hands were clenched by his sides, his eyes glazed with lust, his satin breeches bulging lewdly. Mutely he pleaded with madame, but Grace could not discern whether the plea was for the punishment he craved or for another attempt to pierce the virgin gateway.

Grace, herself, moaned softly, that same yearning within the little swell of her belly, and she made a shuddering movement towards him. Sinuously, she crawled in his direction, reaching up with one pale hand, making her own plea. One breast escaped the folds of the bed sheets and the memory of his cock between her thighs was very clear and poignant in her mind.

'Stop that at once!' rapped madame. 'You naughty pair. Strip, Philipe! Immediately!'

His eyes darting from Grace to his mistress and his sensuous lips moist with spittle, the young aristo did as he was bid. His cockstem sprang from his breeches and Grace, unable to contain her hunger, again reached out with a need to caress the handsome organ.

Madame, muscles rippling with her superior strength, lifted Philipe into the frame at the bed end. 'Hold there,' she ordered, 'until I tie you.'

Philipe stood, arms and legs splayed within the frame, smiling down at Grace, his cock splendidly erect. 'Let me smell Grace's juices,' he said as madame began to wrap the silk ties about his wrists, 'before you bind me.'

Grace hid her head in shame in the tumble of linen, but

peeped up with one eye, to watch as the silk was waved under Philipe's nose. She saw his cock arch with pleasure, saw the little skirt of skin roll back further down the globe and saw the gleam of a bead of juice at the pore.

'Are you ready to be bound now?' asked madame, her tone dripping with sarcasm.

'Quite ready,' answered Philipe.

Grace saw Philipe's lean body jerk as madame tied his wrists to the frame. She saw his toes curl as his ankles were tied, his stem thrust forward in an involuntary movement, and his ball sac draw up with pleasure as the binding was completed.

She sat up, allowing the linen to fall from her breasts. She felt her nubbin pulse and allowed her tongue to moisten her lips at the thought of kissing the salty pinnacle of his upright length.

'I think, young woman, you need something between your thighs,' snapped madame, as if she knew what Grace was thinking and feeling. She took a small satin cushion from a night table and spread the girl's love lips to the full before inserting a smooth and oval pillow. The lips were then closed about it and Grace felt her tip jerk spasmodically.

'Bear down,' ordered madame, 'and keep those thighs spread.'

The sight of Philipe bound in the frame with his cock throbbing into the empty air, and the cushion between her flesh lips, brought tears to Grace's eyes. She began to sob in earnest as she saw madame begin the business of placing his head into the scold's bridle although, as it was fitted about his neat skull, he managed a murmur of pleasure.

'You look so delicious, the pair of you,' said madame, with a broad smile. 'I could just lie here admiring you the whole night.' She threw herself upon the bed, behind Grace, and splayed her knees to cosset her own pleasure place.

Grace tried to close her thighs, but this only made the little pillow press harder upon her burning clitty, and she got a resounding smack on the buttocks for her pains.

'Bear down upon the pillow,' ordered madame, 'and keep those knees fully open.' She sighed as if her world was full of troubles as well as pleasures. She looked up at Philipe.

'Isn't she the most sensual creature?' she murmured, speaking of Grace. 'The little minx enjoyed to the full the tongue and finger placed in her bottom hole. It is time to...' Madame was breathing heavily, and her fingers flashed between her full love lips.

Grace could not help rocking back and forth upon the little pillow, and she felt her nubbin tap again and again on the satin. She felt her pleasure rising. She saw Philipe's cock give a final throb and the veins pulse about the stem. A stream of semen gushed in precious fountains, spurting upon her heaving breasts and belly.

'Time to introduce her to Zeus,' madame finished huskily as she regained her breath and her body calmed from its orgasm. 'What do you think of that, Philipe?'

Grace frowned in puzzlement. Zeus? Philipe could not speak because of the metal that held down his tongue, but beyond the struts she could see his eyes become hooded and his mouth curve about the iron in a grimace of pleasure.

'Yes, Zeus, my pretty loves,' added madame. She nodded and sat up, palpating her heavy breasts. Her mound, between her spread thighs, covered in golden curls, shone with her own dew. 'Doesn't the thought almost make you faint clean away with pleasure?'

Again Grace tried to close her own thighs but was smacked at belly and breasts. 'Open!' rapped madame. 'Always open. And bear down upon that pillow. Enjoy its softness while you can, because there will be something far harder and chillier between those thighs before very much longer.'

A muffled chuckle came from the mask, and she saw the cock begin to fill again, the veins to throb.

Madame bent over Grace and rubbed the spillage from Philipe in sensuous circles around the swell of her belly. The movements were hypnotic, and Grace felt herself bear down upon the circling hand and rock harder upon the satin pillow. 'Good,' breathed madame. 'Excellent, my dear. Do you not think so, Philipe?' But she smiled. 'What a shame you cannot agree with me. But we shall talk later when I decide your punishment is over.

'You must be hungry, my dear,' she said, turning again to Grace. The soothing massage slowed and Grace nodded. Before she could protest she was pulled from the bed, quite roughly, and her body was swept into madame's strong arms, cradled against the enveloping cushion of her breasts. 'We shall use fresh cords and I shall bind you, my sweet. On different occasions it is a task I give to Philipe, but...' She smiled up at the young aristo. 'As you see, he is otherwise engaged.'

From the night table madame brought silk cords, brilliant in their whiteness, and ordered Grace to kneel on the floor.

The girl felt the tiny pillow fall wetly from her sex lips and saw, to her shame, a string of silvery juice follow from her depths. Subservient as she had learned to be, she placed her hands behind her back and, with a glance up at madame, spread her thighs to the full and tucked her heels into her bottom crease. She felt the cords wrapped tightly about her wrists, making her hands and arms quite helpless.

How could she eat, she wondered, when she was bound? She peeped up beneath the dark curtain of her hair, the question in her eyes. It was answered immediately.

A maid entered the room. The girl was pretty and dressed very demurely in black silk and a starched white pinafore and cap. Her style of dress made Grace more than ever aware of her own nakedness, and she hid her burning face in her fall of hair. She tried to slip her bound hands over her bottom to hide the parted and intimate slit, but the maid ignored her, much as she would ignore a pet dog or cat. She ignored Philipe, his head encased in the bridle and his cock stiff, upright and dripping, as she would a painting or a statue.

She set down a tray and Grace felt saliva enter her mouth as she smelled hot food. Madame picked up a steaming bowl and sniffed it, but made a wry face.

'I hate gruel,' she said, but she set it down before Grace and waved the dish under her nose, 'but no doubt peasant girls such as you will find it wholesome.'

Grace stretched her neck, sniffing the air, realising just how hungry she was. The bowl of creamy food was set just out of reach, and how could she use a spoon with her wrists bound so tightly behind her back?

'Like a little puppy, my darling,' said madame, answering Grace's silent question. 'With your sweet and agile tongue and those soft lips which can do such delightful things to both men and woman.' She turned to Philipe and reached up to polish his globe, rubbing the smooth tip until it shone with the repeated exudations he could not seem to stop.

Behind the mask his eyes were glazed with pleasure, bulging in their effort to look down at Grace's buttocks spread by the splay of her knees and thighs. Grace bowed her head, her silky mane falling about her breasts and almost touching the steaming bowl of creamy gruel.

'Madame...' she ventured meekly, raising her eyes.

'Eat, girl, eat!' The mistress stopped playing with Philipe's cock and opened the lush curls on her own sex lips, exposing the flushed folds between them.

Shoulders trembling, Grace bowed over the gruel. Blue-black tresses trailed in the creamy food.

'What are you waiting for?' snapped madame, petting

the tip of her clitty.

Grace tried to toss her hair behind her shoulders, but succeeded only in flicking the upper swells of her breasts with the hot mixture and painting her ruby nipples with the spills.

'I am sure you wish to know about Zeus, my precious,' said madame, her finger busy between her flesh lips.

Nodding, Grace looked up at her gratefully, before trying once more to lap at the warm gruel in the bowl. This time she succeeded in scooping up the creamy food, but her lips, cheeks and chin became smeared with excess.

'Look up, my precious,' ordered madame huskily, prising open the sex lips to expose her hugely erect clitty.

Suffering the pangs of terrible humiliation, feeling helpless and vulnerable in her bonds, Grace lifted her head, her eyes wide, pleading for mercy.

'How sweet,' responded her mistress, slicking her juice soaked fingers in and out of the pulsing slit of her sex. 'Look, Philipe. Her pretty face is spread with cream just as her bottom hole must be when she is presented to Zeus.'

Beneath the coating of gruel Grace could feel her cheeks become fiery red. Her shoulders ached, pulled back by the tightness of her bindings, and her breasts felt stretched beyond bearing, thrust forward as they were. But somehow these discomforts were nothing to the feeling of fullness in her sex pouch, the dribble of juices down her thighs and the itching of her clitty. If those could just be appeased, by no matter what means, she would be content.

'Zeus,' explained madame, 'is the king of the Roman gods, and we have a statue of him in one of the main corridors of the palace.' She leaned back upon her pillows and closed her eyes. 'It is a splendid piece of statuary.' She used a hand to describe its magnificence, a spearing rod from the groin. The size she intimated made

Grace shudder.

'Eat, or must I force you?' Madame noticed that Grace had raised her head, and her face was flushed with anger. She splayed her thighs further and her fingers flashed over the gleaming flesh beneath them as if this calmed her troubled mind.

Grace hesitated a moment too long. Madame leapt from the bed, her face darker than ever. Fingers slick with female juices were dipped into the gruel and Grace felt them force into her mouth.

'You must eat,' urged madame, but her voice was no longer rough with anger, but soft and caressing. 'Suck, my darling. Suck as though you sip milk from a nipple.'

Grace obediently pursed her lips about the fingertips. She could smell the faint tang of female juices, collected as madame pleasured herself, but with her hunger pangs as strong as they were, the taste could have been some delicate sauce prepared by one of the palace chefs.

Chapter Six

The statue of Zeus sat upon a gilt throne in the most gracious corridor in the palace of Versailles. A crown of laurel leaves on his head denoted his place among the gods, and a sceptre in his right hand announced him king.

He was naked, carved from the finest and most unblemished marble imported from the Italian peninsula. But the most notable of all his features was his penis, which was upright and magnificent, smooth as silk, darkened to a livid flesh colour by some secret means of the artist who fashioned the statue. The circumcised globe was bloated, ready to open any delicate orifice to which it was presented. It gleamed wetly in the glow given by the hundreds of candles burning in the chandelier suspended above him. Behind him was a huge gilt-framed mirror, and its twin was suspended on the opposite wall of the corridor, reflecting the massive and sensual image an infinite number of times.

Such was the splendour of Zeus that many ladies, their rustling silk dresses lifted high above their knees, curtsied prettily before him, being sure to prolong the bob so that their dainty heels petted their naked flesh pots as they paid homage to the king of the gods. Some often had to be dragged, shuddering with orgasmic delight, from before the impassive statue.

'What do you think, my darling?' asked madame.

Grace held back, her helpless form shivering with apprehension as the great marble edifice came into view along the elegant corridor. She looked at madame, and tugged feebly against her iron-hard grip on her upper arms. She looked at Philipe, now released from his punishment, but looking sulky as he trailed after madame.

'At least let me...' he began. He wore nothing but a simple loincloth tucked tightly about his waist and slung neatly between his legs.

'No,' refused madame. 'I am still extremely cross with you. You may not penetrate her bottom hole with that rampant cock of yours. But my anger with you is becoming less; I just may have a treat for you.'

Philipe's features brightened. 'Really?' He began to strut after the two women, his step considerably lighter.

'Oh, come now,' whispered madame to Grace. 'It is a statue, my sweet. Nothing more than a statue. What is there to fear?' She caressed Grace, pulling her shuddering form to her and bending to kiss the upper swell of a breast, while her dimpled hand slipped between Grace's trembling thighs to pet the outer lips of her sex pouch.

In the mirrors the vision repeated back and forth. Grace saw her naked and captured form being caressed by madame's knowing fingers. She also saw Zeus, huge and inanimate, naked and ready to receive her in his spread lap.

88

'You are… sacrificing…?' she stammered. She tried to dig her heels into the floor, but it was polished to a glassy sheen by servants and by the hundreds of courtiers who walked the elegant passage every day.

'Your virginity, my darling?'

Grace nodded, feeling the cold wetness of the gruel sliding across the swell of her breasts as tendrils of hair brushed across them.

'Not at all,' madame assured her. Again the swell of her breast was kissed with passionate lips and the erect bud of her nipple was grazed with sharp white teeth.

'That is far too valuable,' added Philipe, driving his fingers into her arm as madame released her. He pulled her forward, shaking her until her breasts quivered and she hung her head in mute submission.

The pair stopped their teasing torment and continued to drag her along the wide and gracious passage. Stumbling, Grace was at last brought to a halt before Zeus and averted her eyes from the sight of the spearing cock, but not before she felt the flutter of pleasure between her thighs and the silky wetness smearing the inner folds of her cunt. 'No…' she murmured, pulling as hard as she could against the grips of her captors, but her denial sounded faint-hearted even to her own ears.

'Perhaps a smear of gruel upon his majesty?' suggested Philipe, thrusting the bowl forward. 'Would that please you more, my darling, to lick the concoction from the royal prick as you did mine?'

With tears beading her dark lashes Grace nodded. If only they would lead her back to the chamber, she thought. They could humiliate her all they wished if it were not in public. Under lowered lids she peeped shyly at the well-dressed ladies of the court who giggled at her behind their fans, and the gentlemen who appraised her willowy figure.

Chuckling, Philipe scooped up some gruel and smeared it liberally upon the huge cock, coating it with the thick white paste that steamed with heat and made the penis seem warm and alive.

Grace shivered and looked from one to the other of her captors.

'Doesn't that look delicious?' said madame.

'Delectable,' said Philipe, and he pushed Grace forward. 'Kneel, girl,' he ordered. 'Pay homage to Zeus!' He pushed her to her knees and Grace felt the hard chill of the polished floor. 'Embrace his majesty.'

A stealing, familiar heat rose up from between Grace's thighs. An unbearable itch centred upon her clitty and she felt it draw out from the fine skin of its enclosing hood.

The marble thighs of the statue seemed to draw her into a chilly embrace. Grace allowed her eyes, the dark verdant green warming to hazel, to flicker up to the upright cockstem which rose so magnificently from the heavy marble balls. The gruel slipped in creamy pearls down the shaft and Grace licked her lips.

'Go on, girl,' ordered madame. 'What are you waiting for? Suck his majesty.' She laughed, a low cruel chuckle. 'Legend has it that if a girl has sufficient talent with her lips Zeus will spurt his juices into her mouth.'

Grace shuffled closer into the marble embrace. She felt the hard fullness of the balls between her breasts and she swayed against them, feeling her nipples harden to tight nubs. She licked her lips, attempting to make them soft and loose. The marble cock was of magnificent girth and speared upwards into the candlelit gloom.

The sliminess of the gruel and her own spittle eased its passage into her straining throat. She managed to make the muscles relax to the full and the length slipped easily into her gullet.

'*Magnifique*!' Madame's voice was ecstatic and Grace heard the clap of her hands as she applauded. 'She has done it, Philipe! She is impaled upon Zeus, and see how she sucks!'

Grace's nostrils were flared as she gasped for breath.

Her tongue flicked with quick little laps up and down the cockstem. With lips stretched to the limit Grace managed to suck upon the unyielding marble.

How silly to even think she could make the god come! It was impossible, she told herself. And yet, was it her imagination that the cock was throbbing between her lips?

'She goes on too long!' exclaimed Philipe testily, and Grace felt his long fingers on her shoulder attempting to wrench her upwards.

'No! *Attendez*! Wait!'

Grace, from the corner of her eyes, saw madame crouching beside her.

'I do believe the balls are throbbing,' she gasped huskily. 'She is working the magic. Zeus is about to come!'

'Oh, what nonsense.' Grace could hear envy in Philipe's voice. 'Stop wasting time!'

Madame sighed. 'Perhaps you're right,' she said. She hooked her hands under Grace's arms and gently eased her to her feet.

Feeling an emptiness as the cock was pulled from her lips, Grace felt tears gloss her lashes, but she also felt a warmth, a creamy warmth, and tasted a bitter saltiness in her mouth. Giving the statue a plaintive glance she was certain she saw the handsome lips curve in a gentle smile.

'Straddle his majesty's thighs, my darling,' madame whispered huskily. Grace was dragged upright.

Zeus sat with his muscled legs open to their limit and, by the time Grace had obeyed her mistress her own thighs trembled with effort, and the fine pale skin was stretched to a transparent tautness.

'Lean forward,' rasped Philipe, 'sway your breasts upon the cock, smear them as if with his majesty's issue.'

With a fearful glance at Philipe Grace did as she was bid. Her fear was that he knew she had indeed done the impossible, but there was no hint of knowledge in his eyes. Only rabid lust and cruelty.

Grace arched her slender back until it was hollowed. Her pert buttocks lifted with this awkward position and they splayed open, revealing the tight little entrance. She felt the cool of her own spittle and... No! She could not believe that she had drawn come from the marble cock!

'Now, my precious,' murmured madame, 'be sure to put a good coating of your spittle on his majesty's organ. A good coating.'

Grace looked up, eyes wide, pleading, though she scarcely knew for what. Her bound arms were thrust hard behind her and high up her back, the position causing her excruciating pain.

'If you do not do as I say,' said madame, her voice losing its soft tone and becoming harsh, 'it will be the worse for you. You will know pain such as you have never known before.' She smoothed the bulbous globe of the marble cock with the pad of her forefinger, slowly back and forth, collecting a scoop of Grace's saliva. The woman frowned and tasted with the tip of her tongue. She looked at Grace, her eyes wide and questioning. The look made Grace quiver with fear, but madame said nothing more. She only smiled a secret smile. Grace shuddered and bent her head, beginning her task at the very base of the huge cock, petting the smoothness with little laps of her tongue and soft kissing movements of her velvet lips.

'Excellent,' murmured madame. 'Continue.'

'Is this the lovely creature we have heard so much about?' Above the murmur of the watching crowd, the scathing comments, a man spoke, a stranger, and Grace wished she could hide away forever. Strangely, though, the tingle between her spread thighs increased and she tried to rub the soft lips of her cunt against something, anything, to ease the aching void, but there was nothing between the marble god's thighs except the cock she was so busy licking. If only she could impale herself upon that!

'It is, Louis,' confirmed Philipe. 'And does she not make one's balls fill, one's prick rise up?'

The man laughed. 'And I notice you are dressed ready for action, *cher frere*,' he said, looking at Philipe's loincloth.

'Madame had something in mind,' said Philipe, looking shamefaced, but rubbing at the tightly bound cloth around his genitals.

'She always has,' replied Louis, giving madame a look that was less than friendly.

Grace, her task completed, eased the ache in her back, hiding her bottom hole as she did so. She was rewarded with a slap from madame, a slap that renewed the fire in her buttocks.

'Smear her anus with more gruel,' ordered madame, ignoring the man's sharp comment. 'A liberal coating.'

'Do you think she's ready for that?' asked Philipe.

Madame grabbed the bowl and scooped up several fingers full. 'Of course she is. Didn't I tell you how she delighted in my tongue and fingers? Bore down upon them? I tell you she is a sensualist beyond all else.'

Grace felt the lukewarm sliminess of the creamy concoction slapped into her bottom cleft. She felt the answering suck of her anal pleats; the warm, swirling feeling in the pit of her belly and the spill of her juices upon her open thighs. A slap of further gruel made her bear back upon the slime and warmth. She felt her bottom hole pout and suck, and open in readiness.

'She is ready,' purred madame. 'Lift her.'

Legs spread, Grace found herself perched upon the cock of the king of the gods. She felt the tight entrance deep in the ravine of her bottom touch the hard globe of the upright cock. She sighed, began to bear down.

'Oh, good, my sweet darling!' cooed madame. 'I knew you would take it.' She whispered confidentially in Grace's ear, 'Many have tried, you know, but have been carried away screaming. I knew you, above all, could do it.'

'May I?' asked the man called Louis, and Grace shivered as she felt the touch of fingers even smoother and more delicate than Philipe's between the velvet slickness of her sex folds. 'When the cunt is stimulated I often find that the bottom hole, with girls such as this one, becomes more giving.'

'Oh, how true, Louis,' agreed Philipe.

It was the king, Grace realised. Her cunny was being petted by the king! She lifted her head, her breasts became more pert, and she tried to stop the tremble of her belly as she bore down upon the royal fingers. There was an easing of her bottom hole and Zeus' cock slipped inside her darkest tunnel.

'I think she is impaled,' sighed Louis. 'Does she not look a picture with her thighs spread and her flesh lips splayed open? And that nubbin is as fine a one as I have had the pleasure to play with for many a year. Do you not think so, my people?' he asked of the gathered courtiers.

Grace saw him wave a hand at the knots of finely dressed men and women who sniggered at her humiliation. It would have been so easy to succumb to the tears which threatened since she had been brought to Zeus, but she held her head high and writhed, very gently, upon the royal fingers.

Louis kept his eyes focussed upon Grace's splayed sex lips. 'Now what did you have in mind, madame? Something imaginative, I have no doubt.' His soft fingers flickered back and forth about her nubbin and dabbled in the steady flow of her juices. The steady petting increased the urge to feel the slender fingers bore into her female opening and she tossed back her head, giving herself up to the glorious sensations created at her front and rear.

'Nothing very inspired,' madame said haughtily. 'I simply thought it would complete the picture if Philipe knelt between the god's thighs to lick at the pretty one's flesh pot.'

Louis lifted his fingers and sniffed. 'Her musk is excellent,' he said. 'You will enjoy it, Philipe. Do not allow me to disturb you further.'

Louis strode away from the sensual tableau.

'He always spoils things,' snarled madame.

'How has he spoiled anything?' asked Philipe, rubbing at the folds of cloth around his loins. 'I cannot wait to kneel before Grace and slip my tongue into her.'

Grace felt the heat of his eyes as he focussed upon the flushed wetness and she bowed her head in shame. Her nubbin was already pulsing from the stimulation of the cock upon which she was impaled, and she felt her juices oozing from her.

'You men always stick together,' snapped madame.

Grace, her rear passage chilled by the marble cock while her flesh pot was hot with need of more fulfilment, waited tensely for the outcome of the argument.

Philipe sank to his knees and kissed the fullness of her mound, tugging at the tight curls with his teeth. His tongue slipped into the upper crease of her sex, caressing the sweet flesh and making Grace wriggle upon the hardness within her bottom. He began to tongue-tickle the fine inner flesh leaves, coaxing them fully open before petting her nubbin, making her breathing fast and shallow.

'I could watch the two of you all night,' said madame, 'but you excite me so greatly I must have Philipe to myself.'

Grace felt the chill of his absence as he was pulled to his feet.

'But madame...' protested Philipe. 'My cock yearns for her.' He licked his lips, tasting her musk. His brother was right. It was sweet and fresh.

'And I yearn for your cock! Come with me.'

'But, Grace...' She saw him look over his shoulder, his face full of need.

'She will not be alone for long.'

Their voices and footsteps faded and Grace was alone, impaled upon Zeus, her sex open to all comers. She was alone for the first time since she entered the palace, but not alone for the giggling crowd of courtiers still hovered around her.

A young man stepped forward from the crowd. Grace had seen his eyes fixed upon her open thighs for some time. His age was no more than her own, perhaps eighteen or nineteen. A bulge was evident in his satin breeches and he rubbed it hungrily.

'Go on, Jean-Pierre!' A woman, her eyes glassy with lust, encouraged the young man. 'They have gone. You said you always wondered what it was like to fuck a virgin.'

'No...' whispered Grace.

Jean-Pierre stood before her, his hands cupping the soft heaviness of her breasts, his fingers rolling back and forth about her erect nipples. 'No?' he whispered in her ear. 'But you delight in the sensations of sex. You are ripe for me.'

'You must not...' Grace's dark eyes filled with tears. She felt his fingers slide down the swell of her breasts, cupping them, lingering at the hard nubs of her nipples before drifting down to the delicate dip of her waist and the shallow hillock of her belly.

'But if I cannot fuck you,' said Jean-Pierre, 'what can I do? My cock aches for relief. How could you be so cruel?'

Sex cleft quivering with her own needs, slippery with the juices which oozed from her hot depths, her body shaking with the orgasms which emanated, one after the other, from the cock so deeply impaled in her bottom, Grace wept.

'Poor girl,' Jean-Pierre murmured softly.

And she realised these were the first kind words spoken to her since she was taken by madame. Oh, the mistress called her by endearments, but she did not mean them.

'I love to see tears in a girl,' murmured Jean-Pierre. 'It makes her look so sweet, so very vulnerable, so ready for a man's cock.'

Grace gave a soft mew of fear and gasped back her tears. Jean-Pierre bent over her, kissing her breasts, her quivering belly and her open sex. She had never felt so open, so wet, and when the young man's tongue flicked back and forth over the slickness of her sex folds she could not hold back the deep-throated moans. She had been on the verge of an orgasm when Philipe was dragged away. The tongue lingered wetly against the hardness of her clitty, rolling back the tiny hood to bare the sensitive tip. She felt her juices combine with his spittle and her body swirled with her mind with forbidden joy.

'Break her, Jean-Pierre!' rasped the woman. 'Thrust your tongue through the precious barrier and then we'll be rid of the little whore!'

Through the mists of pleasure Grace knew she must somehow prevent this final intrusion. 'No,' she managed. 'No... Madame will have me guillotined. I must be pure in all things.'

The chill of Zeus's cock seemed to grow; the size increase filling her bottom hole, spearing upwards and into her soft tissues.

'You must go,' whispered Grace.

Jean-Pierre stood, his face smeared with the slime of her passion and his cock held in his hands, turgid and threatening. 'Very well,' he sneered. 'I shall go, but not before I leave you a little something to remember me by.'

By turning her head Grace received the force of his offering upon her cheek; a pearly droplet which slithered hotly over her pale skin. A second gush spilled over her open lips and more over her breasts and belly.

Laughing and sneering, other men joined in the game and she was surrounded by a semi-circle of men who bared their cocks, holding them like weapons and pointing them at her. Soon she was covered in their spillage. It matted the dark silk of her hair. It coated her breasts like a snail's smear. It dribbled copiously into her pussy bush.

Later that night the last of them trailed away, leaving her helpless, vulnerable and totally humiliated by the way she was used.

The woman who had taunted her so cruelly was the last to leave. Before she left she slapped Grace's bottom and the girl felt the skin sting, redden with the weighty blow. Her flesh quivered about the rod of Zeus's cock, which in turn put pressure upon her female parts. The woman licked a trickle of cock fluid from Grace's trembling nipple and looked the girl full in her dark, tear-brimmed eyes. 'A virgin?' she sneered, before pressing her tongue, with its bitter and salty taste, deep into Grace's mouth. 'Perhaps physically, but a used one!'

Lord Albert Fitzpatrick watched a plume of smoke rise from his cheroot. He lay, one hand behind his dark, dishevelled head, his athletic body naked on his mistress's bed.

'You delight me over and over again, *citizen*,' said Charlotte de Levis. 'Whether you chastise me with hands or cane or cosset me with your lips you make me run with juices.' She smiled and opened her thighs, dipping a finger deep into herself and drawing it out slick with her fluids.

She trailed the same finger down his finely honed jaw, traced the muscular width of his shoulders and both hard pads of his pectorals. The tumbled thickness of her auburn hair cascaded over his taut belly as she lightly kissed the pit of his navel. The kisses trailed down to the lush darkness of his pubis, from which speared the semi-turgid thickness of his cock.

He snaked out a hand and grasped her wrist so hard that

she was flung backwards, her arm thrown behind her as her lithe body was forced flat upon the linen of their love bed, her breasts thrust taut and upwards.

'Don't do that, Charlotte,' he hissed between sparkling white and even teeth. He gave her a thin-lipped smile, still holding her in that painful grip.

'*Mais cher* Albert,' she whispered. 'I thought…'

'That I liked it?' he finished.

She nodded, trying not to flinch as her arm was wrenched painfully in its socket. The position forced her breasts higher, the mounds wonderfully pert. He took another mouthful of fragrant cigar smoke and bent to kiss each rosy nipple in turn, sheathing them in a warm fog. He heard her groan softly.

'I do, Charlotte,' he said at last. 'I love you to pet my cock… but only when I invite you to do so. I cannot abide forward women. Women should be slavish, obedient, pliant.'

His gaze drifted downwards along her contorted body, to where her thighs were splayed open and her calves were forced beneath her firm buttocks, arching the swollen pouch of her sex upwards, displaying the flushed folds and the pert nubbin which nestled in the midst of them.

Drawing on the cheroot once more he blew a plume of smoke between the puffy folds powdered with rich auburn curls. He watched the flushed leaves of the inner part of her sex flutter with renewed need and the peak of her clitty pout up, twitching and moist.

'Are you going to fuck me again, *mon cher*?' Charlotte smiled, despite the pain of his iron grip.

The glowing cheroot waved over her body. It spiralled down to the auburn curls, so close that she could feel the heat of the tip. He laughed as she tried to flinch away.

'I shall never harm you, *citoyenne*,' he promised. He puffed again on the cheroot and smiled through the haze of blue smoke.

'Because you love me?' Her voice sounded hopeful.

'Perhaps,' he agreed, 'but also because you are too useful to me. Useful in my business.' He flung her from him, concentrating upon the enjoyment of his cigar more than her. 'Too useful in aiding me to achieve my ambitions,' he corrected softly.

Charlotte huddled away from him, her slender arms wrapped about her knees, her large green eyes pensive, questioning.

'Useful in what way, Albert?' she asked, her voice husky, almost fearful. 'What is it that you do? Do you help the revolution or the aristos?'

Fitzpatrick swung his legs over the edge of the high iron bedstead and reached to the chair at the bedside where he had hastily thrown his clothes. Not bothering with undergarments he tugged on his buckskin breeches and adjusted his full manhood to his liking. Still saying nothing to Charlotte he pulled on his hessian top boots, for Lord Albert was nothing if not a man of the Ton.

'Why is an Englishman like you in Paris?' continued Charlotte. 'It is not a healthy place to be. There are so many thieves and vagabonds taking advantage of the lawlessness.'

He laughed and bent down, clutching the point of her chin in strong fingers. 'Including you, *ma chere* Charlotte?' He claimed her lips in a hard and punishing manner, his other hand twisting the softness of a breast until she murmured for mercy. Again he thrust her away, his lips twisted in a cynical manner.

'You ask too many questions, *ma petite*. It could be the undoing of you.'

'But I adore you, Albert! Truly adore you. I am concerned when I do not see you for days.'

'Are you?' His eyebrows rose in cynical query as he shrugged into a full sleeved lawn shirt with a high pointed collar. He took great pains to fold his muslin cravat in the twelve pleats as decreed by his friend Beau

Brummel.

Charlotte eased herself on the bed. 'Where are you going, *citizen*?' She stretched until she lay full length, her bottom wonderfully pale and smooth below the long sweep of her elegant back. She rested her chin on her hands, looking up at him with large questioning eyes.

Whirling round, his handsome features dark with anger, Lord Albert pulled from beneath a coat of blue superfine a coiled whip that cracked as he lashed it in the air above Charlotte's body.

'Didn't I warn you, *ma petite*, that you ask too many questions? Why do you not stick to your own business? Do you think I do not know that you are a thief, a footpad, pickpocket?' The very tip of the whip flicked the peak of her buttocks, making the flesh quiver and ripple for several seconds before it finally settled again to quiescence.

Charlotte whimpered, perhaps in pain and perhaps more in surprise. 'I did not mean to be curious,' she told him, and she rubbed the place where the whip had landed.

'Remove your hand.' His sharp tone was like another crack of the lash.

She did so only slowly, revealing the rising weal, the scarlet ridge of beaten flesh surrounded by skin as pale as cream silk.

'Place your hands behind your head, Charlotte.'

'Will you beat me again?' She sounded excited more than afraid, and he saw that she wriggled her sex mound deeper into the linen, and parted her thighs, revealing the moist vale of flushed folds.

'Do as you're told!' He knew how powerful he looked standing over her, fully dressed in his broad-shouldered coat and top boots, and he knew she enjoyed her own vulnerability as she obediently linked her fingers behind her head.

The whip was fine and long. He took slow backward steps until he was far across the room. The sun was going down over the roofs of Paris and the room was all but in darkness. He could see Charlotte's eyes glittering and the hillocks of her pale bottom like twin moons. He drew back his arm, letting the whip trail on the bare boards of the bedroom floor. Drawing his arm forward he lashed Charlotte, flicking the dark ravine between the silky mounds.

A low moan reached his ears, almost a soft purr of pleasure, and he felt his cock thicken in his tight breeches. Again he drew back his arm, moving closer to allow a longer length of the fine leather to snake across the twitching buttocks, which he saw darken.

'*Mon cher*!' Charlotte whispered the endearment and pushed herself up, allowing him to see her full breasts with their erect centres.

The lash whipped across the room and snaked around her arched body, binding her arms to her sides and trapping the soft breast flesh. He strode to the bed and held her helpless form, kissing her long and hard on the yielding flesh of her lips. He groped between her thighs, which she willingly opened for him. He felt the velvet wetness, the hard nub of her clitty and the open silkiness of her slit.

'Take me with you,' she pleaded.

'No!' He thrust one finger deeply into the warm wetness, drawing it back and forth, loving the way she bore down upon his intrusion. 'The theatre pit is no place for a woman these days. It's no safer than a bear pit. When the time comes when I need you, you will know soon enough.' He added another finger and then another, filling her entrance.

Charlotte mewed her appreciation and huddled her helpless and bound body closer to him. She shuddered through a long drawn-out orgasm and he held her until it had faded, letting her fluids spill over his fingers.

'Sleep now,' he told her, drawing the whip from her body and smoothing the fine red weal it left around her arms and breasts. 'I shall be back before you know it.'

His fifteen caped coat swirled about him as he left the small apartment and ran swiftly down the three flights of stairs towards the tall door.

The narrow streets were crowded with the ragged figures of the peasants who had crowded into Paris since the revolution first began to simmer. They huddled over fires, held out grimy hands as he passed, hoping for a coin, a *sou*. He ran on. He was late and the grille behind which he must stand in the pit would be down.

Minette had told him to be at the front of the pit and he would discover something of great advantage. An actress of no mean talent, Minette was even more invaluable to him in his work than Charlotte, whom he admitted to himself with a wry smile, was the best pickpocket in all of Paris. He took the heavy fob watch from his pocket, amazed that he still had it, and peered at it in the light of the sconces and the peasant fires. He was late! He hurried on, scarcely heeding the poverty around him.

'It is time, Philipe!' gasped Madame de Genlis, standing entranced before Grace.

The girl, her beautiful face impassive, but still expressive, her eyes a lustrous and verdant green flecked with elusive gold turning them to warm hazel. They were almost luminescent with scarcely hidden pain. She stood very still before them, wearing only the sheerest of muslin. The slightest breeze moulded the fine material to her breasts, the dip of her waist, the swell of her belly, her whole lovely body. The gossamer was all but transparent, and when a breeze fluttered through Philipe's quarters it made the illusion of nakedness complete.

'Is she not glorious?' Madame de Genlis was enraptured with her finished product.

Philipe was slumped in his ornate chair, one slender leg draped over the arm, looking extremely sulky.

'I think we have gone to a great deal of trouble for

103

nothing,' he said, giving Grace only the most cursory of glances.

'But was she not delightful impaled through her bottom hole upon Zeus? Was she not admired by all the courtiers? Did they not love to touch her, see her tremble in her helplessness? Humiliate her with their spunk?'

Madame de Genlis spun Grace round, admiring her proud stance, the pertness of her buttocks beneath the sheer material, the high-lift of her breasts in the graceful gown.

With her head bowed Grace tried not to look at Philipe's handsome features. She knew he could not wait to penetrate her, any more than she could wait to be penetrated if not by him, by someone who would relieve her of her hated maidenhead. Having tasted him and he having held her so close, she knew their need was mutual. And it was not only Philipe who had this effect on her! Madame de Genlis had awakened fires within her very depths and they would not be quenched except by a fountain of manly issue.

'Wasted our time? How so, Philipe?' asked madame. 'Why do you say that? Grace is charming in every way. Sensual, graceful and ready.' A plump ringed finger lifted her charge's chin, and with dark smiling eyes she gazed with pride at her creation. Her other hand swooped down the curve of the girl's body, admiring the swell of her breasts, the daintiness of her waist, the arch of her hips.

Once again madame walked around Grace, adjusting the fluttering muslin, slipping her hands gently into the girl's bodice, lifting the perfect breasts so that the unblemished hillocks peeped enticingly from the ruffle which bordered the low décolletage. As she did so she gazed into Grace's eyes, smiling a smile of pure lust, but Grace, during the arduous training she endured under madame's tutelage, had learned to be perfectly tranquil, calm, stoic, no matter what indignities she must endure.

At that very moment she felt her breasts become firmer,

fuller, her nipples harden and thrust against the muslin. They seemed to lift so that they were scarcely covered by the tiny ruffle. Worse, the caress, the subtle massage, had set her body on fire once more. Her belly felt molten, liquid. The plump mound at the apex of her thighs became puffed, seemed to open, to flutter, and she knew her cheeks were flushed, her lips parted and she was ready to be used by madame in any way she chose.

'She is not pure, is she?' said Philipe in his sulkiest manner. 'She is sullied, violated and... how can she be pure when she was invaded by Zeus?'

'But only through the bottom hole,' said madame huskily, patting Grace's buttocks. 'The female opening is still whole, pure as driven snow.' She cupped her fingers over the perfectly formed sex pouch and held them there, stroking very gently through the gossamer muslin. Grace could feel an immediate flood of her fluids and could not help swaying her body back and forth against her mistress's fingers, aching for fulfilment. Her nubbin forced its way through the soft velvet of her sex folds, itching to be rubbed by madame's knowing fingers. Grace could feel Philipe's pale eyes linger over her body and she could swear that the look burned into her very innards, seeking out every blemish, every imperfection. She dipped her head, hiding her face, hiding the fire of her blushes. No matter that he found her contemptible, he wanted her above all things.

He had been so excited as he hurried behind madame along the corridor to the statue. She remembered his harsh breathing, his moist lips, the fullness of his loincloth. How could he be so hypocritical?

Grace felt languid in the wake of madame's sensual attentions. Her body felt heavy beneath the sheer and fluttering muslin. She leaned against her mistress, wanting sexual fulfilment above all things.

'And where is my brother?' murmured Philipe, in a voice which was almost a whine. He glared at Grace as though the disappearance of his brother was her fault.

La de Genlis shrugged in her most Gallic manner and gestured that Grace should stand alone. She pirouetted in her own plain white gown, fashioned to mark her as a leader of the Republic with a sash of red white and blue slung loosely over her shoulder and falling over her splendid bosom. 'Be quiet, Philipe. He has gone into hiding, of course. But we have nothing to fear.'

Grace stood very still. It made her fearful, this talk of the Republic, the terrors of the revolution. Having become used to the comfort of the palaces, for all the tortures she had endured to become what Madame de Genlis wanted, she did not wish to have to return to her old ways, scavenging for food and never knowing where she would sleep at night.

'You may have nothing to fear,' said Philipe sharply, 'but there is no guarantee that the same could be said of me or my brother, the king.'

'Perhaps the Black Rose will save you,' said madame with a low chuckle.

'The Black Rose?' Philipe sneered. 'There are some who say he is nothing but a pirate using the revolution to further his own ends. His own fortune. He works both ends against the middle, that one!'

Again, Madame de Genlis shrugged and pulled Grace to her, making unnecessary adjustments to the jet-black corkscrew curls that framed her perfect face. Grace could smell the scent of roses that madame used to hide the odour of her body. It might be fashionable to look like a peasant but the voluptuous woman did not like to smell like one.

'We are going to be late,' said madame.

'I do not wish to go to the theatre,' said Philipe. 'The crowds make me nervous.

'Do not be a baby, Philipe!' scoffed madame, swirling a coat of dark superfine about Grace's shoulders. It made her shudder, the very softness of the luxurious cloth. It brushed her upper arms like a caress and, like any caress since madame's training, it set her belly a-quiver, set it running like a warm stream. 'The peasants cannot hurt you. They are kept behind a grille.'

'But we are late!' Philipe straddled his legs wide, both hooked over the arms of the chair, and he rubbed the growing bulge between his thighs, eyeing Grace lustfully. 'Can we not stay here and play with Grace? You still have not allowed me—'

'Allowed you? Have you forgotten how you tricked me out of my chamber?' Madame pulled the billowing cloak closer around Grace's body, but slipped her fingers beneath it to caress the roundness of her belly.

'You only allowed me to lick her cunt,' he sulked.

Madame stroked a finger down the perfection of Grace's cheek. 'Had I not returned when I did you would have used her fully!' Again she slipped her hand beneath the cloak and lifted the gossamer skirt. Her fingers twisted the ring she found there. 'Push, my darling. Push down.'

'You see?' hissed Philipe. You play and tweak all you like but deny me. And you promised.'

There was that childish whine again, thought Grace, irritated for all her training in submission and pliancy. She kept her thoughts to herself. But for all his faults her experiences with Philipe were only sensual interludes of delightful shame. She enjoyed the humiliation of being at Philipe's feet, kissing and petting his cock, feeling the flood of his juices spilling over her body, just as she enjoyed the feel of his tongue probing between her flesh lips.

'This is her first appearance in public,' reminded madame, 'and I wish to see the reactions she creates. I wish to see how the crowds react to her sweet innocence, her graceful demeanour, her chains.' She turned to Grace and lifted the fine gossamer of her gown, baring the pouting pad of her cunt. 'Are you wet, my sweet? Are you ready?'

Grace thrust forward, rubbing the soft velvet of her cunt against madame's fingers, feeling the delicious and now familiar heaviness in the loins.

'Of course you are!' Madame withdrew her fingers and put them to her lips, sucking them, tasting Grace's musk, savouring it hungrily and smiling at her charge's blushes.

'The grille may be closed,' said Philipe. He sunk deeper into the chair. 'We are so late and I, for one, do not wish to be mauled by the rabble.'

'They would not dare,' said madame in her most positive tone, and she chivvied Grace before her, letting her gown fall and leaving the girl in a frustrating state of readiness. Her full cloak was wrapped about her, hiding all the parts which had taken so long to prepare.

'Come, Philipe,' coaxed madame. 'The play is a comedy and we can all do with something to cheer us up.'

Grace, the hood of her cloak worn low over her face and her hands clasped tightly in front of her, walked with graceful steps as she had been taught. She had grown quite used to the manacles at her slender wrists and the hobbling irons about her slim ankles and she managed to walk smoothly, without a hint of a shuffle.

'I do not wish to go, madame,' grumbled Philipe as they walked across the courtyard to the waiting carriage. The other playgoers, other members of Philipe's court, had departed long since, anxious to be safely behind the grille before it was locked for their safety.

Beneath the billowing cloak of blue superfine, beneath the muslin gown, Grace's body was weighted with other shackles and chains. They were made especially to madame's specifications. The chains were light and fine, fashioned by a jeweller, rather than the blacksmith who could only think of heavy and clumsy loops.

'I order you, Philipe!' said madame, pushing the grumbling Duc d'Orleans. 'I wish us both to be present when Grace is seen in public for the first time. I wish you to pay special attention to her, while I shall watch the reactions of the men in the audience.'

Philipe, at last, began to sound more cheerful. 'I can play with her in public?' He clapped his hands and fairly skipped into the carriage.

'Within reason,' agreed madame.

This revelation had a profound effect on Grace. There were certain parts of her body that were pierced with gold loops that were, in turn, clasped by tiny padlocks. As she stepped, very gracefully considering the numerous impediments, into the carriage, the gold loops which pierced her inner labia caressed the plumper outer lips. It made her sigh. The jewels kept her in a continual state of heightened sexuality.

'What do you mean…? said Philipe, slumping in the corner of the carriage, looking sulkier and more disagreeable than ever. 'Within reason? My cock is aching to thrust into her. We have a private box. I could quite easily fuck her on the floor and no one would be any the wiser.'

Grace sat very straight in the deeply upholstered seats. It was necessary to sit in a certain way, because otherwise the loops, the little chains and the padlocks nipped her tender flesh.

Madame de Genlis shook her head, wagged her finger at Philipe and then, with finger and thumb, parted the cloak and, very slowly, lifted the muslin. 'I knew you had forgotten, you naughty fellow. You may only play with her upper parts, and then very gently.'

Philipe gaped at Grace, revealed as she was. Another rule laid down by madame was that she must always sit with her thighs parted, ready to be displayed to anyone her owners chose.

'Is it not a delicious sight?' Madame de Genlis stroked Grace's sex parts with the very tip of an index finger, tracing the plump outer lips with their mist of blue-black curls and the delicately parted inner lips with the gold loops keeping the parts safe from intruders. Proud and erect, peeping and extruded from its little hood, was Grace's clitoris and, when madame touched the very peak of this, Grace could not help but jerk.

'Oh, Grace!' exclaimed madame. 'That is not how you've been trained to behave, and well you know it!'

The hooded head bowed in shame that she had shown any reaction to the touch of that very sensitive part.

'She's excited!' said Philipe. 'May I feel the seep of her juices, her heat? Just the tiniest feel?'

Madame slapped his approaching hand away. 'How dare you? You know she must be kept on the very edge of orgasm, giving her lovely face that special glow until the right man comes along.'

'But I am the right man!' argued Philipe. 'You acquired her for me... and you.'

Madame shook her head sadly. 'That may have been my intention,' she said, 'but the world is changing. Soon we shall not be the monied and privileged class and we must take riches wherever we may.' She lowered Grace's skirt and closed her cloak as if shutting away the most valuable jewel in the world.

'You're going to sell her!' Philipe was aghast. 'You cannot! She's my plaything.' He glared at madame, who stared him down. 'Our play thing,' he corrected after a moment's hesitation. 'And what do you mean that we may not be the monied class? We shall still have our riches, our palaces.'

Once more madame shook her head sadly. 'Who knows?'

The carriage drew up outside the theatre. Several urchins fought to open the door. Philipe shrank back away from the rabble he hated so much, but the driver and the footmen drove the urchins away with whips and clubs and Grace, Madame de Genlis, and Philipe, stepped from the carriage unhindered.

A young man, ragged like the urchins, stepped forward from the crowd, his filthy hand waving to Grace. 'It is me!' he called. 'Pierre, your half-brother. Grace? Look at me!'

Grace's eyes, the green glinting in the flickering lights of the torches held in sconces on the stone walls, darted towards the voice. Her soft lips trembled in the ghost of a smile. She began to lift her hands in greeting and the glint of gold, the manacles about her wrists, were seen in the dim yellow oil lamps.

'What have they done to you?' Pierre's pinched and filthy face looked horrified, and Grace wanted to feel the warmth and love of familiar arms about her.

'Walk on!' hissed madame. 'He is no one. You do not know him. You have no need to know him.' The voice whispered urgently in her ear and hands pushed her firmly ahead.

'But it was...' Grace became, for the first time, more aware of her total imprisonment, her slavery, and she wanted to run back, embrace Pierre, take up her old life, poor though it was.

Obediently she walked on, head bowed, hiding her face in the hood of her cloak. She was once again the humble slave, owned by a mistress who kept her in luxurious chains; imprisoned by her sensuality.

'I shall not forget that you spurned me,' she heard from the crowd. 'I shall not forget how you treated your half-brother.'

Grace turned her head, looking into the crowd, but she could not see Pierre. The reminder of her old life made her sad and she felt an overwhelming sense of loneliness.

'Forget him, *ma cherie*,' coaxed madame. 'Have I not given you a better and more luxurious life? Do you not enjoy my petting of your most private places?' The woman put her hand gently under the cloak and Grace felt the shiver of sensual awareness as the knowing fingers brushed the imprisoned folds of her sex. She laid her head upon madame's shoulder and allowed herself to be helped into the ornate building.

The theatre was crowded and the ushers were about to close the grilles which divided the court from the populace.

'Wait!' Madame de Genlis called out in her imperious voice. 'Wait, for the Duc d'Orleans and his party.'

The ushers gave grudging bows as madame swept through, followed by Grace and Philipe. Immediately the grilles were closed with a great clanging of iron, and the murmurs of discontent from the crowds grew in volume.

Grace was placed at the very front of the box, in full view of the actors on the stage, the court and the populace. Madame took care to adjust the décolletage so that the pale smooth mounds of the girl's breasts were shown to best advantage. She made another minor adjustment that caused heightened colour to bloom prettily on the pale cheeks. The adjustment caused Grace's breasts to swell the more so, for the labial rings and padlocks were not the only piercing she had to endure; gold rings pierced her nipples, keeping them erect at all times.

'Play with each nipple ring, my sweet,' purred madame, keeping her eyes upon the stage. 'Make sure the footlights catch the glint of gold, but do it discreetly, with grace and subtlety, being sensual but not brash.'

Grace lifted her manacled wrists to the required height and parted her hands as much as her chains would allow. With the tips of her index fingers she agitated the tiny gold loops at her nipples. These were not in full view, but were partly hidden by the décolletage ruffle.

Beneath her skirts juices spilled over the little gold rings that kept her sex lips closed. She felt her nubbin swelling unbearably, butting the labial jewellery.

She became aware of eyes focussed upon her and she stared fixedly upon the stage, although had anyone asked her what was taking place she would surely have been

112

unable to tell them the farcical antics of the actors who dived in one door and then reappeared at quite another.

'A young man...' whispered Madame de Genlis, leaning forward to whisper in Grace's ear. 'Can you see him, beyond the grille?'

Grace allowed her eyes to dip into the pit.

'He is an aristo for sure,' continued madame, 'perhaps English, by his clothes.' The green eyes glistened at the sight of the young man who was darkly handsome, but dressed in the manner of the fashionable London gentlemen. He could not take his eyes off Grace and his excitement was all too obvious, even beyond the thick mesh of the grille.

'And don't get too excited, my girl,' whispered Philipe in her other ear. 'You must fetch the best price for madame.'

'Mind your own business, Philipe.' Madame spoke sharply and rapped her patron with her fan.

The curtain came down for the first act and Grace dropped her aching wrists into her lap. Perhaps the young man would release her from her ownership, but perhaps also she was being unfair. Madame had provided much comfort as well as the little tutelage she devised so cunningly; the sensuality she was taught to enjoy. Indeed she did enjoy it! Her body was a receptacle for pleasure. For pure pleasure.

Chapter Seven

Minette wore only a light basque, laced very tightly at the back by her maid. The garment nipped her waist to wasp-like slenderness and, at the same time, lifted her breasts until they spilled over the satin upper edge. Below the lower margin of the tightly laced garment the slender swell of her belly was pale as porcelain, and below that was a puff of golden curls hiding the moist folds of her sex.

'Albert!' Minette twirled round, her pretty face aglow with pleasure as the young aristo stepped into her dressing room. She held out her arms in greeting, but Lord Albert looked distracted and she pouted at his lack of interest in her.

'There is a girl,' he told her, and he rubbed the crotch of his breeches which sported a large bulge. 'I mean to have her, to use her.'

Lord Albert had entered the backstage dressing room without knocking. As always his whip was coiled loosely in his hand and his expression was mocking, a finely etched eyebrow raised as if in permanent query.

Minette threw her arms about his neck and brushed the fullness of her breasts against his broad chest until her nipples were hard as little beans. 'You have me, Albert, and Charlotte. Why do you need more?'

He claimed her lips, his mouth passionate. 'Because this girl is different; a slave, taught to obey. Pliant and submissive. She would do anything for me. I know. I have seen the glint of her chains and rings that mark her as a chattel.' He drew his hands down her tightly corseted figure until his fingers cupped the fullness of her buttocks. He prised them apart and rubbed them, and into the tight valley between them. 'Even lay down her life.'

'Hmm,' purred Minette. 'When you caress me in that way... I would do anything for you.'

'Introduce me to the girl,' he said, and his fingers drifted to the silky pad of her pussy, slithering into the valley between the delicious lips.

Minette pouted until he thumbed the nub of her clitty. She became heavy and limp in his arms as he rubbed with regular strokes over the receptive little point. 'Where is she?' she murmured, her voice catching in her throat as her breathing quickened.

'In one of the boxes reserved for the royal party,' he

said, smiling at her obvious pleasure. 'I would go myself but it would not do for me to be seen mixing with the aristos.' As her orgasm faded he squeezed her breast and stroked the loops of the folded whip over the hillocks of her bottom.

'I shall go after the next act,' said Minette, leaning back in his arms, bearing back against the stroking movement of the whip. 'The death scene is my final appearance, but will you not reward me for obeying you in this task?'

He laughed. 'And the reward?'

'To feel the sting of your whip on my bottom!' She bowed her head in mock humility, but raised her eyes, looking at him under the fringe of her lashes.

'Oh, I see. You are afraid that my attentions will be permanently elsewhere?' The coiled whip was allowed to fall, the leather making a soft plopping noise on the bare boards of the floor. 'You do not enjoy the whip. Why now?'

'I wish to please you, Albert,' she whispered. 'What must I do?'

'Bend down,' he ordered coldly. 'On your knees, bottom high in the air, and let your breasts hang softly. Your thighs must be fully open and you must tilt your sex so I see every detail.'

'Yes, Albert.'

Minette positioned herself as he required. Never had he known her so submissive, and he chuckled softly. He noticed the slight tremor of the buttocks and the pleasant looseness of the heavy breasts. The folded whip was stroked along the plump pleats of her sex and this, too, caused a quiver that was delicious to watch. He lifted the whip and placed the fold to his nose, savouring the musk of the excited girl.

'Good, Minette,' he murmured, 'perhaps we may train you even yet.'

'I shall do anything to please you, Albert,' she

whispered. 'You know that.'

The whip snaked through the air, whistling as it fell. The next noise in the little dressing room was the crack of leather upon flesh. Minette moaned, her lips pursed in a soft rosebud. Her heavy breasts trembled and the pert buttocks quivered as the leather lashed it.

'Enough?' asked Albert with a chuckle.

'*Non*!' Minette's denial was faint-hearted. 'Do not stop. It is… wonderful!'

'You little liar! A weal as thick as a cow's udder and the colour of a ripe mulberry is growing as I look and I know you are not a lover of the whip.' He chuckled. 'Ever the actress, Minette.'

'Truly! It is wonderful. More. I want more.'

The whip was brought down again and Minette groaned louder, but still she remained on her knees, her thighs open and her sex pouch tilted.

'You are very wet, *ma petite*! The dew drips from your clitty. I believe you are really enjoying it.'

'I am, but I must go back on stage. May I get up?'

'One more to remember me by,' said Albert with a chuckle. 'One more.' The whip cracked about Minette's waist and he drew her upwards, wrapped in its folds.

There was a rap on the door of the box. Philipe and madame looked at each other questioningly, and the cloak was quickly wrapped about Grace's near-nakedness and the manacles and chains which imprisoned her.

Philipe opened the door just a crack. 'Yes?' he said nervously. He saw assassins in everyone in these days of the revolution, but it was a girl; a sweet golden-haired girl, dressed in the costume of a country girl.

'*Ma cherie*!' Philipe flung open the door of the box, his crotch already full and aching. 'Madame… it is Minette, the actress!' He drew the girl to him, one hand dipping into the low cut gown and the other drifting under the full skirt.

Minette moaned and winced as the searching fingers clutched her full buttock flesh. Immediately, Philipe whirled the girl round and folded her over his arm. She tried to hide the darkening bruises and thick welts with her hands. She raised her flushed cheeks to Philipe.

'Who?' he murmured. He had always loved Minette and would have married her had Louis given permission. 'Who whipped you?'

Minette shook her head, her eyes glistening with tears. 'I cannot tell you. I come only to give you a message.'

Again Philipe lifted the full skirt and forced Minette to bend over. His fingers traced the blue-black weals that stood out in stark relief from the pale hillocks. He traced the dark crease of the cleft between the buttocks and gently probed a fingertip into the tight bottom hole. He kissed each bruised and reddened swell and felt Minette shudder as his finger delved deeper.

'Who?' he rasped. 'Who did this to you?' In truth he was not angry. The sight excited him. He wished it had been his hand that wielded the whip.

Minette gave him a frightened glance over her shoulder, but he could see the gleam of pleasure in her eyes beyond the fear. 'The Black Rose,' she whispered. 'The Black Rose loves to tease his girls with the whip.'

Philipe went pale. 'The double agent?'

No one knew just whose side the Black Rose was on. Some said it was the king and the aristos he protected but others said he started the revolution single-handed to further his own ends. This was Philipe's belief as his interest in Minette's body dissipated and he threw himself down on a chair, showing interest only in chewing his nails.

'Never mind that,' said madame. 'You have a message?'

Minette, with a last sorrowful look at her admirer, smoothed down her costume and nodded.

'An admirer?' probed madame. 'For my treasure here?'

She thrust Grace's manacled hands to her breasts, urging her to tweak the gold nipple rings. The muslin gown was thrust high above her thighs and she, without more persuasion, opened her limbs as far as the chains would allow, displaying her neatly locked cunt.

The action brought its usual result; the pleasurable swirling in her belly, the flood of creamy juices which made the midnight blackness of her pussy curls glossy and the swelling of her enclosed clitty. Grace bowed her head, humiliated by her own unbidden reactions.

Minette nodded once more, but lowered her eyes, embarrassed by Grace's forced display. She had heard that many at court were lewd and decadent. This girl, although she acted so submissive, seemed actually to enjoy her own display.

'Are they here? Have you brought them?' asked madame of Minette, taking a glance, first at Grace to check she was showing herself to best advantage and then out into the dim passage behind the box. Shadowy figures lingered there and there was a murmur of voices. 'There was a young Englishman in the pit who could not take his eyes from…'

'I am so sorry, Madame de Genlis,' murmured Minette. Her full breasts trembled over the low décolletage and she twisted her fingers in the looped skirt of her gown. 'It is not the Englishman…'

Grace gasped, her dark eyes wide with fear. Her hands fell from the gold jewellery that pierced her nipples.

The shadowy figures stepped into the box and, in the richness of these surroundings, their clothing, no more than filthy rags, looked more misplaced than ever.

'You filthy little whore!' The rasping voices were suddenly all around her, scathing and insulting. '*Putain!*'

Dragged to her feet by several pairs of hands Grace gave a plea for mercy. Her body seemed torn as if on the rack once more or suspended from the dungeon roof. Her handlers were rough, as were their hands and nails. Her flesh was bruised, her skin chafed and the fine chains tore at the places they pierced. She heard the soft clink of them, one against the other, and heard the hoarse breathing of her new captors.

Her eyes darted to Madame de Genlis and Philipe, pleading for their aid, but Philipe huddled as far away as possible from the newcomers. Grace struggled in the rough hands that clasped cruelly around her bare arms and brutishly thrust down into the flimsy gown to grasp the soft heaviness of her breasts. It was then that she saw Pierre, his face contorted with anger and revenge.

'I warned you!' he rasped. 'I warned you!'

A claw-like hand reached out and Grace felt the sting of a ragged nail as it scratched the full swell of her breast. Her gown fell in shreds about her body. She drew in a long breath as the film of gossamer swirled loosely away from her, leaving her naked apart from the nipple rings and the looped gold chains that shimmered against her pale skin. She stood, head bowed, her midnight hair a silky curtain about her face, not daring to look at the faces turned in her direction.

'Where are you taking her?' Madame stood, her handsome face at once afraid and thunderous with anger. She looked to Philipe for help but, overcoming his fear, he had eyes for no one but Minette. 'I shall call the guards.'

The ruffians laughed and gathered round Grace, mauling her breasts, sucking on the gold rings that pierced her nipples, thrusting their filthy fingers into the lush bush of hair on her mound.

'Has it escaped your notice, madame, that the revolution is by the people and for the people,' said Pierre. 'The guards will do nothing more than join in our games. Come! We must go... Robespierre is not a patient man.'

Madame gave a little cry of fright. 'Robespierre? What does he want with my poor Grace? Will he have her beheaded?'

The men laughed again, pulling Grace by the wrist chains, making her stumble. 'Beheaded? No!' said one. 'There are any number of little games that Citizen Robespierre has in mind for this pretty little miss!'

Grace tried to blink back the tears that gathered under her lashes. 'I've done nothing,' she murmured.

'You are one of them!' grated Pierre. His horny hands, one after the other, whipped across her buttocks. The sudden sting made her cry out. She felt a glow of heat from the blow. Aftershocks made the firm young flesh quiver and her well-tutored little anus sucked joyfully as if on a finger or Zeus's cock.

'I'm not, *mon frere*,' she murmured. 'I was taken against my will.'

Pierre shrugged and gestured that his companions should take Grace, which they did, dragging her unmercifully from the theatre.

Once out in the streets, which were still full with the milling populace, Grace tried to shrink back from the crowds. A roar of approval went up as they saw her, her gown in tatters fluttering about her naked body and her body pierced and bonded by the chains. She hung her head in shame and tried to bury her face on Pierre's thin shoulder, but he pushed her away.

This was worse; worse than anything she had suffered. Worse than the men who tried to rape her in the cemetery; worse than being impaled upon Zeus to be abused by the courtiers.

'These are your people, Grace,' muttered Pierre. 'Not those aristos.'

She knew Pierre was right, but the months she'd spent at Versailles had made her soft, used to comfort, no matter that madame and Pierre tormented her. She sobbed, stumbling upon the slimy cobbles and the remains of rotting food. She wished the ground would open up, swallow her, release her from misery.

'Almost at Robespierre's palace,' said Pierre. 'I believe he has quite a treat in store for you. Oh yes, *ma chere soeur*, we have heard what debauchery you enjoyed in Versailles.'

Grace began to deny it, but in truth, she could not. There were times when she was delirious with the pleasure meted out to her. She enjoyed the warm silkiness of a cock between her lips, the throb of it, the feel of the moist smooth globe at the back of her tongue. And, best of all, the deluge of male fluid that poured into her throat.

And madame had taught her the enjoyment of a tongue between her love lips. She could not resist the shudder in her captors' arms as she remembered the lap of lingual flesh upon her sex; the tickle of it upon her clitty and the resulting joy which welled up within her, made her spiral in a whirlpool of pleasure.

Her captors grasped her arms and dragged her through the imposing doorway of Citizen Robespierre's palace. The ill-clad guards leered at her nakedness as she was shoved ahead of her captors through the entry hall. This was magnificent in its grandeur, but unkempt, the ceilings draped with cobwebs.

'Down!' ordered Pierre as she was pushed through a narrow arch that led down into darkness.

'What is this place?' she asked, peering into the gloom. There was a chill in the air which made her bare skin roughen into goosebumps.

'The crypts,' replied Pierre. 'Robespierre uses these to extract information from those who shield the aristos.'

Grace shuddered against Pierre and, feeling the movement, he laughed.

'Does it remind you of something, little sister?' he asked.

'Versailles,' she murmured. It reminded her of the rooms beneath the king's palace where she was punished when first used by madame. The walls ran with damp and were green with lichen and moss. She heard the low moans of pain and voices begging for death. She shivered in the wet chill.

'*Oui*,' answered Pierre. 'We have heard about the king's debauchery with his subjects.'

One of Pierre's companions stepped forward, coming from out of the gloom. His broad hands were outstretched, his eyes glinting with lust. He pressed her nakedness to him and she looked over her shoulder, pleading with Pierre, but he shrugged and turned away. 'He merely wishes to keep you warm, little sister, until Robespierre is ready for you.'

The broad hands rubbed her belly and trembled as they slid over her breasts, feeling the nipple rings and the chains which connected them. Grace's breasts became fuller, more tender, and she arched towards the man. This encouraged him and the thick fingers entered the space between her parted thighs, gliding over the smooth skin. She shivered as the touch became more intimate, entering the crease of her bottom.

Pierre's friends laughed and moved closer. Their tattered breeches bulged heavily at the crotches. They were muscular, powerful, and she knew there was no point in trying to resist them. Her heart was beating fast as the one who had first touched her pushed her away with a hiss of disgust.

Another stepped forward. Had Pierre called him Raoul? He was tall, well built. 'You must do exactly as I say,' he said.

'I know,' said Grace, letting her head bow in a pliant, acquiescent manner. Had she not been impaled upon Zeus's cock and found pleasure in it? She shuddered within herself as she remembered the hard chill of the organ entering her tight passage, but at the same time she felt a tiny thrill of pleasure in her clitty.

The man laughed nervously and looked over his shoulder at her half-brother. 'Everything!' His voice became huskier and she could see his rigid cock probing through a rip in his breeches. 'Put your hands on your head.' He was so excited his voice was scarcely audible, but he turned to Pierre. 'She is very beautiful.'

'And very obedient,' added Pierre.

Grace held out her hands, showing her manacles and wrist chains. 'I cannot hurt you,' she said.

'Don't argue! Are you trying to make a fool of me in front of my friends?' Pierre's hand lashed out at her shoulder, but his aim was poor and he slapped her breasts, making the fine chains shimmer in the dim lights of the wall sconces, and making the pale flesh quiver. Her nipples became painfully erect and she felt colour drain from her face.

Slowly, she raised her hands and placed them obediently on her head. The chains that connected her wrists swayed over her pale face and made her look more slavish than ever.

Raoul probed a finger between her thighs. His hard mouth curved in a cruel smile that quickly changed to a snarl as he discovered her pussy lips were sealed by gold loops. Grace knew he could feel her dew, warm and slick, dripping on each jet frond and could, perhaps, feel her erect clitty nudging the closed lips.

'What is this?' he asked, tugging the rings as if he would rip them from her flesh.

'I am a virgin,' explained Grace, 'and madame was determined to keep me so.'

Pierre pulled her from Raoul and shook her. 'But you are a *putain* for the court; a whore. I have heard that the courtiers used you.'

'Madame taught me to use my tongue upon men,' explained Grace, 'to drink their spunk and be a receptacle for their come, but I remained a virgin.'

Raoul let his breeches fall to the rough flagged floor and Grace saw the full measure of his bloated penis, which he stroked slowly back and forth. She watched him lick his lips hungrily.

'Nothing else?' asked Pierre with a frown. 'She taught you nothing else?'

Grace bowed her head in embarrassment, not wishing to look at any of the men. Pierre shook her again, causing her hair to thrash back and forth about her pale face.

'Must I whip you to get the truth?' he asked.

Silently, Grace raised her eyes. 'Yes, I have tasted whips,' she told the men. She turned, allowing the tattered gown to open coyly to show the swollen hillocks of her bottom. She waited, expecting rough hands to part the rounded buttocks; to be invaded deeply. She quivered in this expectation.

'So pale,' sighed Raoul. 'So plump and smooth.' Grace stiffened as she heard his voice. It threatened her with everything that was degradation.

It was as if this was a signal. Horny hands reached out and touched her, making the firm flesh shudder. Fingers grasped the smooth swellings of her breasts, tweaked the rings which pierced her nipples, bringing tears to her eyes. Knuckles kneaded her flesh pot, bruising the tender flesh as they tried to part the folds.

'Robespierre will enjoy her,' said Pierre. 'But for now, manacle her to the wall.'

'But we were promised our fill!' Raoul growled out his grievance, his hands busy with his cock, rubbing the tight skin back and forth over his globe.

Two other men pulled Grace towards the lichen-slimed wall and locked her wrists into the rusty iron chains.

Pierre looked round, his eyes furtive, wary. 'We must be seen to obey, citoyen. How did I know about the rings that keep her sex closed?'

The iron was cold against Grace's wrists. It was hard and the edges were sharp. The fine links of her gold wrist chains bit into her skin beneath the iron. She was chained tightly against the wall and her breasts and belly puckered at the damp chill. Her bare feet scarcely touched the rough floor and her arms were strained in their sockets.

'Open her legs,' husked Pierre. 'Hold them open.' She was splayed as far as her ankle chains would allow.

Rough hands grasped her ankles and Grace mewed softly as the jewellery on her love lips tugged at her flesh. She felt her buttocks spread apart and her bottom hole investigated.

'Tight,' murmured Raoul, and Grace felt the tiny pleats spread open and the taut opening touched by a thick finger.

Other hands fingered her breasts, the heavy fullness, the jewelled nipples. There was nothing Grace could do but allow the caresses and taunts. Her very helplessness increased the heavy feeling in her belly.

Raoul penetrated her bottom with his finger, and Grace threw back her head as she felt the fullness in her sex increase. 'She is very willing about the bottom,' he said hoarsely. He withdrew his finger and Grace heard a sucking sound as he wetted it with spittle. The feeling of fullness returned as he thrust into her again, drawing the finger back and forth rhythmically.

'Stop!' ordered Pierre.

'But we were promised,' repeated Raoul. 'Promised.'

'A whore she might be,' said Pierre, 'but she is my sister.' His voice was full of sadness. 'And you are defiling her.'

Grace felt Raoul draw from her and she heard his harsh breathing slow. She gave a small sigh of relief, even though with her legs straddled as they were her cunny felt ready for the soft moistness of a tongue, or the stroke of fingers, but her shame was intense at her profanity before Pierre.

Her half-brother was at her shoulder, brushing her hair from her ears, whispering. 'It is punishment you need, *putain*!'

She shuddered at the intimation in his rough voice; that she could expect no mercy. She heard hate in his tone;

hatred for what she had become. But how could she have stopped the train of events?

'The paddle,' said Pierre. He stepped back. 'Yes, the paddle. That's what you may use upon her, Raoul. Punish her. You seem to set great store by her bottom. I am sure you will find enjoyment in using the paddle upon it.'

Peeping over her shoulder Grace looked at the smooth length of wood, polished to a sheen and whittled to a thin whippiness. The handle was thick and firm, a tube looking not unlike a turgid cock, but tapering to a short neck before flaring out to the blade of the paddle itself. Pierre had the instrument in his hands, admiring the workmanship with his fingers.

Relinquishing his cock, Raoul's eyes became alive as he focussed upon the finely shaped weapon. He took it from Pierre, smoothing the wood, waving it back and forth in the dank air. It made a high-pitched whistling noise that made Grace shiver and press herself closer to the wall.

The last shreds of the gown were torn from her back, leaving her bottom very naked and vulnerable. She clenched her buttocks tightly and was immediately chastised by Pierre.

'No, *ma chere*,' he said. 'Make your flesh loose and soft, otherwise how can Raoul and the other men watch the pretty quivers at each beat of the paddle?' His tone was harsh, full of the hatred he felt for her.

In her nervousness Grace found it difficult to relax her flesh, and she began to tremble against the damp chill of the wall. She turned her head this way and that, looking at the bared stiffness of the cocks of the men who stood so eagerly around her. In the flickering lights of the sconces the stretched flesh of the weapons looked dark and glossy, standing straight from the bushes at their groins.

'Is your bottom soft?' asked Raoul, standing close to her. 'Cool and smooth?'

Grace managed to nod and felt the warm thickness of his cock probing into the crack between the firm hillocks of her bottom.

'Good, *ma petite*,' he murmured, and she felt the whisper of his breath on her neck and through the dark tendrils of her hair. 'Soft and obliging.' She felt the stroke of the paddle over her flanks.

Almost immediately he stepped back and she heard the rasp of excited breathing from the other men. She heard the high-pitched whistle of the paddle cutting through the thick stale air. The paddle beat down, slicing over the softness of her flesh, making it burn with the heat of the blow.

A sound like the prelude to an orgasm whispered around the men. Grace held back her mewl of pain, biting her lips, for she felt a deeper sensation; a pleasurable swirl of warm liquid deep in her belly, a melting which made her beasts feel heavy and her head light.

'Again!' groaned the men almost in unison, and Grace strained her head again to watch them. Their fingers flashed smoothly up and down their cocks and she saw the lengths of flesh throb at each touch.

Scarcely had she chance to draw breath than the paddle sliced through the air once more. The sound of it was sharper in Grace's ears and the landing on her flesh was harder. Her skin burned, for the paddle echoed the first blow. Her buttocks tautened with the pain, closing around her anus, hiding the tiny bottom mouth.

'Is this what you do for the aristos?' rasped Raoul. 'Tease them? Deny them their pleasures?' He lifted her hair, baring the pink shell of her ear, and she felt the slippery wetness of his tongue driving deep into the outer canal. 'Well, we are not aristos,' he grunted, and Grace felt his slimy tongue tip trace the soft lobe. 'We are not refined and you can expect no mercy from us.'

Grace shuddered as she felt him step away from her. She tensed as she heard the paddle whistle as he drew it back. No mercy, he said. No mercy. The words echoed in her head, rang in her ears and her mouth opened, ready to scream just as the paddle beat down upon the same swollen place on her bottom. She felt her body grind against the damp wall with the force of the blow; heard the chains chink against the cold stone. The breath was forced from her lungs and the whimpering sound that whispered on her moistened lips was scarcely audible.

She lost count of the number of times the paddle battered her bottom hillocks. The pain and heat became as one, and in the midst of it came the pleasurable swirls making her cunt become the source of all her senses. Her juices bubbled over the locked sex lips, wetting them with a creamy sheen. Her hidden clitoris was greatly swollen, its hood drawn back, its tip raw and sensitive.

From all around she heard the grunts of pleasure from the men. She heard the clatter as Raoul threw the paddle to the rough floor. She felt the moist silkiness of a cock tip, pleasantly cool after the heat of her beating. It rubbed over the puffy flesh of her beaten bottom; back and forth, leaving a trail of pre-issue as it was smeared across the heated surface.

'Very shortly,' growled Raoul, 'you will feel the spunk of true *citoyens*. It will be more copious than that of the aristos – hotter, thicker.'

She could hear the slap of fists pumping rhythmically, could feel the jolt of Raoul's cock each time he slipped his foreskin up and down the thickness.

'Yes...' she murmured, surprising herself with the sound of pleasure in her voice. 'Yes... I want it... I want to feel it...'

'Good, *ma petite*,' grunted Raoul. 'Perhaps you'll become one of us after all.'

The slime of the first jet of his spunk made her jerk with pleasure as it landed upon the beaten flesh of her bottom. It was like a soothing balm. More spills hit her from every direction until her helpless body shone with male juices.

Breasts swollen with desire, Grace's nipples pained her around the fine gold rings, but even this was a source of pleasure. She almost thanked madame for her rigorous training; the training that taught her to find pleasure in whatever was done to her. The delight grew low in her belly, making it feel full and heavy and her sex very open, despite the rings that held it closed. If only, she thought, she had a lover who would penetrate her to the hilt. Her sex lips would welcome him, draw him in, pet his cock. As it was her cunt convulsed emptily, sucking upon nothing but air.

'Stay very still!' said a low, but very commanding voice.

Grace gasped and strained her neck to look round at the newcomer. He wore a hat low down over his eyes. A long coat with many capes upon the shoulders covered him from head to foot. He held pistols in both hands, and although he spoke French he did so with an English accent.

'*Merde*!' growled Pierre. 'The Black Rose!'

The Englishman chuckled. 'You are correct, *mon ami*, but please remember that you're all very vulnerable with your breeches about your ankles and your cocks covered only by your grubby fingers. My pistols are cocked…' He chuckled again at his double entendre. 'Ready to fire.'

'What do you want with us?' asked a man at the back of the group.

'Release the girl,' growled the Black Rose, 'and take care not to hurt her.'

Who was he, this Black Rose? Grace asked herself. She began to tremble afresh. Her orgasm was just a faint memory, leaving her sex very wet. The chains that held her to the wall had become almost part of her and she was loath to be released.

Rough hands unshackled her and fresh pain made her moan as feeling began to come back to her cramped limbs. She slid to the grimy floor, crouched like a young animal, her paddled buttocks glowing with heat and pain.

'I warn you not to hurt her!' rapped the Englishman, and he used the butt of a pistol to crack a head.

Grace, crouching helpless on the cold floor, reached up to her rescuer. 'Don't hit him again! I moaned because my limbs have been cramped. He did not hurt me.'

She turned onto her side and tried to wrap her arms about her breasts, to curl her legs close to them, hiding their fullness and the puffy wetness of her sex. Her movements were clumsy, far from graceful. She was stiff and slow and the men stared at her open thighs, at the gold rings that kept her outer labia so tightly closed. She began to weep at her clumsiness and her vulnerability.

The Englishman looked at her from beneath the brim of his hat. A strange expression was in his eyes; a mixture of lust and contempt. He threw his coat at her.

'Cover yourself,' he rasped, turning his eyes from her breasts, the delicate slenderness of her waist, and the flare of her hips. 'And follow me.'

It was a struggle, with her chained wrists and ankles, but Grace managed to wrap the full coat around her and pull herself upright on shaky legs.

Walking backwards, pistols in his hands, pointing with threatening steadiness at the sour-faced rabble, the Englishman gestured to Grace to follow him quickly through the dark labyrinths of tunnels that formed Robespierre's prison.

Within seconds they were out in the busy street and Grace found herself gathered into the man's strong arms. She felt her breast squeezed with vice-like fingers and she tried to pull away.

Deep-throated laughter filled the air around her head. 'What's this? Embarrassment? Humiliation? Surely not, from what I hear from Minette.' His fingers became less cruel and he cupped the breast, thumbing her ringed nipple, pulling the gold until tears came to her eyes.

'Not embarrassment, *monsieur*,' she said, lowering her jet lashes modestly. 'And as for humiliation...' She smiled up at him. 'I am trained to take any amount of that.'

He pushed her into the shadows between two buildings and parted the coat, letting the chill night air caress her nakedness. His hand grazed down her silky skin, tracing the curves of her body until it reached the apex of her thighs.

Lips fastened on the upper swell of her breasts and she shuddered, throwing back her head in ecstasy. His kiss was so sweet after the roughness of the men who'd kidnapped her. She felt the quiver which began in her breasts continue down to her belly and further to the downy black curls which grew so lushly on her mound.

His fingers were gentle as they cupped the pad of her flesh pot. They hovered there for long moments, until driving down to the dark slit between the full lips.

'Locked,' he murmured, pulling the loops that fastened the plump flesh of her labia. 'And within?' he asked. 'Is that, too, still locked?'

Grace shuddered as he stroked the moist curls that guarded her sex. His touch was tender and she had an urge to open her legs for him. The stroking was slow and rhythmic and she could feel her clitty behind the swelling flesh of her labia. It was becoming hard, becoming more sensitive. She moaned, arching her body, offering herself to him.

'Yes, *ma petite putain*,' he murmured, a chuckle punctuating his words. 'Come for me.'

His coat fell from her body, leaving her naked, arching against his caresses. Grace could not contain the pleasure he was creating within her. Her whole body felt liquid, heavy, like quicksilver.

'Scream for me,' he urged. 'Let me know how wonderful your orgasm is.'

The release was exquisite. Her body glowed, was on

fire with the pleasure he created. She screamed, letting out all the frustration which had built inside her in the months with madame; all the months in which she was taught to be graceful, delicately sensual.

'Yes, *putain*. Yes!' His voice was hoarse with lust and he turned her aggressively to face the wall. He forced her arms high above her head.

The wall was rough against the fine flesh of her breasts. The stone grated her erect nipples, tugged at the rings. She still shuddered as the aftermath of her orgasm faded. 'What have I done?' she murmured.

'Nothing,' he rasped, and she felt the warm hardness of his cock butting at the crease between her buttocks.

'Yes,' she pleaded. 'Yes, take me in that way.' Escaping Robespierre's dungeons made her feel reckless, inflamed her senses, made her want him to take her harshly.

'Indeed, I will,' he murmured, 'for I have plans for you. Oh, yes. Great plans.' Grace felt her breathing quicken as she wondered what he meant.

He drove all further questions from her mind as he held both her wrists with one hand, held them high against the wall and wrapped his other arm around her waist. She felt the silky moistness of his globe slicking up and down the tight cleft, felt it greasing the pleats of her bottom hole, butting it, opening it with every thrust.

She could hear his breathing harsh and quick in her ears; could feel his cock opening her rear entrance, pressing into the tightness, and she mewed with pleasure.

Within moments he was deeply inserted and she was impaled upon his thickness. The hand by which he held her about the waist slid down to the lush darkness of her sex bush and cupped it gently as he thrust into her. Grace could not hold back the sigh of delight that welled in her throat as he flooded her with gush after gush of his seed.

His harsh breathing slowed and she felt his cockstem withdraw. His hold on her relaxed, and she felt the loss of his warmth as he drew away from her.

With eyes closed dreamily she sensed him fasten his breeches and bend to pick up his coat, fallen to the cobbles in their passion, and then he was gone into the night, leaving her entirely alone.

Chapter Eight

After a few moments Grace peeped over her bare shoulder. She blinked her long lashes as she tried to adjust her eyes to the darkness of the narrow alley. Very slowly, she lowered her arms and hugged them about her as she began to shiver in the swirling night chill.

He had gone. The Black Rose, the Englishman, had gone, leaving her naked and alone. She could hear voices, not far away, but how could she show herself, naked and subjected to bondage, for all this was done with pure gold? A warm liquid trickled down the lower hillocks of her bottom and seeped down her thighs. This was all the Black Rose had left her.

Grace bowed her head and raised her manacled hands and hid her face in her palms, sobbing softly. What would happen to her now? She hadn't even the protection of madame.

She did not hear the footfall and it was a few moments before she realised that the night seemed darker than ever. A huge shadow loomed over her and she scarcely had a chance to scream before she was lifted high into the air.

A great booming laugh made her breasts and belly vibrate. It made the gold chains swing back and forth across the lower margin of her ribcage. The gold wrist cuffs and the chain between them pinched her arms and she wished her ankles were free so she could run from this new terror.

'What have you found, Cava?' The question was asked by a woman with a voice both deep and sensual.

With wide frightened eyes Grace ventured a peep in the direction of the voice. The woman was tall, statuesque, with a great mass of auburn hair piled on top of her well-shaped head.

'A pretty thing,' answered Cava haltingly.

Grace felt the warmth of a huge body and she snuggled into it, grateful for the relief from the chill and loneliness of the night.

'A sweet, pretty thing,' echoed Cava, 'who loves me.' A huge hand kneaded the softness of both Grace's breasts and she felt her body begin to respond to the caress. She urged her breasts into the bruising fingers and squirmed her belly until her cunny fur brushed the big man's palms. Grateful for the relief of the dreadful loneliness she'd felt when the Englishman disappeared into the night, she laid her head against Cava's huge chest and felt his thick fingers drive into her hair, arching her slim neck.

'Oh, put her down,' said the woman impatiently, 'and stop being so ridiculous.'

Grace found herself set gently upon her feet and screamed as she looked up at Cava, who was over seven feet tall and almost as wide as the alley in which they stood.

'You see?' said the woman scathingly. 'She does not love you. She is afraid, as would be most women when they become aware of what you hide in your breeches.' The woman tugged at Cava's ragged trousers, pulling them down to bare his muscular belly. 'You see, girl?' A cock, semi-turgid, and of massive length and girth was waved at Grace. 'Could you take this without being split asunder, eh?'

The woman narrowed her eyes as she noticed the gold chain slung from one pink nipple to the other, the gold anklets and the manacles. 'A slave?' she asked, and

134

began to look excited. 'Are there any other restrictions?'

Grace bowed her head and felt the shining mane of her hair swing down to brush her breasts.

'Well, girl? Answer me!'

'Yes, mistress,' said Grace, remembering her manners.

A hand slipped over the jet-curled mound and into Grace's slit. The woman's eyes widened as she felt the gold rings which closed the soft labia. 'A slave indeed!' she murmured as she drew the heel of her hand, very softly, back and forth over the warm moistness of the sex pouch. The hand was withdrawn and the woman smiled.

Grace glanced nervously from one to the other; the giant called Cava and the woman. The latter was tall, much taller than Grace but shorter than the man. Her muscular body was clad in a simple white gown sashed with the colours of the new republic. A rough piece of stone, hung upon a length of leather, nestled between her generous breasts.

Glancing again at Cava's naked cock Grace could not help but lick her lips, mentally tracing its tip around her mouth. A heavy pearl of dew seeped from the massive globe and she could, in her mind, taste the salt of his seepage. She felt a churning, a wetness in her belly, a familiar heaviness, and she smiled up into the giant's eyes.

'I feel she could take me, mistress,' said Cava, stroking his cock in thoughtful movements. 'She, above all women, could take this monster with which I am cursed.'

'I doubt it, Cava,' said the woman, 'but she does seem very compliant and submissive.' Strong hands, not those of the giant, but feminine in their length and elegance, grasped Grace's arms and peered at her through the mist and the darkness. 'She is a pretty thing, I agree.'

A hand stroked the underswell of her breasts and fingered the chains that looped her nipples. 'Not only is she pretty, she is rich, despite her lack of clothing,' remarked the woman. 'These chains are gold – pure gold.' She paused, looking extremely pleased with herself. 'And she is a slave. Pick her up and take her to my house.' The woman walked ahead and then turned round, wagging her finger in warning. 'Gently, mind. Do not damage her.'

Cava lifted Grace as if she was made of finest porcelain. He bent his head and brushed his huge lips across her own. The sensation made Grace shudder, but not unpleasantly. She could feel the sway of his upright cock, fully erect now, brushing against her buttocks. Its tip, slippery with spunk, butting with every stride into her tight cleft.

Behind them was the woman, her muscular body moving with feline grace over the wet cobblestones.

'Who is she?' whispered Grace, her dark eyes questioning Cava.

'A leader of the new order,' whispered the giant.

'The new order?' The phrase made Grace shudder.

'She and a compatriot were very much to the fore at the start of the revolution,' explained Cava.

Again Grace shuddered. She did not like this talk of revolution. And now she was in the very thick of it, it seemed.

'She is Charlotte de Levis,' said Cava proudly. 'You see the stone she has between her breasts?'

Grace remembered wondering why anyone should wear a piece of rough stone to chafe tender flesh. 'Yes,' she murmured. 'What is it?'

'A souvenir,' murmured Cava. His breathing was quick, the breath rasping in his throat, and Grace could still feel the organ throbbing against her buttocks, pressing eagerly between the plump cheeks.

'A souvenir of what?' probed Grace. Once again she could feel the melting heat of her own growing pleasure in her belly. She longed to splay her thighs for the giant, to feel the huge cock pressing open the soft wetness of her labia, butting against her clitty and, at last, tearing into her virgin sex.

'The people, with Charlotte and her compatriot at the fore, stormed the Bastille, and my mistress picked up a stone driven from its walls by a battering ram.' Cava kissed Grace again, his lips brushing against hers. The kiss was surprisingly sensual, and Grace shuddered.

'Hurry up, Cava,' Charlotte de Levis cried over her broad shoulder. Her eyes darted beneath Grace's cradled body, saw the nestling tip of the huge cock within the girl's bottom cleft. 'Ah, I see. You rampant wretch. I shall have to punish you. Put her down this instant.'

'But mistress...' pleaded Cava, 'she is hobbled. She cannot walk.'

Grace huddled against the giant's chest. Her ankles were raw from the hours of being clasped in the gold shackles. To walk would be terribly painful.

'Down!' There was no arguing with the order. 'I shall help her. We're almost home. I shall make sure she will not be hurt. She is far too valuable for...' The woman paused. 'Far too valuable.'

Grace could not help wondering what made her so valuable. Was it the gold?

Cava, reluctantly, set Grace upon her sore feet, his eyes sorrowful and sympathetic.

'For heavens sake!' screamed Charlotte. 'Stop looking at her with those puppy eyes. Can't you see she's a sex slave, kept to be used by those debauched aristos?' She slapped the giant's cock, first with one hand and then the other. 'And put that away. We have much work to do to retrain this girl.'

Grace shivered. Retrain? What did the woman mean? Hadn't she suffered enough with madame?

'Come along, girl!' Grace felt an arm wrapped about her waist and fingers caressing the underswell of a breast. She winced as a nipple ring was twisted and the gold chain was hefted to feel the value of it. The woman smiled into her eyes, but there was something in the smile that made Grace turn her head away.

Charlotte shrugged and hurried Grace along. She noticed that the woman looked furtive and glanced over her shoulder as if she expected someone to be following. She was too tired to notice where they were and felt only relief when she was eventually laid upon a comfortable sofa.

When she next opened her eyes sunshine was streaming through tall elegant windows, and bathing her naked body in warmth.

'Awake at last!'

The woman she knew as Charlotte was leaning over her and kissing each breast, misted with the warmth of the gracious room. Grace looked around, amazed that a woman who was a revolutionary could afford such luxury.

Charlotte laughed as if she could read Grace's mind. 'I used to live in a garrett and my only luxury was to be visited by my English lover. But when the revolution began and the aristos ran, there were empty palaces for the taking.'

Grace lay, still in her chains, on the damask sofa. Behind her stood Cava, his breathing harsh and rapid, his breeches bulging with the fullness of their contents.

Something glinted in Charlotte's hand. 'I am going to release you from your slavery,' she said, and her voice was low, husky as though with lust. 'Let your knees fall open and be loose.'

Grace trembled. The implement in Charlotte's hand was stroked up and down her belly, leaving a fine red line on her pale skin before it disappeared into the lushness of her jet-black pussy hair. The delicate hillock of her sex mound rippled at the chill touch of the surgeon's cleaver.

'It will not hurt,' said Charlotte softly, 'and your sex will be free and open.' Grace felt the touch of the woman's hands grazing over the crisp dark curls, and she felt the seepage of her fluids at the thought of such freedom.

'Free and open,' echoed Cava, and Grace lifted her eyes, darker than ever with fear, but heavy with longing for him to ravage her.

'Do not move now,' warned Charlotte, 'and keep those knees fully open.' She looked up at Cava. 'Place a pillow under her bottom to lift and make her sex more available to me.'

'Yes, mistress,' and Cava's voice sounded eager.

Grace felt the fumbling of Cava's thick fingers stroking the quivering skin of her buttocks. She felt the cool of a satin pillow and felt her sex lifted high in the air, making her body arched and available.

The surgeon's cleaver sliced through the air towards Grace's offered mound, and her spread thighs trembled as the shining instrument neared her body.

'Be still!' Charlotte de Levis frowned down at Grace. 'Cava!'

'Yes, mistress?' The big man bent over Grace and she could feel his body heat, smell his maleness, and it excited her. His nose was close to her breasts, almost brushing the gold links between her nipples, and his eyes were half-closed with lust.

'Hold her,' ordered Charlotte. 'Arms high over her head and ankles tightly together.'

With any other man the task would have been impossible, but with Cava it was easy. His arm span was as vast as his bulging cock.

'Yes, mistress.' He knelt at the side of the damask sofa and gripped Grace's wrists, thrusting them hard over her head and clasping her manacled ankles in his vice-like grip so that she was held fast.

Once more Charlotte busied herself with the surgeon's cleaver, sawing through the soft gold which held Grace's labia tightly closed. She could feel the heat of friction and the warmth made her tremble with fear that her

139

tender flesh would be cut, but the rings were fine and the task was quickly accomplished.

As the rings were slid from the flesh of her labia, were drawn out of the dark hair, the plump folds fell open, displaying the flushed skin beneath and the erect pip of her clitty rearing up from the silky darkness of her sex.

'Oh, mistress,' murmured Cava, bending over Grace, sniffing the freshness of her virgin sex. 'How beautiful! May I touch it, kiss it?'

'Perhaps,' answered Charlotte, 'but we must release her other bonds so that her legs will be free to be splayed fully open.'

Grace felt her belly become soft with anticipation of that freedom. With her sex lifted by the pillow beneath her buttocks she wanted Cava's massive organ inside her more than ever. She felt her nubbin jerk to become fully exposed from its tiny hood, and she felt a delicious flood of warm fluid from deep within her.

At last her ankles, raw and sore from the hobbling, were free of the shackles. 'Bring some salve, Cava,' ordered Charlotte.

Grace raised tender eyes to Cava as she watched him rise. The bulge in his ragged breeches was more pronounced than ever, and her belly seemed to melt at the thought of caressing it with her mouth and cunny.

She shuddered as she perceived the gentleness of a kiss upon her open flesh pot, the lifted moistness. Her dark eyes flashed open as she realised it was Charlotte's lips sucking upon each plump pussy fold. She heard the hiss of breath as the woman sniffed the growing musk of Grace's excitement. A tongue lapped around the root of her clitty and rimmed her virgin opening.

Grace mewed and pressed her eager and long frustrated cunt against the questing mouth. She felt strong arms enfold her and long fingers squeeze each breast. She tasted her own musk as Charlotte moved up and placed her lips on her own.

'You look so beautiful with chains at your breasts,' murmured Charlotte. 'So slavish. I cannot bear to remove them. At your wrists, too. They make you look so vulnerable, so submissive. Just as Albert would like.'

If it occurred to Grace to ask who Albert was, she said nothing. Neither did she demur when the woman lifted her ragged skirt and straddled Grace. She pressed her naked pussy upon Grace's, who felt the other's crisp cunny curls grating against her own slippery skin. She felt her clitty abraded back and forth and felt her pleasure rising to a glorious peak.

'Yes,' whispered Grace. 'Yes.' She began to move with the woman, increasing the abrasion.

'I can feel you coming,' said Charlotte huskily. 'I can feel the throb of your clitty, the sucking wetness of your cunny. Let it flow, my darling. Pour your juices upon my pussy hair.'

Grace could not help but let out a long scream of pleasure as she convulsed beneath Charlotte. The woman held her, cradling her until she calmed.

'Was that your first time, my sweet?' asked Charlotte, rolling onto her side. Her skirt was still bunched about her waist and her auburn pussy curls were glossy with juices. Her cheeks stained with scarlet, Grace shook her head. How could she say that she was entirely innocent when madame and Philipe had her writhing with pleasure time after time? When Zeus had impaled her bottom hole, and the Englishman had taken her from behind?

Charlotte frowned and, with two straight fingers, opened Grace's female mouth. She arched in pain and mewed plaintively.

'I don't understand,' said Charlotte, removing her fingers.

'I am a virgin,' confessed Grace, 'although I have knowledge of pleasure of many kinds.'

'Delightful,' murmured Charlotte. 'An innocent with knowledge of pleasure. You will be very valuable to us.

Very valuable to our cause.' She pointed to the glossy lushness between her own thighs, which she spread lewdly. 'Press my pussy open with your chained hands, my darling, and place your lips where it will give me most pleasure. I know you understand exactly what I mean.'

The opulent room was filled with Charlotte's rich scent, the sweet aroma of her musk. Grace felt her shudder as the gold chains that looped across her breasts swayed across her belly. The woman shuddered again in obvious delight as Grace's manacles chinked as she used her hands to spread the quivering pussy lips.

The auburn curls were glossy with Grace's own juices, and she smoothed them away from the scarlet cleft before spreading the two plump lips apart.

'A kiss, my darling,' murmured Charlotte, 'and let your lips linger on my flesh.'

Grace buried her nose into the soft wetness and heard the woman groan in ecstasy. Her lips felt the swollen hardness of Charlotte's clitty and she took it into her mouth, rolling back the little hood with her tongue and sucking as if upon a milky teat.

As she sucked, slowly and rhythmically, she let a finger slither into Charlotte's open cunny and felt it clutch as if to imbibe it into her body.

'Two fingers,' groaned Charlotte, 'and push hard, back and forth. You're giving me so much pleasure, my darling. So much. I cannot hold back...' She groaned so loudly that Grace could almost imagine she was in pain, but her body was throbbing with pleasure and she continued to suck and delve into the soft wetness.

Mouth slippery and glossy with Charlotte's juices, Grace was at last pushed away.

'The salve, mistress,' said Cava, standing over them.

'Then use it on the poor girl's ankles,' snapped Charlotte, pulling down her skirts.

Cava knelt at Grace's feet and opened the jar of salve.

His touch was gentle for such a huge man and Grace closed her eyes, enjoying the cool of the cream on her burning ankles.

'She is a virgin, Cava,' Charlotte reminded the giant. 'You would split her asunder.'

Cava's big head jerked up. His eyes filled with tears. The heavy bulge in his breeches became fuller and more prominent. He bowed his head once more and rubbed more salve into Grace's feet.

'But I am sure I could take you, Cava,' said Grace softly.

A warmth swirled in her belly and between her love lips there was a feeling of liquidity. Her clitty was bathed with creamy lubrication and she could feel a pulsing in the pit of her womanhood.

'Let me try, mistress,' begged Grace. 'Let me take him into my body.'

'Perhaps if I greased my cock with the salve...' suggested Cava, pushing the ragged waistband of his breeches down over the muscular flatness of his belly. His cock was iron-hard and standing upright to above his waist. The globe shone with pre-issue, as if it was polished. In the centre of the naked sphere the eye pulsed and drooled. The thickness was such that Grace was sure she would be unable to put her fingers around its circumference, or stretch her mouth to caress it with her lips.

'Well, my dear?' queried Charlotte, her lips twisted in an ironical smile. 'Do you still think you could take this monster?'

The wanting made Grace spread her legs to their full extent, offering her freshly freed cunny to the giant. She let her knees fall open and loose and she could feel her love lips swell and become deliciously soft.

'With the salve, mistress,' she murmured. 'I am sure I could with the salve.'

With a sigh Charlotte de Levis sat back upon a low

damask covered chair. The ragged gown looked incongruous in such an elegant setting. She pulled her skirts over her knees and spread them, giving Grace a hint of her fiery pussy bush. 'It shall be as you wish, my darling,' she said, reaching forward to stroke Grace's flushed cheek. 'Kneel before Cava and smear his cock with a generous layer of salve.'

Grace slid from the sofa and knelt at the big man's feet, taking the jar of cream from him. He had released his breeches and stepped out of them. His muscular legs were spread wide and his magnificent balls were taut in their smooth sac. His cock speared up, away from his big body, swaying and eager, the skin shiny as it stretched over its fullness.

Within her belly Grace felt a warm melting as if her sex turned to molten liquid. Seepage drooled down her inner thighs, lying on the pale skin like shimmering pearls. Her outer love lips felt soft and swollen, and within was the flushed moist bed on which stood her clitty, arching and throbbing.

The salve felt cool as she dipped her fingers into the pot. It was silky smooth to the touch. She looked up at Cava, who smiled down at her and stroked her mane of black hair, the soft curve of her parted her lips. She was afraid, but she had been forced to wait for the feel of a man's cock, had yearned for it since madame had taught her the delights of sex.

'Lie upon the carpet, my darling,' murmured Charlotte. 'It is soft and will not chafe your lovely body.'

Grace could hear Charlotte's excited breathing and Cava's rasping grunts as she spread herself gracefully on the richly coloured Persian rug. She placed her hands above her head, which thrust her taut breasts high. The ringed nipples were flushed and erect and the fine gold chains quivered on her narrow ribs with each breath she took. Finally, she spread her thighs to their fullest extent. Her belly was hollowed and her sex mound, black as jet, was raised and a stark contrast to her pale skin.

'A pillow for her buttocks,' whispered Charlotte, her eyes never leaving Grace's body.

Grace could not help but moan as she felt the cool silk of the cushion against the heat of her bottom. The pillow was plump and forced her legs further apart and her sex mound upwards.

'On your knees, Cava,' ordered Charlotte, 'and be gentle with her, or it will be the worse for you. You are not so big that I can't punish you.' Her voice had an edge to it that made Grace shudder, and she saw Cava's eyes glitter with fear as he sank to his knees between Grace's straddled thighs. The big man shrugged out of his ragged shirt and she saw the reason for his fear; a network of healed scars criss-crossed his broad back.

'Open yourself up, my darling,' said Charlotte, her voice soft and purring once more. 'Show Cava your full delights.'

Grace heard the giant groan as she opened her love lips to show him she was ready and to make his entry that much easier. As she did so her forefinger grazed the tip of her clitty and she sighed with the sudden shiver of pleasure that spun through her body. She dipped her finger into the creamy pit of her entrance and rubbed it over the whole surface of her sex. Cava made and animal-like roar and pressed forward until his globe touched her sex. She shuddered, not with horror, but with joy.

With a slight movement of her hips she arched her sex above the pillow, offering it to him. She felt the pressure of his thickness but her maidenhead did not give. He thrust again, but no matter that she wanted him inside her, there was still a resistance. She began to whimper in her frustration and Cava sweated with effort.

'What's wrong?' asked Charlotte, her voice sharp with exasperation. 'Why is she not screaming in agony?'

The sound of loud voices intruded upon the scene. Grace, with anxious eyes, looked towards the door and cupped her chained hands about her plump sex. Cava had moved away from her and was reaching for his breeches. The door was flung open and a man stood staring at the tableau before him. He began to laugh, throwing back his head and slinging his broad-brimmed hat across the room.

'So you found her, Charlotte!' he said. It was the Englishman. Grace recognised his halting French. 'And I see you have unlocked the gate to earthly paradise.'

He strode across the room and crouched down between Grace's thighs. She turned her face away and closed her eyes as if this would hide her embarrassment.

'Look at me,' said the Englishman. He grasped her wrists, pulling them away from her sex.

Reluctantly, Grace let her lashes flutter open and met his mocking gaze. It was as if he could see into her most intimate places. She could not resist when he bent down and stroked the places where the gold rings had kept her love lips tightly closed. His touch was slow and sensual and promised delights yet unknown to Grace. Very slowly, he opened the plump lips, using the thumb and forefinger of one hand.

She knew her flesh was still sleek from her copious issue and knew, too, that her clitty was hugely erect, its tip bared with the hood drawn back. Once more her cheeks burned with humiliation at his close inspection.

'But the gate is still not open?' He chuckled and grazed the pad of his other thumb over her clitty. Grace could not help but whisper a pleasurable sigh and she felt her hardened pippin judder under his touch. He chuckled again and rubbed the heel of his hand into the wetness of the pit Cava could not enter. 'I'm surprised.'

'I was afraid of hurting her, monsieur,' murmured Cava, miserably.

'And I suppose the idea of opening up those rings of hers was yours, Charlotte,' said the Englishman.

Charlotte de Levis stood and faced him, her rags looking as refined and elegant as the most fashionable of gowns. She placed her hands firmly on her hips and held her head high. 'And why not?' she said. 'Some wretch left her in an alley, naked and chained.'

'Yes,' said the Englishman. 'I rescued her from Robespierre's clutches, but I was called away. I knew you were not far behind me and I knew you would see her value.'

His aristocratic fingers continued to caress Grace's cunny, slicking the sensitive flesh, the puffy folds, the pert and flushed bud, and she could do nothing but writhe under his touch. She remembered some shouting, some screams at the end of the narrow alley, but it was as if they were in a dream world and not real at all. She remembered how the Englishman, the Black Rose, slipped from her and into the shadows of the night.

'Well, now,' he purred. 'Since you have been spared the fate of being torn to pieces by this monstrous pet of Charlotte's, I think you will fetch a pretty price for me, and I know exactly who will purchase you.'

'For you?' Charlotte questioned crossly. 'Whatever she fetches should be given to the cause, surely?'

The Englishman grinned and swept Charlotte into his arms. 'Of course, my dear. That is what I meant.'

But Grace saw the grin fade and a hardness take its place as he released Charlotte and turned his gaze to her.

Chapter Nine

The small ship dipped and plunged perilously into the grey waters of the English Channel. Grace clung to the rail, the spray soaking the fluttering muslin of her gown.

'You will catch a chill.' The Englishman placed his hands upon her shoulders and tried to guide her below.

'I don't care,' murmured Grace. 'I feel so ill I don't care if I die.'

He pressed her to him and she could feel the chains and rings which adorned her nipples pressing painfully into his chest. His hands gripped the cheeks of her bottom, the fingers digging into her flesh. Her buttocks were wrenched apart and his fingers slid up and down the tight cleft. The pain of his cruel grip at least made her forget the misery of her seasickness.

His lips pressed against hers. His tongue ravaged her mouth as his fingers sought her intimate places. Her muslin gown was so wet and transparent, moulding to the rich curves of her slender body that she might as well have been naked against him.

'What is he like?' she murmured when he at last freed her. 'This man to whom you will sell me?'

'Dark, very handsome, and foreign,' he said, with a strange smile.

'Foreign?' Grace forgot, for the moment, her nausea. 'You mean French?' It would be so wonderful if she was to be sold to a Frenchman.

'He speaks French among other languages,' he said enigmatically. 'And you will not be alone.'

'No,' she said happily. 'I shall be with him.'

'And other girls.'

Suddenly the deck pitched as the small ship was flung high on a huge wave and then plunged into a dip so deep that Grace screamed, thinking they would be thrust down into the depths of Hell itself.

But he held her tight and she felt safe, even in this terrible sea. Breath caught in her throat as her cunny, under his less than tender probing, became moist. She wished with all her heart that he would touch her on its most sensitive peak, but he deliberately skirted around the silky root.

'Is he kind?' she asked above the scream of the wind in the rigging and the noisy flap of the billowing sails.

He chuckled and shrugged. 'As kind as any husband is to his wife,' he answered.

Grace's eyes fluttered open and she tried to see him clearly through the mist of streaming rain. 'Husband? I am not to be his slave, but his wife?' She could not believe what she heard.

'Does that distress you?' His mouth quirked in a strange sardonic smile.

'No,' she murmured, but she laid her head wearily on his chest, unable to believe that her slavery was at last over. Despite her denial a frisson of fear niggled at the back of her mind. It was the fear of the unknown.

She had known poverty and she had known slavery. But marriage? That was something else again. Now she was to be a chattel.

'Don't be afraid,' he said, holding her close. 'Perhaps it won't be as bad as you think – to be a wife.'

She frowned up at him, blinking into the sea spray. Why did he hesitate?

'Come below,' he murmured. Once more he drove his fingers into the firm flesh of her buttocks, first prising them widely apart and then squeezing them together. 'I have just the cure for *mal de mer*.' He smiled, a twisted smile which made Grace quiver against him.

He helped her down the steep and narrow companionway. Grace was unable to stop the shivering which wracked her body. Her muslin gown clung wetly to her sea-soaked body. True, she could feel the sensual warmth of his hands and it was in direct contrast to her own chill.

On the last step she stumbled and fell into his arms. Her gown ripped, baring the water-slicked heaviness of her breasts, with the trembling adornments of gold pierced through the flushed nipples surrounded by the creamy pale mounds. He laughed and brutally completed the tear in her gown, allowing the muslin to fall in tattered curtains on each side of her body. His eyes went immediately to the neat triangle of pubic curls, black as jet and glossed by the sea water. With a low growl he

149

swept her up and walked steadily into his cabin.

Once there he set her down, but kept a close hold on her wrist and reached up with his other hand to the top of a locker.

A lantern swung from a low beam with every movement of the ship. The flickering light cast eerie shadows upon both of them, and Grace's dark eyes widened as she saw his hand close upon a shadowed item on top of the locker. Her lips parted, apprehensive and trembling, but no sound came from them.

'No need to fear my little friend,' he said in a low voice.

Grace tried to tug away from him, but he held her fast. And if she did break free, where could she go? Into the sea?

'Your little friend?' she said at last in a voice no more than a whisper. 'The whip?'

In his free hand he held a beautifully fashioned length of leather. The handle was intricately plaited and tapered to a single length which was so supple that it moved on the cabin floor as though alive; a serpent, hungry for prey.

'But why?' Grace could scarcely enunciate the words. Her tongue was stiff and her lips dry with the fear of the unknown.

'Oh, come now,' he chided. 'You took whippings gladly at the palace, and even took the paddle in Robespierre's cells. And here...' he stroked the whip between her legs, letting her pussy lips fold around the thickness of the handle '...here there were all the signs that you enjoyed every moment of it.'

Grace felt two patches of heat flare on her cheeks and she dipped her head in embarrassment. She could see the cylinder of leather disappearing between her thighs and she could not stop herself bearing down upon the plaited tube, encouraging him to saw it back and forth between her love lips. She felt the leather chafe against the sensitive folds, opening them out, baring her most secret place. She heard him laugh, a low chuckle deep in his throat, as if he was enjoying some secret joke.

Moisture, warm and creamy, dripped onto the leather. Grace could feel the tube becoming slippery and could feel her clitty tip butting against the slowly moving handle. She clutched her buttocks, urging him to move the leather faster. She mewed and flung back her head, tossing her sea-soaked hair back from her face and allowing it to sway heavily across her shoulders.

'So sensual,' she heard him murmur, 'so deliciously sensual. Come, my darling, come. Let your clitty throb upon the leather, soak it for me. Let your juices seep into it.'

Grace could smell her own musk as she became more and more excited. Her body writhed from side to side as he thrust the cylinder back and forth, but never once entered her.

'I want... I want...' murmured Grace, her legs trembling with need.

'What is it you want?' he asked, halting the sawing motion of the rod. 'Tell me, my darling.'

'I want...' Grace was breathless. Her breasts were thrust out, her back bowed and her long legs straddled widely apart. 'To be rid of my maidenhead.' The last words tumbled from her lips.

He slid the plait of leather from her, even though she was still hovering on the brink of orgasm. He laughed, the same cruel, sardonic laugh. 'Is that so, my darling girl?'

'Oh, please!' She was so close to her peak of pleasure, but he drew her back. 'Please, don't stop!'

He grasped her wrists, both in one of his strong hands, and pulled her across the narrow space of the cabin. He grasped so hard that he squeezed the gold manacles into the tender flesh of her wrists, squeezing and bruising. It was a relief when he released her, but the relief was short-lived as he pulled her upward by means of the chain between the manacles. Her body was stretched, her breasts flattened, her belly hollowed. Grace gave a soft scream as her feet left the floor of the cabin and the chain was looped over a hook in the bulkhead. She was suspended, swinging helplessly.

Her orgasm was so close. The movement of the ship caused her to chafe her breasts against the polished wood of the cabin wall and she moaned, pleaded, but he said nothing – did nothing. She knew his eyes were on her, watching her breasts flatten against the cabin wall, perhaps admiring the smallness of her waist, caressing the swell of her buttocks, the dark place between her legs.

Above the creaking of the timbers, above the whistle of the wind in the rigging, above the sound of the waves crashing against the hull, Grace heard another sound; a high-pitched scream. It was not her own. It was unearthly, inanimate. It was as though a knife cut the air itself.

In the very next moment a sharp knife sliced the plumpest part of her bottom flesh. At least, the pain was so intense that was how it seemed. Her body arched on its suspension as the whip stung her bottom. A branding iron could not have burned her skin less.

He stood close behind her and she could feel the thickness of his cock, hard and rigid, through his buckskin breeches. His breathing was loud in her ears, harsh and rapid.

'And are you coming now, my darling?' he whispered hoarsely.

Grace could scarcely breathe for the smarting pain across her bottom. It felt as if her skin was flayed from her flesh and yet, strangely, her cunny was moist, dew mingled with the sea spray, and it trickled down her inner thighs. She tried to speak, but could only make a feeble whimpering sound.

'Nothing to say?' he said, and the words were growled.

With her clitty greatly swollen, itching and more erect than she had ever known it, Grace's need was to place her fingers between her thighs, spread her cunny lips and ease the terrible ache, but she could not. Her hands were held fast by the manacles and the chain. She was helpless, swinging back and forth.

She did not hear him step back, but she felt the chill of his absence. Twisting her head, her cascade of shimmering wet hair whipped from her back to her captured breasts. She saw the pallor of his handsome face, the flush of his full lips and their thin smile. She saw him draw back the whip, heard it whistle through the air, and felt again the sting of its lash.

This time she managed a barely audible scream. She felt the first flush of supreme pleasure and hoped that her orgasm would consume her; would negate the burn of the whip, or even better, enhance it. She concentrated hard upon the itching tip of her nubbin. She focussed all of her thoughts upon that burning little bud. Such was the pleasure she drew from her thoughts that she managed a smile; managed to trail her tongue tip about her lips. In her mind's eye she saw her swollen bud throbbing in its inflamed bed of silky flesh.

'And now, my darling,' he whispered, standing very close to her, 'your climax is upon you, is it not?'

His deep voice startled her from her thoughts. Could he read them?

Another flush of pleasure flooded through her body, made all the greater by the touch of his finger on the swelling weals brought up by the whip. The waves of pleasure broke on her faster and faster and she mewed as each one consumed her. If only the thick rigidity of his cock would plunge into her pulsing cunny, but it seemed doomed to clutch upon the empty air.

'You will appreciate my little friend all the more,' he said, rubbing the folded whip back and forth in the running valley of her cunt. 'Your pleasure will continue until you can bear it no longer; until you beg me to stop.'

Wrists rubbed raw by the gold manacles, lower arms aching and upper arms almost wrenched from their sockets, Grace flung back her head in a gesture of weariness. Her bottom felt swollen. He was truly an expert with the finely tanned leather whip.

Again he stepped back and Grace heard soft rustlings. Once more she dared to look over her shoulder and blushed as she saw him fully naked. He was a magnificent man. Broad of shoulder, narrow of waist and hip, chest dark with hair, he was bigger in manhood than any man she had seen apart from Cava. As she looked, he smiled, and stroked the whip up and down his cock.

'Soon, my darling,' he murmured, 'very soon.'

Grace bowed her head again as she saw him draw back the whip. Try as she might she could not relax her buttocks to take the sting of the lash on spongy flesh. Instead her bottom was tight, the two hillocks drawn together as if to hide from the cut of the leather. She could not hold back her squeal of pain. The lash landed across the cuts he had already made.

'Just a few more, my darling,' he said in honeyed tones. 'Believe me, you will thank me for it when we lie together.'

Breathing was almost impossible and Grace attempted to take great gulps of air, but the small cabin seemed devoid of it. It felt stuffy, and she could only gasp like a fish out of water, her mouth open and her lips parted. Did he say 'lie together', she asked herself. Did he mean that in the fullest sense of the word?

Once more her flesh pot prepared itself; became soft and open. Warm driblets of cream gathered on the flushed and puffy folds. The thick outer portals, covered in the crisp dark curls, were glossy with her juices. Grace moaned, not in pain but in need of the ecstatic mixture of the pain and pleasure he seemed to have promised.

Glancing over her shoulder she took another quick look

at his naked magnificence. His trunk-like thighs were spread apart. From the dark mound of his pubis speared a cock that made her quiver with its splendour. It was fully turgid and she could see the dark shadows of its pulsing veins clambering like vines about its thickness. She licked her lips, hungry to feel its silkiness between her lips. At its pinnacle she could see the shimmer of its globe, polished and naked, its foreskin drawn back beyond the glans. It sprouted from balls that were full and perfectly round, hard and spherical, pressing against a taut sac.

With a narrow smile, no longer sardonic but lustful, he drew back the whip, allowing it to fall with a slap upon the bare boards of the deck. Grace tensed, ignoring the pain, although it was not easy to ignore the sting of cuts across her bottom. These brought the thrill of sensual pleasure to her sex, made them pout and wetted her nubbin. The shrill of the whip cutting the air behind her seemed endless and she heard her own voice, as if beyond the ship, far out on the sea, sobbing piteously, hiding the pleasure wave which soared through her body.

At last the fine leather touched her body, not on her tortured bottom, but at her waist, snaking around it, pulling at it vigorously, whittling it to unimaginable smallness. Grace felt the breath knocked from her as her lower body was lifted from the deck and further strain was placed on her wrenched arms.

Suddenly the sense of being stretched beyond endurance was over and she was in his arms, the whip still wrapped tightly about her waist, bonding her to him; skin upon skin, sex upon sex. They lay, very close together, on the bare boards of the deck.

'My beauty, my gloriously innocent beauty,' he murmured. She felt his lips melt against hers and felt his hands take her breasts as if he would drag the flesh from her bones.

Between her thighs Grace could feel the smooth

warmth of his cock, sawing back and forth in the same manner he used the handle of the whip. She felt it become slippery with her juices, slick with her cream. She felt its ridges, pulsing like her own flesh. It teased her, brushed against the tip of her clitty, made her shudder with unbelievable delight.

He still had not penetrated her and Grace shivered against his broad chest, needing fulfilment.

The two were so engrossed in each other that they didn't hear the commotion of docking; the dropping of the anchor and the lowering of the gangway. Neither did they hear muffled voices, growled angry words, the harsh blows of knuckles upon flesh.

Grace felt only the smooth moist head of his cock nestle between her love lips, soaking in her dew. As they kissed she could not help the moan which whispered from her lips.

The door crashed open and a chorus of cruel laughter filled the small cabin. Grace's murmur of pleasure became a scream of horror and she tried to pull away from the Englishman, but the tight coils of the whip locked them.

Once more Grace felt the sweet taunt of denial. The Englishman was so close to fucking her and now these ruffians had interrupted that potentially glorious moment.

'What a precious sight!' murmured one. Grace could tell by his voice that he was young and she felt his eyes on her bruised and swollen bottom, on her slightly parted thighs and the moist nest between them.

Such was the depth of her training from madame that it was only natural to part her thighs, displaying the cleavage between her buttocks and the fullness of her love lips. There was an ache between her legs that refused to be ignored, and a continuous throbbing in her sex.

'She's asking for it, lads,' said an older man. 'We've been sent to the right ship, that's for certain.'

The Englishman was suddenly on his feet and Grace felt herself flung from him as he uncoiled the whip from her waist. Her thighs fell fully apart, her whipped bottom faced the open door and her cunt was evidently in a full state of sexual tension.

'Who are you?' he snarled. The Englishman held the whip at his side, ready to let it rip on his would be attackers when the moment was right.

The intruders scarcely paid him attention. Their eyes were fixed on Grace's vulnerable body, the raised weals on her pale buttocks, her cunny, the manacles on her wrists and the chains that swayed from her breasts. She closed her eyes, shutting out their leering faces.

The whip slashed the air and its fine tip caught the older man about the cheek, laying it open. Grace screamed and rolled away, but she was trapped against the bulkhead, vulnerable to the men who shuffled forward ready to fall upon her.

'I asked who you are,' hissed the Englishman, ignoring the man who tried to staunch the flow of blood from his cheek, and totally oblivious to his own nakedness.

'We were paid...' said the younger man haltingly, 'by a French woman.'

The Englishman snarled. 'Charlotte de Levis?'

'Yes, sir,' said the young man, shamefaced. 'I think that was her name.'

Grace hugged her knees close to her breasts, making herself small. The pain of the beating seemed a hundred times worse as the heat of her passion faded and she began to shiver. The cabin was cold and bare and she felt dreadfully vulnerable with the inquisitive eyes staring down at her.

Two other men pushed into the narrow doorway, straining their necks to look at Grace and not hiding the fact that their cocks were fully erect in their breeches.

The young man, the one who had spoken first, pushed the rest behind him. 'Our orders are to take the doxy's

157

maidenhead.' He spoke firmly, his eyes steady, focussed on Grace's huddled figure.

She moaned softly and tried to hide her sex with her hands.

The Englishman laughed. 'Had you been a few minutes later that deed would have been done.' He reached down and pulled Grace upright and forced her hands to the back of her head, indicating that she should link her fingers together. He tapped her inner thighs with the whip he still held in his hand, indicating that she should straddle her legs. 'She's ripe for it, lads.' He pointed to the chains that linked her wrists and those that were attached to the fine rings through nipples that were erect and pointed. 'She was trained by an expert at the royal court; an expert who required her to be both sensual and intact when she was sold to a husband.'

Tears came quickly to Grace's eyes. What was he doing, displaying her like this? He was tempting the men, almost offering her to them.

'You?' asked the young man.

The Englishman gave a wry smile and shrugged noncommittally. 'Look at her large and heavy breasts,' he said, ignoring the question. 'Open those legs wider!' he snapped at Grace. Tears spilled down cheeks made hot with embarrassment but she did as she was told, sweetly pliant and obedient as always. 'And arch yourself so I may demonstrate your qualities to these gentlemen,' he continued.

Through her tears Grace saw his cock thicken at his own words. The shock of the ruffians' intrusion was forgotten.

She arched her slender body so that her pussy was thrust towards the men. She knew they could see her nubbin, fully extended and peeping from her dark curls. She knew those curls would be shining with dew and somehow this knowledge increased the feeling of wantonness growing in her belly; the feeling of delicious shame.

With the folded whip he peeled her sex lips open and tapped her clitty. 'Notice how prominent this is. The training, of course, is the root cause.'

Grace could hear the ruffians' breathing change; become faster and more ragged. She dared to open her eyes and saw their rising excitement; the glittering eyes, the parted lips and the thickening bulges in their breeches.

'Could you not get her to lie down?' asked the young man. 'So we could see her qualities more clearly and get on with what we were paid to do?'

The Englishman nodded, smiling, and pressed Grace's shoulder, forcing her to her knees and then to lie prone. 'Keep your hands on your head and your head thrown back,' he ordered, 'but spread your legs, knees bent and loose so they fall outwards.'

The position was not new to Grace. It was madame's favourite, and Charlotte's too. She positioned herself as he demanded.

The men sighed. The Englishman let the whip move lightly over her belly. Grace shuddered.

'I assure you, gentlemen,' said the Englishman, 'that this girl wants nothing more than to be fucked.'

Her wantonness was uncontainable. Grace, keeping her knees bent and open, could not help but arch her body upwards. She heard the whisper of lust that hissed from the men.

'You see, gentlemen. Quite delightful.'

There was something in his tone that gave Grace an inkling that he was encouraging them. She willingly lifted her beaten and bruised bottom from the cold hardness of the deck and spread her thighs further. Their breathing was harsh, animal-like, rapid.

'But perhaps it would be only fair for one of you to explore her with your tongue,' the Englishman continued, gently probing between her sex lips with the whip. 'And fingers would not go amiss.'

Grace felt her sex quiver at the sensual stroking and felt her clitty ease further from its hood, felt it throb intolerably. The slow stroking brought her juices bubbling from the pit of her belly and, at the same moment, the Englishman slapped her inner thighs with the fold of the whip, reminding her to keep them fully open.

The rabble grunted their approval and the young man threw himself to the deck. Grace could smell his masculine need, feel his breath, warm and damp on her bruised buttocks, and then a tongue pushing against her bottom mouth, licking the tight and wrinkled opening until she moaned with delicious shame. The tongue tip slithered up and down the tight cleft.

'No one else?' asked the Englishman, his eyebrow quirked in mockery.

The older man, the pain of his slashed cheek forgotten, knelt between Grace's thighs, his tongue flicking about his slack lips. She moaned again as her sex lips were taken one by one into his slobbering mouth and gnawed as if they were delicious morsels. She shuddered as a fingertip grazed back and forth over her quivering nubbin.

'And surely, you men,' queried the Englishman, 'will not deny these glorious breasts the pleasure of your hands and mouths? You see how they beckon you? Would you not like to suckle these hardened paps as if you were drawing milk?' The other two needed no second bidding and Grace gasped as hands kneaded her breasts and mouths clamped upon her teats. She felt her belly tighten as all these sensations combined and a warm swirling drew her up into a vortex. It was impossible to resist moving with her tormentors, contorting herself to feel each suck and touch more intensely.

'I am sure you will feel each pulse of her orgasm,' said the Englishman, and Grace raised her eyes to meet his.

He was smiling, his arms folded across his chest and his cock turgid, spearing from the base of his belly, but unheeded.

Grace's clitty palpitated unmercifully. Her bottom convulsed upon the tongue that drove softly in and out. She felt a warm creamy wetness spill on her belly and drool down to the crisp curls of her pussy nest. Looking up she saw the men who had sucked her teats standing over her, their cocks in their hands, spilling their seed all over her.

She heard muffled groans and the men who had been so busy between her thighs were rubbing their cocks to the same effect.

A boot, soft from years of wear, was pressed into the cushion of her belly and Grace felt a deeper shame, a defilement greater than anything she had felt before. The sole of the boot spread the viscous spillage over her breasts and belly, showing their contempt for the use of her.

Laughter, loud and triumphant, filled the cramped cabin. 'I think you'll agree, gentlemen,' said the Englishman, 'that my turn has come.'

Grace, her body trembling from the many orgasms and wet with sweat and slick with come, looked up at him. Her eyes were heavy with weariness and her arms ached from the forced position on her head.

'But we...'

'It isn't fair!'

'You cunning wretch!'

The angry cries were somewhat distorted by the rasping breaths and the groans of pleasure.

'But be assured, gentlemen,' said the Englishman, calmly and coldly, 'I shall carry out your appointed task to the letter.'

Suddenly he whirled the whip about his head, his face dark with fury. The lash cracked about the younger man's head and, almost immediately, thrashed the other three in, what appeared to Grace, one movement.

'Get out,' he ordered in a voice as cold as ice. 'Get out of my sight, and you...' he turned to Grace, his expression still cruel and tight-lipped, 'get up. Clean yourself... over there!'

They were left alone in the cabin and Grace walked, unsteadily, to a jug and bowl set in a hollow in a wooden washstand.

'And when you've finished dress in these clothes.' He began to dress himself, grunting with discomfort as he tucked his still turgid cock away in his tight breeches.

Grace shivered as she sponged the drying spunk from her breasts. The water was cold and her skin puckered in tiny goosebumps. The come was thickest at her pussy bush and she soaked the curls many times with the water until they were, once more, glossy black.

When he was dressed and she had washed as well as she could, he insisted on inspecting her very closely.

'Excellent,' he said, as he prised open the tightness of her bottom hole and, that done, petted open her sex lips until he was satisfied that each fold was smooth and clean.

'Now the boots,' he said.

The boots were very long and had heels that were so high they threw her forwards. They were laced, front and back, with leather thongs that tickled her bottom and probed between her sex lips at the slightest movement.

'You look very beautiful, my darling,' he said, turning her round to admire her from all sides. He slung a cloak about her shoulders and the soft wool tickled her breasts and belly, while the bootlaces pricked her cunny and bottom cheeks, keeping her in a state of high sexual tension.

'Where are you taking me?' she asked nervously as he led her from the cabin and out into the narrow alleyway that ran from bow to stern of the ship.

He said nothing, but merely led her to a carriage

waiting at the dockside. 'In you go,' he said.

The boots made her clumsy and she found it difficult to mount the two steps into the carriage.

'Hurry!' he said sharply. 'Hurry! We have a long journey ahead.'

At last they were on their way and the Englishman stared straight ahead for some moments. His eyes were always upon her across the carriage, boring into the voluminous folds of her cloak.

'On your knees,' he said at last. 'Unfasten my breeches.' His voice was low, hoarse, urgent – but still commanding.

Submissive and pliant, she did as she was ordered. The boots were new and stiff and they made it difficult to kneel, but anxious to please, she managed the task. Kneeling before him, she awaited his next command.

His large hands felt gentle at her throat and Grace allowed her long lashes to droop over her eyes. It was only after long caresses that she realised his intention was no more than to release the fastening of the cloak. As it fell from her shoulders and drifted about her thighs her tear-filled eyes raised to meet his.

'Do you know what I require?' he asked.

Grace nodded, wondering when her own needs would be realised.

He stroked his fingertips across her lips until she was forced to open them. 'Place your hands upon your head,' he commanded, 'for I adore to see you looking so easily controlled and vulnerable.' He paused, merely admiring her at his feet. 'But wait...' His breathing was harsh and rapid. 'I want your hands working on my breeches to release my cock.'

Her hands trembled and the lump beneath the buckskin made the breeches tight. He wriggled impatiently, thrusting the swelling against her dainty hands as they worked. The heat of him was enormous and his male musk strong. She supposed this was because he had been forced to wait so long for relief. Despite her trembling the buttons were at last released and his cock burst forth.

He held her tightly at the back of her neck, keeping her mouth steady and close to his thickness, in spite of the jolting of the carriage over the rough road.

'I want you, Grace,' he said as he forced his cock deep into her mouth. She could feel the smooth slickness of his stem sliding over her tongue and she felt, even though tears spilled down her cheeks, almost joyful as he spoke her name.

'I want you fully,' he murmured roughly, pushing her head harder onto him. 'Not like this.'

Her lips brushed his balls and Grace thought for a terrible moment that she might gag at his extraordinary length, but at that very moment he wrenched away and let his spittle-moistened cock rest lightly against her cheek. The movement of the carriage made it saw back and forth against her cheek. Breathlessly, she looked up at him, wondering what he would ask of her next.

'Yes,' she said meekly. It was what she wanted most of all.

'But not now,' he said, 'in this jolting carriage where we cannot spread ourselves. When I take you it will be in a bed; the biggest, softest bed in England.'

She heard him groan and felt the silky warmth of his come splash on her upturned face. Gratefully, she lapped the spillage, delighting in the salty bitterness. When it was over she laid her head upon his knees, dozing briefly despite the jolting movement of the carriage.

'Wake up.'

It seemed to Grace that she had slept for only moments when the Englishman placed a hand about her breast and slung the wool cape about her shoulders. She gave a murmur as his fingers stroked the heavy underswell and a thumb teased her nipple to hardness. She looked up with wide limpid eyes, questioning why she had been woken. Aware that the laces of the high boots prickled her buttocks, she swayed her body to ease the sensation.

'The path is narrow for the next stage of our journey,' he said. 'We leave the carriage here and continue on horseback.'

It was then that Grace realised that the carriage was at a halt. He placed his hands under her armpits, lifting her. She felt his fingertips kneading her breasts as he drew her to her feet. Her nakedness brushed against his fully clothed body, making her feel more than ever vulnerable.

As they left the carriage Grace heard the night sounds; an owl hooting, sea crashing against the rocks, wind whistling across moorland. 'Where are we?' she asked, as he swung her up onto a horse tethered at a stunted tree.

'Across the sea from your beloved France,' he said enigmatically. He drew his hands under her cloak, letting the night wind caress her breasts, seep between her straddled legs. His gaze upon her was so intense that it was some moments before Grace realised the horse was not saddled and she sat astride it bareback.

The pelt tickled her spread sex lips and the open flesh pot between them. She tried to lean back to ease the sensation but he swung up behind her and pushed her hips forward and slapped her inner thighs, making her spread them further. His fingers worked into her sex folds, slicking the black hair from the wet crease. Satisfied that she was fully open, he palpated the folds until Grace was sighing with pleasure. He tapped her nubbin with a fingertip, stroked it, dipped the same fingertip into the pool of her sap and dabbed the pulsing bud with her juices. Grace arched her neck, throwing her head back against his chest. She felt her breasts swell, become tender, and her breathing quicken until her pleasure burst within her.

It was almost daybreak when they entered the rambling Manor House. She tried to walk gracefully, keeping the cloak wrapped tightly about her, but the high boots and the continued stimulation he had given her on the horse caused her to move unsteadily.

They were greeted by a manservant who eyed Grace lasciviously, making her bow and hide her eyes in shame.

'This is John,' said the Englishman. 'He will prepare you.' With that he left the room, leaving her terrified and alone with the manservant.

Prepare you. The words echoed in her mind, made her tremble. Hadn't she been trained by madame to the full? What other preparation could she need?

The manservant beckoned her to accompany him upstairs and took her into a room furnished only with a crude wooden bathtub and a strangely shaped stool. John slipped the cloak from her shoulders, but when Grace bent to unfasten the boots he wagged his finger, warning her to leave them on. He beckoned her and, obediently, she took a step and then another until she was close to him. He smiled with satisfaction and knelt at her feet. He began to unfasten the laces, and at every stage Grace could feel his breath wafting over her sex. She felt her whole body flush with shame, not at his nearness, but at the feelings that washed over her; the softening in her belly, the moistening of her sex, and the throbbing of her clitty.

It was over at last. The boots were slipped from her feet and legs, but she was ordered to keep her legs apart. Small slaps delivered with the very tips of the servant's fingers made her spread them to the limit. He pinched her sex lips and bit her trembling belly. He fingered her bottom, pressing the hillocks fully apart and probing the tight hole experimentally.

'You need oil,' he told her.

Grace tried to pull away from him but he held her close.

'No need to be afraid. Oil will make you loose and supple.'

He pulled her to the stool and positioned her in such a

way that her bottom was cupped by the curves of the stool and her thighs were lifted to show her sex and bottom hole to the full.

'My master has begun the preparation,' said John, and he traced a smear of oil over the bruises which coloured her bottom. 'Keep these thighs wide,' he added, pressing her legs fully open and again slapping the tender inner skin. The strangely shaped stool hollowed Grace's belly and made her flesh pot and bottom hole receptacles.

Across the dimly lit room she watched the servant warm the phial of oil over a flame. His face, as he walked towards her, was an impassive mask, but within his livery Grace could see a thickening, a bulge at the tight satin crotch, and it made her shudder, not with fear but with longing. She wanted to be rid of the nuisance of her maidenhead so much.

The servant tipped several drops of oil onto his fingers and worked them into her offered anus, gently at first, and then more vigorously. He smiled lewdly at her between her open thighs and added more oil into the twitching pit.

Despite the fact that she found her position shameful, a forbidden wantonness simmered in the pit of her belly, and when John placed two fingers into the entrance she sighed pleasurably and tautened her flesh about the intrusion.

'Good,' he murmured. 'Now we must prepare the front.' He had set down the oil and picked up a polished ivory rod. It was smooth and shiny and perfectly cylindrical. Its thickness was no more than a slender finger. Grace was very close to an orgasm and she quivered as she wondered what he might do to her next. Would he push the ivory inside her, deep into her bottom, which he had so carefully prepared with oil? Or most wonderful of all, break her maidenhead, freeing her at last?

With finger and thumb he separated her flesh folds and

Grace shuddered and became tense.

'No!' he rapped, holding her sex lips wide apart. 'You must be supple, loose. Relax!'

She felt so vulnerable with her thighs spread in this strange position and her sex and belly cupped. She waited for the pain in her funnel; the pain she was sure would come when her maidenhead was broken.

The ivory rod was slipped up and down Grace's silky slit and then the servant pushed the cool smoothness lengthways between her lips. He moved back as if to admire his handiwork, but her juices were copious and the rod slithered from her.

'No! You must hold it there!' He moved forward and folded the swollen lips about the slim stick until Grace could feel it butting against her bud.

He pressed it hard and Grace looked between her thighs and watched her lips fold over the ivory as if it was becoming part of her.

She shuddered as he bent between her thighs to kiss each nipple. She felt the bulge of his cock, encased in satin livery, butt against her tortured sex lips. He grinned at her as if he knew her orgasm was very close. He rubbed the bulge against her again and this time she could not contain her pleasure. A swirl of heat made her melt. She felt herself drawn up in a vortex that made her murmur. Her nubbin throbbed against the rod, which slithered from her again.

Tears beaded her lashes and her lips trembled as she waited for his sharp reprimand and chastisement. She had tried so hard to obey and was so close to completing the task.

Her legs were fully spread as he dictated and she knew her sex pouch was completely unfolded. Her clitty still bobbed within those folds. To her shame she could see its erect state, its flush and upright posture. She could see it boldly peeping from its hood, standing proud between the scarlet folds, slick with her juices. Yes, she would surely get a reprimand.

'This is excellent,' said John, to her surprise, and he squeezed the hot bud. 'And this, too,' he added, tapping two fingertips at Grace's female opening, 'is good. Ah, yes! My master is going to delight in you.'

She closed her eyes in shame as she felt the trickle of warmth ooze down her spread bottom cheeks, but it was a wanton, very pleasing shame.

'He uses me to prepare his girls,' said John, and he sounded sad. 'Not that I don't enjoy it, for I do. Very much so.' As he spoke he stroked a finger, slicked with her own juices, down the clenching crease of her bottom. Grace wanted to ask if his master had many girls. She wanted to believe he did not.

She felt her bottom hole clench upon something much smoother than John's finger, and she felt it slither deep inside her. Was it the rod, the ivory rod she'd been forced to hold against her nubbin? The feeling of fullness increased as the manservant pinched the opening closed. Grace felt her belly tighten as it was stroked by a gentle palm.

'It's a good thick candle I have placed inside you,' said John hoarsely. 'My master likes his girls to be satisfied in every direction.'

Grace's belly felt full with the cylinder of beeswax inside her bottom, and she felt light-headed as John helped her to her feet. He sat her upon the stool with her thighs apart, smoothing his fingers up and down her spread slit. He bent to plant a kiss upon the very point of her nubbin and then sucked it between his lips. Grace felt a wanton desire to press forward on his kisses, but he seemed to realise her needs and held her hips fast so she could not move.

'You are ready for the master,' he said, rising to his feet and pulling her upright. He brushed his lips against hers and Grace blushed as she tasted the strength of her own musk.

Chapter Ten

If Grace expected the master to be lying at ease upon the bed, she was much mistaken. Naked and pacing the floor impatiently, he turned to face her as John showed her in. His face was dark with anger and the fire in the grate cast scarlet shadows on his body, highlighting the bulges of his well-developed muscles and deepening the shadow of his slender waist. His cock was massively turgid and his balls were drawn up tight to his body, showing only a slight curve of his sac.

'She is prepared, master,' said John, pushing Grace further into the room.

A soft whisper made Grace look towards the wide four-poster bed. Nestled deep into the swansdown quilt was a girl. The exact opposite to Grace in colouring, her hair was reddish gold and spilled over the lace and satin pillows. Her creamy arms were stretched taut above her head and her wrists were tied with silk ropes to the oak posts. Her long shapely legs were spread wide and her ankles were tied as tightly as her wrists. Beneath her back was placed a thick bolster that arched her belly and thrust up her sex mound, which was frosted with red-gold curls. The sex itself was open, the folds pressed back and the nubbin erect and shiny with juices.

The girl's sapphire blue eyes, despite her bondage, glinted at Grace, full of triumph as though she had succeeded where Grace had not. The dark girl bowed her head, hiding her tears. Had the master not said that he wanted her? Meant to have her? Why was this girl here?

'You are such an innocent,' said the Englishman, his voice butting into Grace's thoughts of the girl on the bed. 'Perhaps that is why I find you so intriguing, so delectable.'

His anger was fading and the shadow of a smile softened the handsome features. His cockstem looked thicker and more erect than ever and it brushed against Grace's belly, made taut by the inward pressure of the candle. The touch made her shudder pleasurably, especially when his hands slid down her arms and caressed the manacles clipped around her wrists. It seemed to Grace that they were now part of her, that she had worn them all her life. His fingers touched the chain that linked the gold wrist cuffs in a tender, almost loving, manner. It reminded her of her slavery to him, to madame and Philipe, but she no longer cared.

She delighted in her slavery when it led to this. He cupped her breasts and made a shiver of pleasure run through her. The touch made her very aware of the cylinder of wax that filled her bottom hole. Like the rings in her nipples and the chains at her wrists it was part of her slavery. The thought brought a delicious heaviness, a melting around her sex lips, even though a wicked wantonness filled her with shame.

'Because you are so innocent,' he said in a voice as soft as velvet, 'I feel it is only fair to teach you by demonstration before I take you as a woman should be taken.'

Muffled giggles came from the bed and Grace turned her limpid eyes towards the sound. Tears spilled from her lashes and fell heavily down her pale cheeks.

'You wicked creatures!' snapped the Englishman. 'You naughty girls! Do you see how you have upset your new companion?' He let his hand rest upon Grace's belly, his fingertips hovering about her pubic curls. The touch was sensual and Grace felt her skin pucker with forbidden gratification.

A second girl, redheaded and her face and voluptuous body sprinkled with freckles, turned her face smeared with sex juices towards Grace. She was free of any bondage and her head nestled between the spread thighs of the other.

'Forgive them,' he said. 'I'm afraid I have rather

spoiled them.' He looked at the two girls as a doting parent might when his charges were particularly disobedient. It was a look full of love but tainted with disappointment. 'Yes, they are spoiled. I have used them as my own special playthings rather than sending them to...' He shook his head. 'But let us not dwell on such matters.'

He cupped his hand over Grace's mons and allowed his fingers to stray, very lightly, over the lips that were swollen from John's preparation with the rod. He allowed his middle fingertip to slip between the lips and linger there. Grace gasped, her breathing quick and shallow, and he smiled down at her, delighting in the reaction. The finger slid deeper and rested upon her nubbin. He brought another finger to rest in the same place and used the two to slide back her hood. Her belly shook and she was very aware of the pressure of the beeswax deep within her bottom.

'Although Carla has been with me for two years and is highly trained, she should know better.' His gaze was fixed on the wriggling bottom of the redhead. Grace felt a strange mixture of shame and pleasure. Her shame was that he seemed not to be thinking of her as he tickled her nubbin, made her spread her legs and bear down upon his fingers. But her pleasure was so intense it could not be ignored.

Despite her shame her gaze wandered to the bed and she noticed that the freckled hillocks were marked. Fine stripes of varying hues from purple and dark blue bruising to fading yellow criss-crossed the twin spheres.

Her attention was forced back to the fingers between her thighs. With his other hand he used his strong fingers to spread her sex lips, making them gape and her dew spill copiously. Was it his caress that was causing this melting, or the sight of Carla's whipped bottom? Madame had made her used to pain; to accept it in the same way she did pleasure.

172

'Arlane,' he continued, indicating the bound girl with a slight toss of his head, 'is being prepared by Carla. Sit up, my dear,' he ordered of the latter. 'Let us see how Arlane is progressing.'

Grace's eyes were drawn to the bound girl; to the pushed up belly and the open flesh pot. The girl smiled again at Grace, that same triumphant gleam in her eyes and her nipples drawn to points by the pleasure received from Carla.

Carla sat back on her heels and Grace blushed as she saw her wipe Arlane's glistening juices from lips and cheeks with the back of her hand. She lapped her tongue as though drinking some delicacy.

'You see how Carla leaves the cunny smooth and clear of juices, but still delightfully moist?' His forefinger slid down the valley between Grace's moist labia and her erect clitty as if it was a tongue. She closed her eyes, allowing her thick lashes to flutter to her pale cheeks. She could feel the warmth of a tongue tip sipping her juices; could feel it lash her nubbin. It made her belly quiver unbearably. Her eyes opened and pleaded for mercy, and a soft whimper whispered from her lips.

The Englishman chuckled and tapped the tip of his forefinger on the very peak of her nubbin, and she felt it throb under his touch. 'Does it excite you?'

He stood very close and she could feel his thick cockstem swaying against her sex, tickling the dark curls. Its tip swayed against her belly at the lower margins of her ribs. Slick dew dribbled on her skin and became chilled in the air.

She whimpered as he again spread her sex fully open, held them that way and allowed the warm air of the room to whisper over the sensitive flesh.

'I see it does. I am sufficiently experienced to know a girl's mew of pleasure when I hear one.' His voice was low, caressing.

He chuckled again and pinched the sex lips closed.

'And now let us see how this pleasure zone is faring.' He arched her over one arm and drove his fingers into the yielding flesh of Grace's bottom, and she moaned softly as more pressure was placed upon the beeswax so deeply inserted there. The chuckle faded to a sigh of delight and he allowed one hand to remain lightly on a buttock while the other strayed over the curve of her hip and down over her belly. It rested there, testing the pressure from within created by the candle before travelling down to drive again between her sex lips.

Grace bowed her head, letting her long black hair hide her blushes. It was not the man's actions, his caresses that shamed her, but the knowledge that those other girls were watching her every reaction.

'How dare you hide your head! Hold it up! Look across the room, meet Arlane's eyes and Carla's.' His voice was strident, angry. The hand which had rested so tenderly on her buttocks flashed downwards to slap her bottom so fiercely that she almost fell, but he held her steady.

'Stand up... look at me,' he hissed. 'I'll have no false modesty in this house. You have been trained to accept pleasure, have you not?'

Grace nodded and did not try to stem the fresh tears that dripped once more from her lashes.

'I like that in a girl,' he said huskily. 'I like tears very much.'

Once more he was tender, caressing her breasts and thumbing her nipples. His lips sipped at her tears and he smiled into her eyes. His fingers strayed down again over her belly, feeling it quiver under his touch. Grace was careful to keep her head high as his fingertips tickled the upper margin of her black pussy curls.

'So plump,' he murmured, pinching the pad of flesh beneath the curls, 'so proud.'

He allowed a finger and thumb to trace the margins of her sex before going inwards to press back the folds.

'How could a wanton like you remain so innocent?' he

174

asked, flicking her clitty back and forth with the tip of a forefinger. 'You were born to be a sex slave. Born to it! A valuable commodity in a girl. Very valuable.'

His voice became clipped, although not harsh. He was like a schoolmaster reprimanding a naughty student. 'Do you think I cannot see how Arlane's slick sex excites you?' A forefinger drifted down her cheek, tracing its oval line.

Grace gasped as the tenderness changed to harshness and he pushed her from him. 'Tie her to the frame, John,' he said. 'Facing the bed, and if her head droops in that irritatingly modest manner, I am sure you'll deal with the matter in the appropriate way.'

'Indeed, master,' said John, and Grace felt her shoulders grasped by bony fingers. She had a sense of being rushed backwards, of stumbling clumsily over the polished wooden floor.

Her elbows were wrenched behind her while her wrists were still captured in the gold manacles with the fine chain between them. The servant pulled her to the wooden frame between the bedposts. She struggled, remembering how madame and Philipe had kept her imprisoned in such a device, but she was no match for John's strength. Quickly, he pulled her arms high above her head and she felt his skilled fingers tie them, one at a time, to the wooden frame. Because of the tight bindings the gold manacles cut more painfully into her wrists. Her lips stung as she bit back the faint moan that rose from deep in her throat, and she despised her weakness.

The servant busied himself at her ankles, pushing her legs wide apart and tethering them as tightly as her arms. Grace was forced to clench her bottom very tightly to keep the cylinder of beeswax in place, but this had the effect of thrusting forward her pussy and tilting it in such a manner so that the inner folds could be plainly seen by the two girls and the Englishman. It was only natural that she began to bow her head to hide her shame at such a lewd exposure.

A smack upon her cheek made her head rock from side to side as John chastised her as ordered. Grace held her head erect, swallowing back the tears which threatened to spill over her fluttering eyelashes.

The frame was a simple rectangle of wood and Grace's buttocks were as fully exposed as her pierced nipples, her belly, and the triangle of curls that guarded her cunt.

When the full amount of her exposure became clear she again felt the sting of chastisement, the whip across her buttocks, the burning heat as the skin flushed in a long and raised weal. This time she could not hold back the tears that filled her eyes. She heard the two girls giggle at this new humiliation.

'Does that amuse you, my pretties?' asked the Englishman. 'Shall I ask John to punish the new girl again?' He clicked his tongue in mock disgust. 'You are truly wicked little creatures!'

Grace saw Arlane pout at the mischievous reprimand and saw Carla draw in her brows in an annoyed frown.

'Not wicked,' denied Carla.

His hand strayed to his cock and Grace watched him caress it as tenderly as if it was a woman's breast. She saw it pulse, become more upright, saw the veins throb.

'No, perhaps not wicked – just naughty.' The tip of his thumb slicked over the bead of spillage at his globe and he smeared it over the full surface until it shone as if polished. 'Would you truly like to see this lovely creature beaten further?'

'Oh, yes!' squealed Arlane, and Grace saw her raise her golden cascade of curls from the pillow and saw her slender arms straining against the bonds. Carla clapped her hands, her eyes glittering in the candlelight, and nodded vigorously. Her agile tongue flickered about her lips like that of a snake's scenting the musky air.

'You would?' His voice was calm and cold, but mocking and smooth as silk. His eyes danced with mischief as he caressed Grace's body from breasts to pussy. She was mortified, humiliated.

'John!' The name, spoken so sharply, was a command.

Grace felt her breasts become more tense, although her belly quivered softly with anticipation of the pain. She tensed her buttocks but this only made her more aware of the beeswax cylinder clutched between them.

'Soft,' he rasped. 'The buttocks must be kept soft to take the smacking satisfactorily.' She heard the manservant breathe more harshly.

She heard him crack the whip upon the bare boards of the floor and, after an age, heard it whistle through the air and felt the heat of its sting on her rippling buttocks. She could not help but arch her neck back at the sharp pain. Her long jet hair swung back and forth over the painful hillocks, tickling the soreness.

'Again,' whispered Carla. 'She looks so pretty when she strains against the bindings. Her arms look so slender and her breasts so full.' Through her spilling tears Grace saw the red-haired girl kneeling with her plump thighs spread and her hands stroking the fiery red curls on her open pussy lips, spreading the slick flesh to show the erectness of the clitty, proud against the scarlet flesh.

Once more the Englishman tutted in annoyance. 'I suspect you are jealous, Carla, and I believe you have a task other than to gloat over others' misfortune. Get to it, girl!' He glared at the redhead and she shrank away from him and, obediently, buried her face between Arlane's spread and bound thighs.

The whip sliced the air behind Grace and once more her body swayed back and forth with the force of the blow while her buttocks burned with the continuing lashes.

The pain was nothing to Grace as she fixed her eyes on Carla's bobbing head. She could almost feel the stroke of the small hands drifting over her own thighs. Her sex lips yearned to feel the touch of those gentle thumbs. If only they would part her own jet curls just as they parted

Arlane's. Wantonly, she let her mind dwell on the shameful delights she knew Arlane was feeling.

Was Carla using her spittle to moisten Arlane's cunny or had she spread oil or some other unction both back and front to grease the path of fingers, lips and tongue? In her mind's eye Grace could see the slick nubbin rising proudly from a flushed bed of fine sex skin. She could see it throbbing and driving upwards from the little skirt of skin. She had to close her ears from the sounds of pleasure that came continuously from Arlane's throat.

She was certain her sex lips were gaping and she could feel her flesh pot drool and weep. Yes, the pain faded with the wanton thoughts of delight that clouded her mind.

'Now you are excited, Grace.' The words intruded into her lewd thoughts and she gasped with dismay that he could read her mind so clearly. He stood before her, smiling at her loveliness held helpless in the frame.

He placed his arms on hers. Her soft lips formed a perfect O as she felt the heat of his maleness brushing between her thighs, his broad chest caressing her breasts, teasing the ringed nipples.

She could not meet his eyes and she stared over his shoulder at the two writhing figures on the bed. She could hear the liquid slurp as fingers slipped easily in and out of moist entrances, back and front. The sounds made Grace's toes curl and her fingers moved involuntarily in their bindings.

'It is all so delicious, Grace, is it not?'

She had a very strong desire to bow her head, to close her eyes, but within her body the liquid and wanton swirling could not be ignored. She felt her bottom, still stinging from the swing of the lash, tighten about the candle. She felt her nubbin twitch against his cockstem, which he sawed back and forth between her slick sex lips. It teased her unmercifully.

'Answer me!'

178

Grace could scarcely breathe. Her breasts felt overfull and the nipples tight. Her belly churned and her bottom felt raw. Her arms ached and her wrists were chafed by the silk bindings that pressed the manacles into her skin.

The Englishman sighed and drew away. She felt tears sting her eyes. She wanted to cry out: 'Come back! Touch me! Take me!'

With his eyes still upon her, he returned to the bed and threw himself upon the two girls who welcomed him with squeals of delight. She watched him fasten his lips around Arlane's teats and watched her strain against her bonds in ecstasy. She watched miserably as Carla closed her oil slicked hands around his cockstem and slid them down to caress his balls nestled so snugly in their sac.

Grace licked her lips as though it was her mouth which would envelope the master's cockstem; her tongue which would curl about its thickness and dip into the oozing pore to sip away the delicious cream. But these were such shameful thoughts she had no right to contemplate.

She dared not droop her head in shame or misery perchance John raised the lash to her once more. It was not the pain of the lash she feared but the wantonness it brought upon her, the lewdness that made her nubbin swell and itch.

'John,' said the Englishman, 'our new maid looks lonely strung upon the rack. Perhaps a caress – gently, mind you – will keep her warm and interested.'

'Yes, master,' responded the servant immediately, and Grace could hear the eagerness in his voice.

'But I think we shall hood her,' added the master, 'for my antics with Carla and Arlane seem to excite her beyond bearing. There's a sheen of juices coating her thighs and I find it unladylike.'

Grace felt hot spots of colour stain her pale cheeks, which deepened when the servant sponged the driblets of female cream away. She dared not look down, nor close her eyes, and she dreaded the hood the master mentioned.

Was she to be hooded like a falcon, to be used however the servant desired?

John stood before her, his thin face wreathed in a beaming smile. He had stripped off his livery and the blue satin shimmered at his feet like the skin of some exotic snake. His cock was not as large as his master's, but it was full and turgid, the globe swollen and bursting out of the skirt which was wrapped in folds at the base of the swollen sphere.

Grace pulled on her bonds and looked pleadingly across the room to her master. If she was, at last, to be relieved of her virginity she wanted, with all her heart, to feel him pierce the hated barrier, not John. But the master was plunged deep within Arlane's bound body, while Carla, spread-eagled between both their thighs, used her agile and expert tongue. Grace saw her dip to caress Arlane's petted nubbin and sip the excess juices that were squeezed out of her vagina as the master plunged into the helpless girl. She saw Arlane tug at her silken bonds in ecstasy as she was fucked completely by him. She saw how he thrust more vigorously as Carla licked the root of his cock and his throbbing balls.

'No,' murmured Grace. 'Please, no.' She thrashed her head from side to side in anticipation of being plunged into darkness.

'Be quiet,' rasped John. From behind his back he brought a thick leather hood which he pushed over Grace's head, before she could protest further. It was as if she had fallen into some dark pit, heated by the fires of hell itself. To struggle was to increase the heat and feel more vulnerable than ever in the darkness, but weakly, she tugged at the wrist bonds. Within the hood at the precise level of her mouth was a plug of leather, and such was the fit that it forced her to open her mouth and the plug slipped into her throat, gagging her.

But far from the discomfort making her feel less wanton, it only increased the liquid warmth which cosseted her flesh pot. The lips felt more swollen and warm. It was as if a blanket of the finest wool was wrapped between her spread thighs. She longed to rub herself against some object, hard and thick, and to press it to her itching nubbin. She longed for the ivory rod John pressed between her sex lips, longed for it as for an old friend.

Unable to see and scarcely hear, barely able to breathe through the tiny holes at the nostrils, she was prevented from protest. All her senses, apart from touch, were denied her. Every nerve in every part of her skin seemed, as a consequence, to be especially sensitive. A hand stroked between her straddled thighs. Grace purred with pleasure. The touch was very light, only brushing the ends of her pubic curls. A panic seized her and she tried to struggle, but only succeeded in bearing down upon the heel of the hand which gradually caressed her sex lips, moulding them like putty, spreading them one from the other. Fingers nipped her erect clitty, squeezing until it throbbed and drew out of its hood. Grace felt her juices flow, soaking the fingers that teased and played.

A voice muffled by the hood whispered in Grace's ears. 'It is well past the time when you should loose your innocence.' She struggled again, thrusting against her bonds and against the probing fingers. She wanted to scream, but the gag, the plug of leather, only drove deeper into her throat. She wanted more, much more.

Hands stroked the swollen hillocks of her bottom, caressing the scorched flesh. The hands were gentle but firm, petting and wanton at the same time. The motion became circular, soothing, and made Grace's flesh soften and relax. To her horror she felt the candle extrude from her bottom and heard a low laugh as the tube of wax was twisted and turned, driven in and out by the unseen hands.

'That is how a cock will feel, but in your front hole,' said the voice. She felt the slick of cock flesh wiped over her belly and, almost immediately, over her bottom.

Were there two men taunting her? Could the master have finished with Arlane and Carla and again be rigid? Ready for her? Was this the time, the time she had been forced to wait upon?

Her hands were released from the frame, and then her feet. She ached from the long bondage, and her limbs were weak to the point of collapse as she was led, stumbling and tripping, across the room.

No one spoke, and what soft sounds there were – the crackle of burning coals in the grate, the tinkle of glass as someone poured wine into a glass – were muffled by the hood.

Her tongue was dry and compressed down behind her teeth by the plug. A terrible thirst made her throat contract and she would dearly have liked to cough, but even this was denied her.

'On the bed,' ordered a voice.

That was surely the master, but didn't Arlane and Carla already occupy the bed? Grace struggled weakly in the vice-like grip of the hands which held her, but the struggle was in vain. Was she to be laid against the other girls? Her taunted sex became full at the thought, her clitty pouted, a drool of juice trickled from her. The thought of the women caressing her, kissing her most intimate places, brought on a naughty lewdness she found both delightful and shameful.

Suddenly she was free, flung high in the air, suspended in nothingness. Grace longed to scream at the frightening disorientation, but it lasted only a moment and she sank into the enveloping softness of the feather bed.

The feeling of comfort lasted only briefly, and once more her arms were wrenched high to be bound to the bedposts. Likewise her legs were spread and tied in that position.

The bed dipped as another person crawled across the feather-filled expanse. Tears filled her eyes and were spread across her cheeks by the tightness of the hood as her nipple chains were pulled and tension was put upon her sensitive teats. A resounding slap reached her ears and a soft whimper followed it. Grace knew that one of the girls was at the receiving end of the reprimand.

She strained her ears, for the room seemed full of whispering. 'You know what is required,' said one voice. 'Open her, kiss her until she is ready for me. Until she begs for me.'

Grace shuddered. Begs for who, she asked herself, the master or John?

Feminine fingers spread her sex lips and she tensed, waiting some other spiteful act from Carla, for she was sure it was she who twisted her nipple chain until she wanted to cry out at the exquisite pain.

A tongue tip stroked each side of the slippery valley in which lay her nubbin. It slithered down until it circled the still-closed entrance to her sex. A small hand cupped her mound and little fingers spread her swollen sex lips. Other fingers, strong and masculine, cupped the weighted heaviness of her breasts, gathered them up until the valley between them was a tight ravine. A different tongue lapped at her paps and fingertips slapped the fullness beneath and at the sides. Grace could feel her breasts wobble, and she was unsure whether this was from the smacking or from the many sensations that came from all parts of her body.

She knew above all things that her sex gaped, exposing the brightly flushed flesh.

'I think she is ready, master.' That was John, thought Grace.

'Yes.' The word from the master was no more than a whisper. 'I believe she is.'

Grace tugged on her bonds in eagerness. She wanted to welcome him, to smear back the jet curls so that nothing impeded his entrance. At last his cockhead, swollen and smooth, wet with his spunk, was coaxed about her entrance. Grace wanted to arch up in offer, but her bonds were too tight. He pushed, expecting resistance, but she was so well prepared, so excited by the long years of waiting and the night's games, that she drew his length deep into her body. Her own copious juices soaked his balls, smearing them with the blood of her virginity. Her tight sex contracted about him, sucking him in until his globe pressed against the wall of her womb.

His middle finger probed her bottom hole, replacing the candle, and Grace arched her neck, wishing she could scream her joy, but the gag caused her to remain silent.

He began to thrust into her very fast and hard, and she knew that soon she would be flooded with his sex milk. But as Grace thought her pleasure would be completed he withdrew his cockstem and the finger that plugged her bottom. The hood was removed and she opened her eyes, expecting to see John slide from her, sweating, his cock thick and smeared with her blood and juices. She cried out and tears spilled down her hot face.

'Master,' she murmured, pleading, joyful.

The Black Rose knelt between her spread thighs, his cock still spearing from its dark bush of hair, but slick with juices. He cupped her sex and let his middle finger slither into her.

'Beautifully open, silkily wet,' he said. 'You are ready for him now, but I should not have taken you. You were so valuable.'

'Valuable?' He spoke of her as if she was a precious jewel.

'But you are so very beautiful, that I could not resist my own urges.' He put his head in his hands. 'I had no right! You were not mine to use.'

'No,' she cried, and wished she could hold him close, soothe him. If his words puzzled her he put the questions at the back of her mind. 'It's all right. I wanted it. Needed you. I think I have needed you all of my life.'

Grace could not stem her tears, but they were not tears

of pain or unhappiness. They were tears of joy. If only he knew how long she had waited, how many years of frustration had been spent caressing her own sex.

Chapter Eleven

'My name is Lord Albert Fitzpatrick.'

The identity of the Black Rose was revealed! And to her! Grace was honoured.

And a lord, thought Grace, and she bowed her head, not in shame but in reverence. Even so, her manacled fingers tried, in vain, to hide her pussy bush. Her virginity was taken by an English lord, she reminded herself. She must be especially respectful.

He lay back on the pillows, and she noticed that he held and twisted a thin but short leather whip, split into several tongues.

'I am going to take away those fetters,' he said, and smiled as Grace's head snapped up, her eyes wide. She felt a flutter of joy in her heart. He was going to free her!

She was overcome that he should trust her. These past months she had been trained, disciplined and punished to a measure of severity she could not have imagined in her old life. It was an act of kindness she did not expect, and she allowed her lips to curve into a gentle smile.

He beckoned to John, who waited to attend his master's wishes. The servant was again liveried, but Grace could not prevent her eyes from darting to his crotch, and she shivered, remembering the previous day. She thought of the other girls who delighted in her humiliation as they murmured their own pleasure. But most of all she thought of that moment; the moment of such perfect release when her pleasure consumed her and her master took her purity.

John's fingers brushed her breasts as he manipulated

the key in the manacles.

'Come here,' said the master.

With head held high and hands free at last, Grace walked with effortless beauty to the bedside.

'Turn round, hands behind you.'

Grace felt thin binding being wrapped around the base of her thumbs, and felt cool aristocratic fingers touch her in the tight valley between her bottom cheeks. Again she was bound, and all she had gained was freedom from the gold manacles.

'On the bed.' Lord Albert's voice was flat and impassive.

The bed was high. Grace was forced to lift each leg, one after the other, to lever herself up. She blushed, knowing she was displaying the gap between her flesh lips, the nubbin as hard as a pea and burnished to scarlet, and the newly opened doorway to her body, which was dewed with her meltings.

She knelt before him, thighs slightly parted and head erect, looking directly at him.

The long fingers brushed her downy pubis. 'Open wider,' he said, in that same impassive tone.

Grace shuffled her knees apart.

'Wider.' His voice was terse and he slapped the inner sides of her thighs until she could feel the heat making her glow.

The smacking stopped and his touch became more tender. Fingertips grazed across the taut swell of her belly before he kissed it lightly. Grace parted her lips, a moan trapped in her throat, tantalised at his gentleness.

Lord Albert again lay back on the pillows, no longer touching her, but Grace felt his eyes upon the open darkness between her thighs. It was as if he touched her there, kissed the protruding tip of her nubbin, sucked at her wetness. Her legs trembled at his intimate gaze.

'I do not require you again, John,' said Lord Albert. 'You may leave us.'

'But…' The servant spluttered his protest and Grace glanced over her shoulder. She gasped, noticing that his breeches were open and his cock was erect. The look he gave her was venomous and promised tortures at any opportunity.

'Leave us!' Lord Albert hissed the command.

Grace could not help but whisper a sigh of relief as the servant left the room. But why did his lordship require her alone? Was he going to merely gaze between her open legs for the whole night? Her thighs trembled at the forced position.

'Sit upon your heels,' he said as if he read her thoughts. 'Let them cosset your bottom and your open quim.'

He wore nothing but breeches that bulged lewdly at his groin, and he stroked the bulge slowly and lovingly with one hand while the other slipped under the piled feather pillows upon which his head rested. His broad chest had a line of dark hair that disappeared into the waist of his breeches as if pointing the way to his cock.

'I have a gift for you,' he said.

'A gift?' whispered Grace, and a tear spilled on one heavy breast. No one had ever given her a gift before.

'Hm,' he murmured, and the sound was a caress that seeped between her thighs like a physical thing.

'Knowing how you love pain…' He paused and let his lips curve into the familiar sardonic smile. 'Oh, don't be coy,' he continued, and flicked the many-stranded lash from one hand to the other. She listened to the soft slap of it on his skin and shuddered as she imagined it whispering over her bottom, grazing her belly or tickling her breasts.

As the English lord inched towards her clutching the whip lightly, first in one hand and then the other, she tried to shimmy away from him. She did not fear the soft strands of leather – it looked too delicate to cause severe pain – but she feared her own reactions to it.

He swiped it back and forth in the softly lit air and she

watched the muscles ripple in his powerful arms and broad chest. She did not dare look down to his crotch from which speared his freshly turgid cock for she knew it would affect her deeply, for all that he still wore his breeches.

'Where shall I slap you?' he asked. But the query was pretence, Grace knew, for she heard the beginnings of a chuckle in his voice.

'Wherever you wish, milord,' said Grace, surprising herself at her boldness.

'Oh, you wonderful creature,' he whispered, and knelt before her, his bulge brushing her cunny curls. He slid the leather straps across the upper swells of her breasts. They felt cool, almost soothing, and Grace threw back her head in ecstasy, letting her hair spill like a river of jet down her back.

'May I smack your belly like this?' he purred.

'If it pleases you,' murmured Grace. Her belly quivered from the smack, and she felt the heel of his hand between her thighs rubbing back and forth, irritating the heated flesh.

'Oh, it pleases me very much.' His voice was a husky growl coming from the very depths of his chest. 'Or perhaps here?' He stroked the edge of the straps under the weighty heaviness of her breasts. 'Could you take that?' His free hand, the one not holding the straps, twirled the ring that still adorned her nipple. When Grace showed no reaction he pinched the flushed bud of flesh, delighting in the immediate erection his fingering caused, the opening of her lips and the widening of her eyes.

'I only wish to please you, milord,' said Grace.

'Just as a slave should,' he said with a nod, 'but I shall not smack these.' He hefted each breast and squeezed the pliant flesh.

Grace allowed herself a small sigh of relief as he threw the straps to the floor and jumped lithely after it.

'I am hungry,' he said, and he padded lightly across the

room to a table on which there was a covered silver platter. 'As I am sure you are.' He lifted the cover and Grace could smell the delicious savoury aroma of vegetables and meat of some kind cooked in wine. She licked her lips at the thought of food.

Her hunger became greater as he approached the bed with the platter and the delicious smell of hot cooked food became stronger. She shuddered as his weight made the feather mattress sink. Unconcerned, he settled himself comfortably on the pillows with the silver platter beside him.

'Some food?' he asked, and stabbed the point of his knife into a piece of succulent meat.

Grace tugged at the bindings about her thumbs and let the very tip of her tongue peep between her lips. She felt her heels nestle into the moistness of her cunt and felt shame as her own flesh excited her nubbin.

As he chewed he unfastened his breeches and allowed his cock to spring out, stiff and throbbing. 'Which would you rather enjoy, my darling?' he asked, stabbing another morsel of meat and holding it above Grace's head. It dripped warm gravy on her trembling breasts.

She stretched up, her lips open like a hungry bird, her nostrils flared. Her tongue probed out in an attempt to catch the savoury drips.

'Oh, you disappoint me,' he said in mock dismay. A strong hand pressed the back of her neck and she smelled his maleness as she was forced to bow over his upright cock. 'Drink your fill of my meltings, my darling,' he said as her lips brushed his tip, 'and then perhaps I shall allow you to share my plate.'

As Grace's lips slid down his shaft she was conscious of another hunger, perhaps even greater than in her belly, and she felt shame at her own wantonness.

His male milk oozed onto her tongue and slithered down her throat. She tasted his salt, the bitterness of his juices, and began to suck more greedily, rolling her lips about the taut skin, feeling the veins which throbbed in tortured tension along the shaft. She heard him groan and this increased her inner hunger. Her thighs parted until her spread labia brushed the tumbled bed linen.

At last his fountain burst, spurting warm cream into her throat, and Grace swallowed it all to appease her own hunger as much as his. She held his shaft, still thick and throbbing with aftershocks of his come, between her lips, not wishing to relinquish the dribbling length. He pushed her away and lay back on the pillows, eyes closed, enjoying his restitution. So copious was his come that Grace's lips were coated with it, and no matter how she lapped she could not reach the full measure.

In time his eyes opened and he stabbed another morsel with his sharp blade. He grinned and licked the succulent piece of meat, sipping the seasoned gravy. Grace stretched her neck, reaching hungrily for the piece of food, tasting his spunk and wishing to add to the flavours. She heard him chuckle and felt something very warm and soft enter her flesh lips, felt it being smoothed around. Looking down she saw the morsel of meat touching the inner lips of her flesh pot and her eyes fluttered up, pleading that he should end the shame. She could see driblets of her own juices against the darkness of the meat, felt the touch of its warmth against her sensitive flesh and felt her nubbin twitch as the meat brushed its tip.

In the flickering candlelight she saw the flash of the knife blade as he drew it from her. 'Head up,' he ordered, 'and mouth open.'

Grace, her cunny still fluttering from the stroke of the meat, stared at him.

He shook his head impatiently. 'Come now, did you not say you were hungry? You wanted food?' Head lowered, Grace gave a tentative nod. 'Then stretch up your neck and take this meat.' He wiped the morsel back and forth against Grace's lips. She could smell her own musk along

190

with the spices and wine absorbed by the meat. She opened her mouth fully and felt the food on her tongue, and her hunger was such that she could not help herself but chew it.

He fed her in this manner many times more, sometimes allowing the juices to dribble on her breasts, and sometimes sipping them before gently inserting the morsels of meat between her flesh lips to absorb her silky sap.

'And now wine,' he said, pushing the platter beneath the bed.

Grace shuddered, knowing and dreading what he might do. She heard the trickle of wine poured into a glass from a crystal decanter on a bedside table. He held the glass to his lips, looking at her over the rim with twinkling eyes. She heard the faint sound of his swallow and licked her lips. It made her thirst all the greater to hear him slake his own.

He swirled the wine in the deep crystal goblet. It was a rich ruby red and, as the candlelight caught it, Grace shuddered. Like blood, she thought, the blood that spilled from her at that glorious moment when he took her hated virginity.

'Come, drink,' he said, and held the goblet to her lips. It spilled from the corners of her mouth – so quickly did he tilt the glass – onto her breasts, trailing like tiny rivers over the pale mounds, gathering in the pit of her navel and swilling down into the lushness of her bush.

Grace gasped for breath as he finally released her. Her head spun from the deep draft of wine.

'Lie back,' he said, setting aside the glass.

The bindings on her thumbs seemed tighter and she struggled against them. She heard him chuckle as he pushed her shoulders and was helpless to resist. She felt herself falling back into the tumbled, wine-stained linen, her bound thumbs and her long legs folded beneath her.

'Glorious woman,' he murmured. He stroked her sex,

made open by her spread thighs and thrust upward by her own feet trapped beneath her buttocks. She sighed, a plea for the completion of her pleasure. She fixed her eyes on his cock, again fully erect. He spread her cunny lips open. Again she moaned. She had an urge to writhe beneath his hands, but he held her still as if he knew her need and had no intention of allowing it.

With the ball of his thumb he pressed against her jutting bud. The pressure was gently released and he rolled it from side to side, stroking back its hood and dribbling more wine on its sensitive rawness. Her bud was hot and throbbing, but the wine was cool, as were his fingers. The mixture of sensations was unbearably exquisite in their torture.

'Let go,' he murmured. 'Let me see you come.'

Her pleasure was so great there was no room in her for shame. Boldly, she looked into his eyes, just as her belly quivered. She was pleased to submit to this latest humiliation and she felt her nubbin pulse with glorious release, and felt liquid seep from her core.

As the glow faded so did Grace feel her boldness fade, and she closed her eyes, letting tears spill from them.

Helpless in her bound state she did not protest when he lifted her up, held her head to his chest for a moment, and flipped her face down on the bed. She felt him spread her legs and scoop her juices onto his fingers.

'Now I have two openings,' he said and his tone, chill and flat, made Grace quiver with fear. 'And I shall take them.'

A pillow was pushed beneath her quaking belly and her juices were rubbed between her buttocks. She felt him working the creamy liquid into the tightly wrinkled pit until he was satisfied it would give pleasurably about his cock.

His fingers slid down to the uplifted and pouting entrance to her sex. He used a finger and thumb to stretch her open and then allowed the tight opening to snap shut.

The movement caused a greater trickle of liquid from her honey pot and he worked this deeply into both openings until he was satisfied that both would give him pleasure.

His hand touched Grace's tethered thumbs, squeezing her numb fingers. 'Use these to pleasure my cock as I thrust,' he commanded.

No protest passed her lips, although she was unsure whether her fingers, with the prolonged binding, were capable of movement.

'If you do not please me...'

Grace, with questioning eyes, twisted her head to peep at him over her shoulder.

'This little beauty will work upon you until you do.'

In one hand he held the black leather straps and Grace's buttocks, still bruised from the previous night, felt the playful caress of the supple implement.

His turgid globe butted against her open wetness. Grace fumbled for his shaft, thick and unyielding, but her fingertips merely brushed the stiffness and she heard him growl in anger.

'Is this how you show your gratitude for taking you in?' He drew back and she heard the harshness of his breathing as the straps were drawn back in readiness for thrashing her vulnerable bottom.

Grace cried out in a most piteous manner, throwing back her head and arching her neck.

'Cosset my shaft!' he rasped. 'Don't fumble!'

'I'll try,' she murmured, fighting back tears, and as he thrust into the velvet wetness she tried with all her might to stroke the entering cock in a graceful and sensual manner.

'Better,' he grunted. 'Much better.'

His shaft opened her fully, sliding into her on her own slickness, in to the very limits of her womb. She bit her lower lip to stifle the moan of pleasure which welled up inside her, but almost at the peak of her ecstasy he withdrew, leaving her bereft, her fingers fluttering emptily. She waited, wondering if she had displeased him.

'You have done well,' he whispered, and she felt the dark line of chest hair brushing her shoulders. She felt the gold rings tauten as her nipples came to full erection against the bed linen. 'You are so wonderfully submissive. You excite me beyond all bearing.'

Grace felt his thick shaft caress her backbone and slide down to her bottom crease. The numbness in her fingers brought about by the tight binding of her thumbs and the ache in her shoulders from the long bondage no longer mattered.

His cock globe butted at the tiny pore of her bottom and she bore up towards it, mewing with gratitude. She felt his fingertips press into the pouted entrance of her sex, scooping up her liquid. He drew back and worked the juices into the tightness, spreading the tiny wrinkles and pressing the ball of his thumb into the easing orifice. The weight and length of his cock spread her bottom cheeks, opening them out until his smooth globe again spread the tight entrance wetted with her honey.

Grace sighed with pleasure as she felt him enter, opening her rear passage as his fingers massaged her sex. She felt a thumb pet the tip of her clitty and a long finger slide into her female passage. The soft walls clutched at the invading digit and she felt the web between his fingers brush her sex lips, swollen with her need.

The room was full of liquid sound as he drove into her; the sound of his cock being sucked into her welcoming bottom hole and the sound of his fingers petting her sex. She smelled the scent of their combined musk, heavy and hot, becoming stronger as their excitement grew. She moaned into the pillows, wondering how much longer this pleasure would continue.

She could not hold back a scream as he slid from her, leaving her empty once more, but almost immediately his thickness filled her female passage and his thrusting

194

became faster, frantic. She heard his rapid breathing, which echoed her own. The throb in her clitty grew until she could not hold back the scream that welled up in her throat. His grunting was loud in her ears and the solid four-poster shook with their passion.

At last she felt the first flood of his come. It swilled into her, overflowing, soaking her pussy curls and trickling down her thighs. Grace was consumed with her own orgasm, which made her helpless body shudder from head to toe.

Chapter Twelve

When Grace awoke next morning she was alone in the huge bed. Sunlight streamed through the leaded windows, dappling her naked body with golden light and sensual warmth. Her breasts felt full and tender, her flesh pot sore and much used by a large cockstem. A smile curved her lips as she remembered the previous night.

Far beyond her dreaming she heard a soft knock on the oak door. She allowed the linen sheets to remain down the bed and spread her thighs invitingly as she waited for her lord to return to her.

'Come in,' she said haltingly. The English language was coarse and came with difficulty to her tongue.

The door opened and a maid hurried in with a laden breakfast tray. The girl was plump and plainly dressed, not at all like the pretty girls who romped with his lordship the previous night.

The crimson stain of shame flushed Grace's cheeks as she dragged the sheets to cover her nakedness. But the girl showed no such embarrassment.

'Will my lord be joining me for *petit dejeuner*?' asked Grace, attempting at some normality. She looked with some dismay at the mountain of ham, hot rolls, eggs and mushrooms.

'I doubt it, miss,' said the maid, setting down the tray. 'He set sail for France early this morning.'

It was as if a heavy weight settled within Grace's belly. All the pleasant feelings she experienced as she awoke were dispelled. '*Non*!' she cried. '*Quelle dangereuse*! Oh, he cannot have done so!'

The sheet fell and her breasts were bared again. 'Bring me my clothes and… and… a horse!'

'No, miss.' The plump maid looked stern. 'Master left orders that you must not leave the manor house.'

'But I must!' Grace threw back the covers and swung her legs over the edge of the bed. Such was her panic that she didn't notice the maid staring between her thighs.

'I've got my orders, miss. You stay here and eat your breakfast or I've been told to bring John to teach you how to behave.' The plump maid ran to the door and Grace heard the click as the key was turned in the lock.

'John,' murmured Grace. John with the cruel eyes and pinching hands. She ran to the door and pounded on it until her fists hurt. 'Let me out!' she sobbed. 'Please! I wish to go to my lord.' She sobbed so hard she did not hear footsteps in the passage beyond the door and scarcely heard the heavy key turn in the lock.

'Now, miss,' said a rasping voice, 'what's all this, eh?'

Grace fell away from the door. To her shame she knew her jet curls hid nothing of the fleshy portals. Fear made her limbs stiff and she made no attempt to hide herself as she looked up into glinting eyes, staring from a leather hood favoured by the executioners on the steps of the guillotine. Despite the hood she knew it was John; she recognised the cruelty in the voice.

'A pretty sight,' he murmured. 'A pretty sight indeed, and I am ordered to make it prettier yet.'

He wore only a short leather apron, held in place by a thong between his buttocks. One of his hands strayed beneath the square of leather and Grace knew his fingers rubbed at his thickening cock.

'What do you mean?' Surely after last night the master would not send John to harm her. She tried to hide herself by curling her arms around her breasts and drawing her knees up to her chin. But bony hands dragged her to her feet and took the opportunity to feel the yielding flesh of her breasts. She shuddered as fingers combed through the dark silkiness of her pussy hair. 'No,' she murmured. A fingertip rolled the tip of her bud until she felt every nerve stretched to breaking point, but she did not quite reach the peak of orgasm. She moaned softly, arching her body against his caresses, hating herself for doing so. She wanted her master to touch her intimately, not this fiend he ordered to replace him.

'Do I give you nice feelings?' said John huskily. 'Tell me. Let your liquid flow over my fingers.' First one finger was thrust into Grace's freshly opened passage and then a second and a third, stretching her, driving into her wetness. She bore down upon the feeling of fullness, for to her shame it brought back the sensations of the previous night.

'Don't hold back,' hissed John. 'This is why you are here; to give pleasure.'

Without wishing to Grace arched against the thrusting fingers. She could feel his thickened cockstem beneath the leather apron. She bore against it, wanting it, but hating him at the same time.

With her breasts full and tender, pouting upward from her bowed body, Grace suddenly shuddered through an exquisite orgasm.

'My master said you were sensual,' whispered John, slipping his fingers from Grace and examining them, admiring the gathered pearls which slithered down to his palm. He grinned and thrust the fingers deep into her open mouth. 'Suck,' he ordered hoarsely. 'Suck as you would suck a cock.'

Grace, tasting her own musk, felt her cheeks redden,

but she obediently sucked every drop of her own juices.

'Good,' said John. 'Walk ahead of me.' He pushed her trembling form forward, sending her stumbling into the passage outside the room. 'Hands on your head and no hiding your face. Head up.'

There were servants polishing silver and dark oak furniture in the shadowy passage. Grace heard sniggers as she walked ahead of John. She felt her cheeks burn with shame. She cried out as her bottom felt the caress of a leather strap. She felt heat as the welt left by the leather swelled proud from her pale buttocks.

'Don't cry out,' ordered John. 'I'm well aware how you enjoy chastisement.'

Grace felt his cruel fingers on her shoulders, whipping her round, arching her over the polished oak of a trestle table. Trying to save herself she let her hands fall from her head, but was rewarded by light slaps of leather on her breasts.

'Up! Up and legs open,' he said, in a tone that would take nothing but obedience.

The ancient polished oak felt cool and smooth under Grace's bottom. It soothed the strapped and heated flesh. She slid slowly forward, her legs high and spread. Pinching fingers coaxed her ever-willing nipples to perfect points. The leather apron swayed back and forth across the open cup of her sex, and she could feel his erection beneath it.

The fingers slid down over her belly and hovered about her sex. 'This hair must go,' said John, and she felt the fingers comb the silky darkness of her nest.

'No...'

'By order of the master,' he insisted, spreading her sex lips with finger and thumb. 'It must all go. It will increase your sensitivity and your appearance of innocence.'

'Does he truly wish it?' She bore down upon the probing fingers as if her English lover stood between her legs, and not this servant who seemed to delight in humiliating her before the other servants of the house.

'Of course.' John sounded very certain. 'And it will be my task to keep you sleek every day.' With one last caress John helped her to her feet and guided her on down the passage.

The air became more chilled as they descended into the cellars of the old house. But they were nothing like the dungeons beneath the palace of Versailles, nor were they like those beneath Robespierre's headquarters. There was one cell, noticed Grace, with a studded iron door several inches thick. The floor was bare earth and it was furnished only with a rough wooden bench.

'You wonder why I have brought you here?' John unfastened the leather apron and let it fall to the floor. 'Does this explain?' He stroked his erect cock. 'Does it?'

Glad of the flickering single candle, glad of the dim light, Grace bowed her head and tried to hide her blushes. 'What do you want of me?' Her voice was no more than a whisper.

'Be free with me,' said John. 'As you are with the master. Be voluptuous. You are a slave, after all.'

Madame's training had been such that in the presence of a needful man Grace could be nought else. She sank to her knees and let her tongue slip between her lips. It lapped and coiled around the tip of his thickness, dipped into its pulsing pore and sipped the ooze of sap that beaded from it.

'Yes,' groaned the servant. 'Be free.'

Grace slipped her fingers into the depths of her sex and worked them deep until they were coated. She eased them under the servant's ball sac, stroking them gently. She heard him moan, felt him thrust towards her, felt the slime of his tip brush against her lips. She sucked and drew the fine skin back over the bulb. She stroked his inner thighs, making them tremble. With fingers taught by madame she pressed the cock a little behind the bulb and dipped her tongue tip into the pulsing opening. She felt him thrust rhythmically until most of his length was within her throat and she could taste his salt. He could not hold back. She heard him grunt and felt the creamy spurt of his come slide down her throat.

Gently, her lifted her to her feet. 'You are a slave,' he mumbled thickly, 'a slave to give pleasure to men. My master has found someone who will…' He paused, his fingers smoothing her breasts and his thumbs rolling the hard pips of her nipples.

Grace shook her head. 'No.' She was something more than that now, surely. Hadn't Lord Albert taken her for his own? Made her his? 'No, I am no longer a slave.'

The servant chuckled. 'Did my master tell you this?' He drew off the leather hood and grinned at her. He stroked the garment between her thighs and she could smell the leather blended with her own musk. It made her bear down.

'Not exactly,' she admitted.

'But that is what you are. A slave, to be used by men for pleasure. And my master has instructed me to continue your training. You will obey me now?'

Grace bowed her head, and meekly yielded. 'Whatever he wishes, I shall do.'

John nodded with satisfaction and led her to the bench. He eased her down upon it, and Grace remained stoic and compliant. It was a trick, a lie, she was sure. Lord Albert was a gentleman. Why did he wish to shame her further by denuding her sex? Why? John was taking advantage of his absence, she was sure.

'Spread your thighs.'

It was as if she was back in madame's clutches, to be shamed and humiliated.

She felt a light smack on her belly when she hesitated a moment too long, and she opened her thighs the width of the bench.

'No! No! Not like that!'

The smacks became harder and slid down to her inner thighs, making her spread her legs so they hung down loosely at the sides of the bench. Her feeling of vulnerability was increased with the knowledge of her lost maidenhead. The tears flowed. What did Lord Albert have in mind?

Fingertips brushed her curls and strayed down to her sex lips.

'Too thick,' murmured John. 'This hair is far too thick and lush for a girl such as you.' He smoothed his palm over the curls, making her tremble with a delicious, although unbidden, wantonness. 'Women are always more desirable if smooth. It makes them more open, more available, you see.'

He left her and she heard him moving about in some corner of the small chamber. She heard sloshing sounds and lifted her head, straining her eyes in the gloom.

In a moment he was back at her side, the leather apron lifted lewdly by the stiffness of his cock beneath it. In his hands he held a cup and a soft brush.

'Remain very still,' he ordered, 'or you will find your pleasure rising more than is good for you. But keep these thighs spread.'

A slippery coolness was slopped between her legs and spread upon her sex. The brush wiped upon the very tip of her nubbin, making her buck with the wanton pleasure of it. A new awareness of the rings still pierced in her nipples and the chain that slid about her ribs and weighted the fullness of her breasts came upon her. Looking down her body she saw the creamy mound of suds which hid the dark lushness of her pussy curls, and fresh tears spilled upon her the upper swells of her breasts, shimmering like crystal on the pale flesh.

He left her again and she heard a new sound; the sound of leather being stroked back and forth. When he approached she saw the glint of polished steel in the flickering candlelight. She whimpered and tensed, and made a hesitant attempt to roll from the bench.

'Oh no you don't, my pretty missy!' He laid the razor down and took two lengths of rope from a hook on the bare wall. Before she could complete her roll from the bench he was beneath it, grasping her wrists and ankles. She felt the roughness of the rope as he bound all four limbs together so that she was bowed, her breasts and sex mound lifted by the tightness of the binding.

'Now, the master said I must not truss you unless strictly necessary.' He shook his head as if in sorrow. 'I did not want to do it, but...' He stroked the leather apron and the bulge rose. 'I could not take the risk that you might escape.'

'I am sorry,' said Grace truthfully, but she knew the binding made her more vulnerable and she felt the swirl in her belly which heralded her pleasure.

The servant took up the razor once more and held it at the widest part of her triangle of curls. Grace shuddered as she felt the coldness of the steel and the edge of the blade on her flesh.

'Be still now,' he warned again. 'Very still.'

He placed a piece of white cloth on the bench and cut the first swath of curls. His movements were light and precise as he wiped the cut hair and white suds upon the cloth. Grace felt the chill of the air on her freshly bared skin.

'Naked,' he said, smoothing the last curl away. She heard him squeeze a cloth in water and felt a new coldness on her intimate parts as he wiped the last of the suds away. He patted her dry with another piece of cloth and bent over her, his fingertips caressing the smooth skin of her sex folds. 'How does it feel?' he asked, as a forefinger rubbed beneath the arch of her mound.

'Very open,' she told him, her eyes closed in her shame.

'Yes,' he said, 'of course. That is how it was meant to feel for the men who wish to use you. Very open and very

202

wet.' His fingers remained within her folds. 'Are you wet?'

Grace said nothing. She knew she was very wet indeed. His fingers slid downwards, and hovered at the entrance newly opened by Lord Albert.

'You are very wet,' he said, answering his own question. 'Very welcoming and smooth, just as men like.' Two fingers slipped in further and Grace felt her opening clutch the intrusion. 'Beautiful,' he murmured. 'Let me feel you do that again.'

The movement had been quite involuntary and Grace was unsure whether she could repeat it. She arched up, knowing her silky smooth mound was close to his questing lips.

'I think you are ready for a cock,' he said roughly.

Grace, in her newly bare state, felt her pleasure very close, but this man was a servant at Lord Albert's beck and call; surely it would be wrong to allow him her body? 'No, please. It would be a wrong against the master.'

John twisted the square of leather to the side and allowed his cock to bob and spear freely to his waist. He laughed. 'I do it on my master's orders, and he instructs that I may use you whenever and wherever I care when he is away. This is to accustom you to your new life.'

With a thumping heart Grace resigned herself to the fact that there was nothing she could do to resist the servant, but what did he mean; new life?

He climbed onto the bench, his knees pressing against her inner thighs, his cock waving over the swell of her belly. He grinned down at her and placed his hands flat on the ancient wood to steady himself. He pushed within her and she heard him grunt as he began to thrust in and out. He groaned louder and his body stiffened as he flooded her with his seed.

'Did you deliver her?' asked Charlotte, lying back on the pillows. She was drowsy, having just been roused from sleep.

The Black Rose shook his head. 'I took her to the manor house on the Kent coast,' he said, unfastening his caped coat. The crossing had been worse than usual and he was weary beyond all telling.

Charlotte, naked, her heavy breasts quivering with rage, sat up. Her handsome face was a mask of fury. 'And could not resist her, I suppose! I knew this would happen! That is why I tried to save her from you when the Channel boat docked at Dover.' She hissed with anger. 'You took her, didn't you? What kind of money do you think we can get on used goods, even a beauty like Grace?'

Lord Albert, naked apart from his breeches, shrugged. 'She was so sweet, so innocent,' he said, 'in spite of all they did to her at Versailles, that I could not bear the thought of the Sheikh taking her maidenhead and then turning her over to his guests. She would never have survived the harem as she was.'

Charlotte, sitting very straight, her knees pressed by her own hands to fall outwards, threw back her head and laughed. 'You are becoming soft, Albert!' Her smile faded quickly. 'You have lost the cause thousands of francs by your softness.'

Shrugging out of his breeches he threw himself on the bed between the inviting knees. 'Perhaps I am, as you say, becoming soft,' he admitted. 'But I have vowed to wreak vengeance on that harridan and her consort who ruined the girl in the first place.' He sucked first one of Charlotte's sex lips into his mouth and then the other. What did he care for the cause? What Charlotte did not know was that he worked not for the cause of France but to increase his own fortune.

She groaned, leaning back once more upon the pillows. '*Oui*, Albert, *mon cherie*!' His tongue drove into her wetness over and over again. It flicked upwards, caressing the taut bud of her nubbin. 'Tell me it's me that you love,' she groaned. 'Only me, and not that milk sop of a girl.'

The Black Rose lifted his head from the depths of his lover's thighs and wiped the cream of her sap from his lips. His rugged features were a mask of fury and he grasped her thighs, driving into the flesh with iron-hard fingers. Charlotte murmured, begging for mercy. 'She is no milk sop!' He twisted her long limbs until she lay on her belly. 'Remember that Charlotte, and if you cannot remember it then I must find ways to imprint it in your mind. Shall I do that?'

'*Oui*! Do whatever you wish to me, Albert.' She spoke with a tremor in her voice. 'Only say you love me.'

'I love all slaves,' he said tightly, 'you included.' He jumped from the bed and, just as Charlotte was about to run towards him, he lashed out with his whip. It coiled about her thighs and tumbled her to the floor. She whimpered as he dragged her towards him. He rolled her over by uncoiling the whip. 'Admit you are a slave, Charlotte!' The whip cracked again and caught the creamy hillocks of her bottom. A weal rose up, a diagonal scarlet line across the twin peaks.

'I am a thief!' cried Charlotte, her lips compressed in a determined line. 'A pickpocket!'

The whip cracked across the room again, the tip teasing the underswell of a breast. 'Not good enough. Tell me you are a slave to my cock.'

'I will admit to that!' agreed Charlotte, turning over and kneeling in a provocative manner, her buttocks inviting him to whip them.

Chapter Thirteen

'I'm afraid,' said Madame de Genlis as they hurried down a narrow alley in the back streets of Paris.

'Dreadfully afraid.' Her heavy breasts were partially bared by her torn gown and her feet were naked, her shoes stolen while they slept in a narrow alley.

Was it only three days ago when she and Philipe took Grace to the theatre? Only three days! How her world had changed, and not for the better. Philipe was right. They should never have left the palace that night simply to show Grace to the world. It was then that their troubles started. But she was so beautiful, so glorious, and she should have fetched a tidy sum had all things been right with the world.

Madame shuddered and clutched her torn gown to her bare breasts.

'There must be somewhere we can go,' said Philipe. 'Somewhere warm and away from these… creatures.'

'Oh, stop whining, Philipe!' She hurried ahead of him.

'Well, I'm afraid too, and I have more right than you to be so.'

Madame sighed. He was whimpering now – whimpering like a child.

'Don't you realise I could be beheaded?' he said, hiccoughing with fear.

Madame tried not to think about Philipe's plight, but hurried on. Her hands itched at the thought of that gloriously sensuous creature in her arms. She closed her eyes as she thought of the girl coming to orgasm, the glow of her pale skin. So delicious! But now their only source of potential income was lost to them.

She shook her head, remembering.

There was a little fuss, of course, when she ordered the jeweller to pierce the flushed nipples and the virgin flesh lips. It was necessary to discipline her. It was such a pity, because madame was quite certain he had trained her to be entirely submissive, and then the little wretch screamed!

As madame stumbled along the filthy cobbled streets she tutted in annoyance at the memory. It was necessary for Philipe to smack her bottom and thighs until they glowed, not that that made a deal of difference. The girl continued to scream until Philipe plugged her mouth with a wad of silk.

Madame did her best to explain that the bondage came within the training advised by Rousseau, but did it make any difference? It did not! The little wretch continued to squirm and mew behind her gag.

Her eyes! Madame would never forget her eyes over the white silk. Full of tears, shimmering with them, and pleading. It made madame want to spread the girl's legs and suck her nubbin until she was again calm and entirely pliant.

She gave a grunt of disgust. That she should come to this – homeless and hungry. Her white muslin gown was stained and torn, and some thief of the night had stolen her shoes. Every step sent pain to which she was quite unused; her every pleasure was in giving rather than receiving pain.

'And you have good reason to be afraid, too,' said Philipe, interrupting her pleasant memories. 'And why are you still wearing that ridiculous stone between your breasts?'

Madame de Genlis clutched her torn gown, trying to hide the pale mountains of her breasts, and touched the stone held by a leather thong about her neck. 'It is part of the Bastille,' she said, fingering the rough edges. 'I hoped it would bring us luck. A young woman gave it to me and said as much.'

The Duc d'Orleans laughed bitterly. 'Well, it has not, has it? And where is the famous Black Rose? Did you not say you had made arrangements for him to save us?'

'Yes, when we slipped out of the palace. One of the footmen promised...' She felt a strong arm wrap around her ample waist and squeeze the pliant flesh of her bared breast. She screamed. 'Philipe! Save me—!' A hand muffled her cry.

'Let go of me!' yelled Philipe, who had troubles of his own.

'Be quiet, aristo!' snarled a harsh voice.

'Wh-where are you taking us?' asked madame.

The man who had grabbed her so roughly ripped her gown open completely and hefted each heavy breast, one after the other, and gave a grunt of satisfaction. 'Just what we need,' he said, ignoring her question. He pinched each nipple until she moaned in pain. 'Big and juicy,' he added.

'And we can have fun with this one,' added another voice, a woman, ripping Philipe's breeches open to bare his cock. 'Not bad for an aristo,' she said. 'We can have fun with both of them.'

Madame was pushed and chivvied along one dark alley after another. Hands, rough and clumsy, slipped under what was left of her gown, feeling the soft wetness of her sex, opening the lips and driving deep into her passage, between the cleft of her bottom and the tightly pursed hole between the hillocks. She tried to cry out but a filthy rag was jammed between her lips.

After what seemed like an age she was pushed into a brightly lit room. She blinked in amazement at her luxurious surroundings.

The woman who still held Philipe pulled him down on a sofa. She held him face up and used a thumb and finger to slick up and down his cock. Madame was not surprised when the limp shaft became erect and the woman slipped the rim of skin down below the shining globe. Philipe lay back on the woman, writhing under her caresses.

'Kneel!' the woman ordered. 'Suck him!'

'That's it, Charlotte,' hissed a rough voice. 'Let him die happy.'

Madame struggled. It was the end – the end for both of them. 'Philipe!' she cried to her lover. 'Goodbye!'

A balmy evening, and the gypsies gathered round their camp fire waiting for the women to prepare their meal.

'Listen!'

As one, the men turned in the direction in which Veranti pointed. 'Someone approaches,' he whispered. 'A woman. I can hear the swish of her skirts.' His head went up and he sniffed the still air. 'Young,' he murmured, 'ripe. Very ripe.'

One of the younger men rose up from his seat by the fire and stood close to Veranti. The wise one cocked his ear again. 'She wears jewellery. I hear a chain sway against flesh. She draws closer.'

'She is beautiful,' said the young fellow who was called Peli.

She had stepped into the clearing. The black servant's gown she wore sat ill on her. The swell of her breasts strained the bodice and the waist was loose, hanging about its slenderness and drooping untidily over the curve of her hips.

'Who are you?' asked Peli, and he walked towards her. The blue-black hair was like his own; thick and lustrous, catching the cold light of the full moon which made it shimmer like jet and the flickering firelight which turned it to bronze.

'Help me!'

She was foreign, by her voice, thought Peli.

'Careful, lad,' warned Veranti, plucking at his sleeve. 'She could be a decoy for the Peelers, and we've got those kegs of brandy...'

Peli shrugged away from the older man and went towards the girl. Green eyes shimmered with tears and the full breasts heaved, almost bursting from the too tight bodice. The gown was not hers, Peli knew that, and he ached to have her beneath him, naked, her breasts free and her thighs outstretched. There was something about her. She was submissive, but courageous and sensual in the extreme. He sniffed the air, trying to catch the aroma of her ripeness noticed by Veranti; the female musk.

'I have run away,' she said haltingly.

Peli's eyes flickered from the heaving breasts to the girl's sweet face; so innocent. Veranti must be wrong, surely. This one must be a virgin.

'From where?' asked Peli. He stood close to her now, at the edge of the clearing. He took her hand and tried to draw her into the circle, by the fire, but she held back and he noticed there were faint scars at her wrists. She had been manacled; a slave.

'The manor house,' she murmured.

Peli's breath caught in his throat. 'One of Lord Albert's girls?'

'He is in danger!' Her eyes darkened as they became wider.

Veranti stood beside Peli now, and he laughed. 'In danger? Him? What danger could he be in? He cares only for himself and the fortune he has amassed.'

The girl bowed her head and Peli saw tears fall upon the pale slopes of her breasts, glittering like crystals in the moonlight. 'They will kill him,' she murmured, choking back her sobs.

'Who?' asked Peli. The girl's beauty and her distress, as well as his own need, tore at his cock.

She raised her head. 'The revolutionaries.'

Veranti laughed, throwing back his head. 'The man is a smuggler, a spy for both sides in France, and a dealer in women…'

The girl's face, already pale, became as white as the chalk on the cliffs below their camp. 'A dealer in women?' she asked, and her tongue tripped over the words.

'For the harems in Morocco,' explained Peli. All the fight seemed to go out of the girl and she collapsed in his arms.

Veranti's hearty laughter followed them as they walked into the thick stand of trees.

She made no murmur as Peli lifted her skirt and trailed his dark fingers up her thighs. The full skirt impeded his hands and he growled his anger, his frustration. To his surprise the girl gathered her skirt and lifted it over her head, to stand before him naked. Had his cock not been fully turgid in his breeches it would have become so immediately he saw her body.

'Will you scream if I touch you?' he asked. His own eyes widened as he looked down at her full flesh pot. Her sex was shaven smooth and added to her air of youth and innocence. She shook her head and the movement made the chain slung from one breast to the other quiver. The chain was looped through two gold hoops pierced into the flesh of nipples, which were permanently erect and flushed to a rose-pink.

Peli threw the discarded gown on the woodland floor and eased her down upon it. Without a word from him she opened her thighs and lifted her knees, giving him full freedom. He gazed in wonder at the sight revealed to him. With trembling hands he reached out to the delicious sight, but her eyes hardened and she cupped her fingers over the smooth mound.

'If I let you do anything you wish to me, will you do me a great favour?' she asked. Her voice pleaded with him and no matter what the favour, however impossible, he vowed he would oblige her.

'Anything,' he said.

'On your father's life?' she asked, opening her fingers and revealing the inviting folds.

'On my father's life,' swore Peli.

The girl lifted her arms and beckoned him. Clumsily, Peli shrugged out of his brightly coloured waistcoat, his shirt and breeches, and sank to his knees between her open thighs.

'I need to go to France,' she said. 'Soon... on the tide.'

'I will arrange it,' he said hoarsely. 'Somehow I will arrange it.'

When he touched the silky smoothness of the outer flesh lips, Peli felt his cock jerk with the delicious innocence of it and yet, within, the hot flesh was slick with sap. This was no innocent! His thumb slid along the arch of her nubbin and back again, drawing the hood to form a little skirt at the root and leaving the tip a polished bead.

She turned her head and Peli followed her gaze. 'Go away!' he ordered huskily. 'She is mine.'

The three men were his friends, one the son of Veranti and they, too, were naked, their cocks stiff and upright. Ignoring them, Peli pushed his dusky middle finger between the plump flesh folds, sighing with pleasure as it sank into smooth silkiness such as he had never known in a woman. The moist flesh sucked at his finger, much as a child's mouth would suckle a nipple. She smiled at him and, with his free hand, he stroked his cock. He had reason to be proud of his organ. It was thick and ebony black, much darker than the tawny skin of his face and torso. It throbbed under his touch and he stroked the skin back from the swell of his globe.

'She is one of Lord Albert's whores,' growled Veranti's son, whose nickname was Mule, for the hugeness of his shaft.

Peli heard the girl gasp as she strained her neck backwards, making her breasts pout upwards as she looked at Mule and at the length that speared up from his groin.

'Maybe she is,' agreed Peli, lifting the fine gold breast chain and watching how the pink nipples rose to follow his pull. But the girl didn't whimper or complain as many would. She remained stoically silent. 'But she is beautiful and her quim oozes silken fluids, beckoning me.'

'My father says Lord Albert's women do not enjoy sex unless it is accompanied by smacking,' said Mule. His cock jerked and throbbed, lifting to his waist.

'Or whipping with leather,' said another of Peli's

friends, whose name was Banu. He had a length of leather, blackened by age and wide as the cock he stroked with it. The leather was supple and thin, and Peli reckoned it to be from the workbench in his caravan where he made simple sandals.

'Or caning,' said the third, Ricco, who held a birch twig, pale and stripped of its bark.

'Is this true?' asked Peli of the girl.

She closed her eyes and turned her head away from him. A sudden anger made his face flush under his swarthy skin and his hand lashed out to smack the pale oval of her cheek.

'Yes,' she said at last, gazing up at him with eyes full of tears.

He watched her cheek redden and could not help but feel sorry for his chastisement. She let her knees fall further open and her sex folds part yet further.

'I am open and ready for you, master,' she said meekly. 'So long as you abide by your promise, I will do anything that pleases you.'

'All of us?' asked Ricco, who was small and wiry, unlike the other young men in the group who were muscled and tall. He knelt at the side of the girl and stroked the birch twig across her breasts. The green eyes turned upon him and Ricco felt a tightening in his groin, a drawing up of his balls. 'Anything which pleases you, masters,' she said.

He rose to his feet and prodded the swell of a breast with his bare toe. 'She isn't a witch, is she?' he asked, and the others laughed as he cupped his balls, letting the birch twig fall to the ground.

Peli snatched it up. 'No,' he said, 'she isn't a witch.' The twig was drawn across her sex and he switched it in the night air, making a whistling sound before bringing it down upon her belly.

'You see!' he cried in triumph. 'Not a sound, but see how the weal appears on her skin. No, Ricco. She isn't a

213

witch.'

'I am trained,' said the girl, placing her hands behind her head and letting her knees drift flat upon the woodland floor. The young men stared at her fully open flesh pot and watched the weal across her belly darken to the colour of blood. 'Trained to take pain and to give pleasure... Who will be first?'

Banu prodded her hip with a foot, pushing her over until she lay on her belly, her bottom pouting up into the night. 'There's a sight that begs for a supple piece of shoe leather if ever I saw one. Open your legs, girl. You've been very open with us so far. Don't spoil it now.'

Keeping her hands at her head, her thighs splayed and her bottom slightly raised, the girl awaited the promised blows.

'A smack or two with my hands first,' said Mule, holding up palms as wide as dinner plates. 'I don't need any twigs or straps, I think you'll agree.'

'Do it!' said Ricco.

Banu smacked his piece of leather across his own palm while Peli softly smacked the birch twig against his muscular thigh.

Mule sank to his knees and smoothed his huge palms over the milk-white hillocks. He allowed a thick finger to invade the crease between the two buttocks, and they all watched in awe as the finger was drawn into the depths of the girl's bottom hole.

'She does not object,' grunted Mule, 'and my finger...'

'The smacking!' reminded Banu.

'Very tight,' murmured Mule, as he drew his finger out of her bottom. 'It grips delightfully.' One of his big hands drew back and came down upon the offered buttocks. The smack resounded through the woods and as Mule drew back his hand the three young men watched the smacked flesh quiver under the force of the blow.

'Oh, again!' said Ricco, his eyes fixed upon the slight but rapid motion of the bottom mounds and the reddening

214

flesh.

'But with your other hand, Mule,' said Banu, 'which is fresh and full of power.'

Peli bent over the girl and whispered in her ear. 'Does it hurt?'

Her head was hidden in the crumpled folds of the servant's gown and her words were muffled. 'It stings a little, master,' she said.

'Continue,' said Peli.

The sound of the smack was louder this time, and when Mule drew back his hand they saw the whole bottom glowed scarlet. He was about to administer another blow when Peli stopped him.

'Let us see if it's as they say,' he said.

Mule frowned, his hand resting on the heated flesh that trembled under his touch. 'What do you mean?'

Peli crouched again, his cock spearing upward from his groin, the veins pulsing and eager. 'Allow me to feel within the girl's sex, feel its wetness, the readiness.'

Mule grumbled as he moved back to make way for Peli, who began to stroke at her ankles. He noticed the slight scarring of the skin where the anklets had been. The girl shuddered, but opened her thighs to their fullest extent. His fingertips trailed up the inner sides of her thighs and then his palms cupped her smacked bottom. He felt his cock throb and he wished with all his heart that his friends had not found them, that she was his alone. He felt the tightness of her bottom crease open and tickled her bottom hole with his fingertip. It was tight, but she seemed to take great pleasure in this place. 'It is true,' he said to the other three. 'Lord Albert's girls seem to delight in being smacked.' The sticky wetness coated his hand as he used his palm to spread the plump lips. His fingers sank into satin flesh, which drew him in. It was made even more pleasurable by them being shaved to a silken smoothness. He groaned. If only he could just fling himself upon her just as she was and pump his come into her.

'Let someone else take a turn,' said Banu, his voice full of envy. He bent down and roughly pulled her head back by grasping a handful of hair with one hand. With the other he cupped a breast and flicked the pierced nipple. His face creased in a cruel grin as she winced at such outright cruelty. 'Let me use my strap on her. That will tell us exactly how much she enjoys pain.'

Reluctantly Peli stepped away from her, but Banu let the strap lie idle upon the ground as he opened the girls pouting sex folds. 'All women should be shaven,' he grunted, pressing the leaves open with his finger and thumb. The girl wriggled as he teased the inner lips open and kissed each soft wall of the pouch with the touch of a fingertip.

'We're testing for pain,' reminded Peli coldly. He slid his fingers up and down the ebony shaft spearing up from his groin. He used his thumb to smear the drop of moisture that beaded at his globe. It would slide into her like silk, he thought.

Banu scowled at Peli, but picked up the strap. 'On the bottom only?' he asked, looking down at the reddened hillocks.

'Where else?' asked Peli impatiently. His groin felt tight and heavy. He had to have relief.

Banu grinned and prodded her with his toe. 'The belly will shudder nicely under the strap. The breasts, too.'

'Just the bottom,' said Peli firmly. He wanted this over. Wanted to take her and fuck her. Whether he fulfilled his promise to get her to France, that remained to be seen.

Banu knelt at the girl's side and drew back the strap, bringing it down again and again on the girl's buttocks. He wanted to get some whimper from her, some cry of pain, Peli could tell, but she remained stoically silent, her bottom raised in offer and her sex posed in such a manner that the men could see the nubbin fully erect.

'Nothing!' said Banu in disappointment. 'Not a sound.'

'But look at her bottom!' Ricco had picked up his cane and he prodded the mounds, which darkened beyond scarlet to dark wine colour. The girl mewed softly, and the sound was muffled as if she had dragged the gown into her mouth. Her hands were still clasped obediently upon her head. As one, the young men groaned.

'What now?' asked Peli. His impatience grew by the second. 'We cannot beat her more. Her flesh will not take it.'

'The belly,' insisted Banu.

'Yes, the belly,' said Ricco, swishing the birch cane through the air. 'And the breasts.' He looked at Banu, who nodded agreement.

Peli lifted the girl's head by her hair, but although his action was rough, his expression was full of tenderness and sympathy. 'You said you would allow anything,' he reminded her.

'Yes, master. Anything.' Her voice was steady although her eyes glittered with unshed tears.

He let her head fall. 'Go ahead,' he told Ricco. 'A few strokes of the birch on the behind and then turn her over.' He stood back, his arms folded. He did not dare touch his cock for fear he would not be able to hold back his pleasure.

The birch made a fearsome noise as it was brought down. It was like the scream of a wounded animal. Peli noticed how soft the bruised buttocks were. The flesh enfolded about the thin birch twig, drawing it into her, becoming part of her, but only for a split second. Ricco drew it back and then down again. He did this many times and Peli could only stand there mesmerised that the girl could take such punishment without wailing for mercy.

'Turn her over,' he said at last.

Ricco, his cock dripping with pre-issue, stared at Peli, his eyes glazed. At last he stretched out his leg, ready to prod her with his toes, but the girl rolled over of her own

217

accord, hands still behind her head. Only then did she allow a tiny whimper as the stones and dead twigs on the forest floor pained her punished buttocks.

She looked so slavish with her breasts chained and her mound shaven. Obediently, without being ordered, she splayed her legs, bending them a little at the knees to make the sex pouch open and available.

Ricco drew back the birch, ready to smack the soft swell of her belly, but Peli grasped his wrist. 'That's enough,' he said, and he threw the birch to the ground.

'But you said…' Ricco's face was dark with anger.

Peli grinned. 'Now's the time for pleasure after the pain.'

'You mean we can fuck her?' Mule caressed his organ with both hands.

'Well, look for yourself,' said Peli. The girl had arched her body and her sex was lifted from the ground in a delicious gesture of offer. He could see the bruised buttocks and wondered whether the gesture was simply to ease the pain of the rough ground upon the punished flesh.

Banu slipped the leather strap into her open sex, rubbing the edge up and down the cleft. The leather was supple and he folded it into a tube. 'Try this for size, little whore,' he said, and spread the sex leaves as he fed the tube of leather into the girl's creamy entrance.

'See how she clutches,' cried Banu.

'Always a sign of a professional,' murmured Ricco.

Peli saw the girl's cheeks flush with inner shame, but he also saw her part her lips, moistening them with the tip of her tongue. With a great roar Mule sank to his knees behind her head and thrust his huge organ between those irresistible lips. 'Swallow,' he grunted. 'Swallow it all and do it pleasurably. No gagging.'

'Take it out!' ordered Peli. His breathing was fast and ragged and his cock was throbbing unbearably.

'What?' asked Mule, thrusting his hips, stretching the

girl's mouth. 'You dare tell me what to do? A knife between the ribs is what you're asking for.'

'No, I mean Banu; I want her,' said Peli. 'I want her cunt.' He pulled Banu from between her thighs and slipped the tube of leather from her sex. The black leather was beaded with her sap. He threw himself between her lifted and opened thighs and his hands trembled as he guided his cock into her.

'Hey!' cried Ricco. 'What about us?'

'You can wait your turn!' said Mule, his big hands on his thighs. He grinned up at the two others, allowing his attention only to wander from the rhythmic sucking of the girl's mouth.

'No, one of us can have her,' said Banu. He slithered beneath the girl's lifted buttocks and spread them. He gave a low chuckle as he saw her tightly pleated bottom hole press out in invitation. He tickled it with a fingertip and felt it give delightfully. He pushed into it and felt his own hardness become even more rigid. With his hands upon her hips he pulled her down and brushed his globe against the little secret bud. 'Ah...' he groaned, as she gripped him in the delicious tightness.

Peli could feel Banu's cock enter the girl and this increased his own pleasure enormously. 'Don't come yet,' he gasped to Banu. 'This is too good to spoil by a short time.'

'It is too good,' grunted Banu. 'I don't think I can... She grips me so tightly. It is beautiful.' To add to the glorious tightness he could feel the heat of the girl's punished bottom on his belly. The heated flesh caressed him as much as her bottom caressed his cock. He felt the first wave of his orgasm and felt consumed by it. He groaned and pumped his spunk into the girl's bottom.

Peli knew then that he couldn't hold on either. He had to give those last thrusts into the warmth of her vagina. She clutched him and he knew that she, too, was spiralling upwards in a vortex of pleasure. He rolled from her. 'Your turn, Ricco,' he panted.

The girl looked up at him with yearning in her eyes, but she welcomed the young man, Ricco, enfolding him in her arms. Peli noticed how the girl clenched her thighs about the lad until he groaned.

'She sucks me,' sighed Ricco, 'she draws my seed.' He bucked in the girl's clutches and Peli noticed that Banu was still beneath her, inserted within her bottom, and Mule was working his cock once more between her succulent lips.

They had treated her badly, thought Peli. Her bottom must pain her, and yet she took Ricco as though he was a long lost lover, giving him pleasure such as he'd never had before.

Ricco's frantic movements stilled and he lay upon her, his hands clutching the softness of her breasts.

'She has drained me,' groaned Banu, and he pushed her from his body. The movement dislodged Ricco who growled his anger. Mule shook his still spurting cock and the pearly liquid sprayed the girl's face. Peli saw her swallow and lap at the spillage around her parted lips.

He helped her up and shook the leaves and twigs from her gown and settled it over her head. The girl turned away, her face red with shame, and used the ruined gown to wipe away the spillage from her chin and which ran down her legs.

'Your promise?' she whispered.

'It will be kept,' said Peli, dragging on his breeches.

Chapter Fourteen

Grace bowed her head unhappily, and even this slight movement caused her pain.

'Oh, please let me go,' she murmured. Her wrists were shackled between her legs.

The man who watched over her spat onto the filthy floor of her prison. 'Aristo!' he hissed, and spat again.

'But you don't understand—'

'We *paysans* understand only too well, little mistress,' said the man, picking his teeth with the point of a sharp knife. He leaned against the rusty bars of her cell, grinning at her.

Grace held back a murmur of pain. A further chain led from the manacles and parted the soft folds of her sex and the taut hillocks of her bottom.

'I am not an aristo,' she wailed. 'Truly!'

The chain held her wrists between her widely splayed thighs. It was tightly held and the merest fraction of a movement cause it to chafe between her sex lips.

'I am a *paysan*, like you!' she added. She tried to shift her stance but the links of the chain rubbed over her nubbin, causing it to become painfully erect. They rubbed her rear bud.

'Lies! The evidence is against you,' he hissed, thrusting his face against the bars. 'You lived in the king's palace and an English aristo's manor house.'

The chain chafed again between her sex. She felt the swirling of pleasure in her belly and Lord Albert's face swam before her fevered eyes. She moaned.

The guard threw back his head, laughing hugely at her plight. 'You were one of the palace whores,' he said, his grin fading to a grimace of hatred. 'Our informant gave us all the details.'

'Who? Who is your informant?' As she lifted her head to stare at him through the bars, the chain chafed again and drove deeper into her bottom cleft.

Her ankles were held wide apart by a rigid iron bar and the chain that was slung between her spread thighs was also fastened about her waist, nipping it painfully. It travelled up between the deep valley of her breasts to her throat.

The guard tapped his nose knowingly. 'That would be

telling, little mistress.' He looked hungrily at her breasts, and looked down at the knife he used to pick his stained teeth.

There was no escape. She was naked, chained, vulnerable. He lifted one of her breasts with the flat of the blade. The metal felt cold against her flesh. The chill made her nipples become sharply erect, painful about the gold rings which pierced them.

'Pretty titties,' he growled, and with his free hand he worked his grimy fingers into the soft flesh, kneading it, hefting the weight by means of the gold ring.

She had been captured at the very outskirts of Paris and brought here. It was as if the revolutionaries were waiting for her.

The gypsy, Peli, arranged her voyage across the Channel. She'd begged him to accompany her, but he refused, shaking his head sorrowfully. He held her tight, thrusting her body tightly against his, swaying his rigid cock against her. His mouth bruised hers in a last passionate kiss.

'Do you think Lord Albert would welcome me?' He threw back his dark head and laughed. 'More likely take his pistol and blow my head off!'

The voyage was rough and the road to Paris was long and stony. By the time she reached the city her feet were torn and bruised. She asked at the first tavern where she could find an English lord, and that was her undoing.

Lifting her head, she smiled at the man who guarded her. He frowned. 'Why do you smile?' he asked suspiciously.

'Does it please you to touch my breasts?' she asked. Could she dare hope that she could trick the guard into letting her go? Dare hope that her hardened nipples could tease him into releasing her chains? Hope that the swell of her breasts under his fingers could bait him?

'When I move,' she told him in a low voice, 'the chain rubs back and forth in my sex slit.'

The guard's face flushed with eagerness and his dull eyes brightened.

'It rubs my clitty, presses back the skin of its hood and bares the most sensitive part,' she continued in husky tones. 'Shall I show you?'

The guard's expression hardened. 'I know what you are doing and it won't work!' He stumbled away from the bars, his eyes never wavering from her bonded body.

Grace moaned and he grinned as he threw himself back in his chair.

Deliberately, she sawed the chain back and forth between her sex lips. 'It rubs my nubbin,' she said, and arched backwards to show him, gritting her teeth against the pain of the bond cutting into her sensitive flesh. The guard groaned and fumbled with his breeches, rubbing the bulge that grew there. 'It presses back the hood. Can you see? Can you see how hot and inflamed my tip is?'

He groaned again and his cock was in his hands, rubbing the bloated flesh. 'It will not work *citoyenne*.' His globe was polished by his dew, naked of foreskin which was pleated behind the swollen tip. 'It will not work!'

The chain slipped painfully back and forth, becoming glossy with Grace's dew. It rubbed her nubbin again and again. 'What? What will not work *citizen*?'

'What... you... are trying to do to me,' he groaned. 'But it will not work!'

'Perhaps,' she murmured.

The thick shaft throbbed in his hands and Grace could see the shimmer of pre-issue dribbling on to the dusty floor of her prison. Through her pain she felt the wave of an orgasm engulf her. Shudders rippled through her captured body and caused the chain to catch her clitoris. She moaned softly as another pleasure wave rode through her. She tried to hide her enjoyment, keeping her face a beautiful, but inscrutable, mask.

Head thrown back, the guard tossed his length to his

own pleasure peak and then, to Grace's dismay, drifted into a heavy slumber.

Many hours passed. Grace had no idea how many. Time seemed to have lost its meaning.

'Water,' she gasped. No food or drink had passed her lips since she set foot on the road to Paris.

'Water?' He stirred and got up. 'Water? It will be wasted on you. It is only hours before Madame Guillotine will kiss you.'

'But I am not an aristo!' she repeated. 'Why won't you believe me?'

'Because our informant tells us different!' He touched her soft lips with a fingertip and shuddered as if thinking what the lovely mouth could do for him. 'You were looking for the English aristo, Lord Albert, and she...' He stopped abruptly, gnawing his lower lip.

'She?' asked Grace. 'Who?'

He shook his head. 'It doesn't matter, little missy.'

The guard traced the press of the chain in the valley of her breasts. 'Does the chain hurt you?'

'Only a little,' she lied. 'A very little.'

He grinned and his rough palms stroked the slopes of her smooth breasts. 'What a pity these will die with you when the guillotine falls!'

Grace shuddered under his touch and at his words.

'We have a few hours,' he reminded her, 'what say we use them pleasurably? More pleasurably than when you tried so hard to beguile me.'

'You will release my chains?' Grace's heart pounded. Perhaps even yet she could find Lord Albert.

The man laughed. 'Do you think I'm a simpleton?' The grin faded and he smacked her breasts, making them quiver and the chain that connected the hardened nipples shimmer against her heaving ribs.

'No, citizen,' said Grace meekly, 'but if you loosen my chains, just a little, I could give you so much more pleasure.' She was prepared to do anything to find Lord

Albert. Anything.

A rough finger slid under the chain that cut into her belly, causing greater tension within her sex and the cleft between her buttocks. Grace bowed her body in an attempt to decrease the tension but he pulled tighter and the links bit cruelly into her most sensitive parts.

'Do the links bite at your nubbin as they did when you taunted me, *citoyenne*?' He spoke with an assumed air of sympathy, but beneath the soft words there was cruel sarcasm.

Grace bit her lip and bent lower, again trying to ease the tension, but he tugged at the chain, making her cry out.

'What a graceful bottom,' he said, smoothing the curves with a rough hand, 'but it is marked!' He pulled her upright by placing a finger under the point of her chin. 'What did they use?' His voice was hoarse with lust. 'What did they use?' He rubbed at his groin and bent closer to her. His free hand grasped her breast, pressing the nipple ring into the malleable hillock.

'Their hands,' she said, trying to swallow back the tears that hovered on her eyelids.

Again he smacked her breasts, making them quiver about the chain which cleaved them so tightly. 'Lying aristo!' he rasped. 'They used much more than their hands and it's my guess it was not done for punishment, but for pleasure.' Crimson spots of colour daubed Grace's cheeks. 'Did they fuck you? How many were there? Did they come into you one after the other?' The questions came rapidly, assailing her ears, increasing her shame, but what choice had she? Her quest depended on the young gypsies. She had to please them.

'And this?' The man stroked the soft stubble of hair returning to her sex mound. 'Why was it done and were you smacked there as well?' He bent down examining her intimately. He rubbed the chain back and forth across her nubbin, irritating the tender tip until Grace had to bite her lips to hold back a moan of part pain and part pleasure.

'No, citizen,' they did not smack me there,' she said, her eyes downcast.

'Perhaps my mistress will enjoy that task,' he said, sliding his hand up her belly, feeling with apparent pleasure the way the chain cut into the little swell.

'Your mistress?' Her mind went immediately to madame and her alternately tender and cruel ways.

'She is a leader, a prominent *citoyenne*. She leads the people in the revolution.' There was no coyness now. He revealed that his superior was a woman boldly. He stood proudly, as if about to salute, but Grace shuddered.

His eyes flickered back to his captive and his hands cupped her shoulders, shaking her until the chains rattled ominously. 'She ordered your execution. But we were not discussing my mistress. We were discussing how you could give me pleasure.'

'Who is she?' Grace shivered. She was sure she knew the answer to her own question.

The answer came in the form of a hard smack upon her buttocks. With the bruises scarcely healed from the gypsies' onslaught upon her flesh, she cried out, but she felt the chain vibrate against her clitty and bottom mouth and the cry was part pleasure.

'Is that what they did?' He spoke softly in her ear, standing behind her. 'Did they do it many times until you begged them to fuck you?'

'They used a strap,' admitted Grace, 'and a birch twig until my bottom was black with bruising.'

'And then they fucked you?'

Grace nodded, her cheeks aflame with her shame.

'Was your cunt sore with the shafts dipping in and out?' The man was enjoying his interrogation.

She shook her head.

'No?' he questioned, laughter in his voice. 'Did they have the cocks more suited to be within the sac of mice?'

Thinking of Mule's thickness, she shook her head

vigorously. 'They did not only thrust into my...' she hesitated, not wishing to speak the word he used.

'Your cunt?' He sounded excited and allowed his thick fingers to drift into her bottom crease, parting the bruised hillocks. 'Did they come in here?' He moved the chain and put a greater tension on her clitty, making her butt against the link that pressured its raw tip. She felt his finger prod her rear bud.

'*Oui*, monsieur,' she admitted, her head bowed and her black hair hiding her shamed cheeks. 'One of them.'

'And where else did they fuck you?' She could feel his cock hard against her buttocks. He breathed harshly against her ear and the noise was like the hard breathing of a horse reined in from a fast gallop. His hands held her breasts, kneading them, parting them, thrusting them together. Her nipples pained her at every movement as he pulled against the gold rings and the chain that looped across her ribs.

'Your mouth?' he rasped. 'Did they come in your mouth? Did you swallow the spunk?'

'I swallowed,' she admitted.

'Good,' he growled. 'You were well used and I am sure you would enjoy to taste more come before you die upon the guillotine.'

'What does it matter?' murmured Grace. Over the past year men and women had used her body alike. She was a vessel for them – nothing more. 'If you will allow me to lie down, *monsieur*, you may use me all you wish.'

'Thank you kindly, *citoyenne*.'

He grinned, but she felt his hands tremble in excitement as he unfastened the bar which kept her ankles wide apart. Grace's legs trembled as he slipped the shackles from her ankles. 'Nothing more,' he said, 'I am loosening nothing more. My mistress warned me that you would try to escape.'

'But, if you fuck me, will not the chain which parts my sex and bottom pain your cock, which is so *magnifique*?'

The guard grinned again. 'I have no intention of damaging my prick on your bonds.'

'You haven't?'

'Lie down,' he growled.

'But...' Grace frowned, wondering what he had in mind.

'Lie down!' The hard fingers smacked her breasts, making them quake, one against the other.

The chain holding her wrists so tightly between her thighs cut cruelly into her as she tried to do the guard's bidding. She gasped as the smooth loops dug deeply into her female opening.

'Spread your legs,' he said, and his voice trembled as he gave the order.

Grace could not straighten her back because of the tension of the chain, but this made her sex an inviting vessel, a cup, spread open at the apex of her splayed thighs.

Standing with open legs at her head, he gave his order. 'Suck my cock,' he said, and he sank down on his knees, unfastening his breeches and baring his taut belly, his full groin and ball sac drawn tightly between his muscular thighs.

Supporting himself upon his hands he nuzzled his globe between Grace's moist and parted lips. She felt the warmth of his breath upon her shaven mound, felt his lips brush the soft fuzz upon it and she felt her flesh shudder, not from fear or distaste, but from the inbuilt pleasure brought about by madame's training.

'Suck me, damn you,' he growled.

Grace took his globe between her lips, drawing his length deep into her throat until his groin curls tickled her sucking lips.

She heard his sigh, felt the warmth of his tongue as its tip slipped into the sex cleft deepened by the chain. She felt it lap and tickle open the fine inner lips. She drew upon his cock, feeling the veins throb against her lips and

228

tongue and feeling the length pulse with pleasure. His lips closed about her nubbin, petting it and drawing it out to a fine sensitive point.

Thrusting deep into her mouth the guard flooded her with his spunk. It came in creamy bursts and triggered Grace's own pleasure. Her sex quivered in his mouth and her own issue bubbled from her depths, musky and rich.

'Well, now!' said a female voice, one which Grace recognised. '*Maintenant!*'

Arching her neck, the guard's cock still held gently between her lips, Grace looked behind her, through the open door of the cell. She saw neat black leather boots with spiked heels planted squarely apart. The boots were long, seeming to clad the whole length of the legs they covered. Above the boots was a skirt of an unseemly short length, also made from black leather. The odour of leather was strong.

The cock was withdrawn from Grace's mouth and she watched the guard scramble to his feet, trying desperately to put his clothing to rights. This done he began to help Grace up.

'No, leave her!' The woman crouched beside Grace and smiled. 'Remember me, ma cherie?'

'Charlotte de Levis,' murmured Grace, wishing her wrists were free of the manacles so she could wipe the spillage of the guard from her cheeks and lips.

'*Oui, ma cherie.*'

A shining breastplate encased the woman's firm and well-shaped breasts, and supple black gauntlets clad the long fingers and wrists. These slid the length of Grace's body, drifting lightly over the quivering breasts and the trembling belly.

'*C'est moi,*' she said huskily.

'Madame is a soldier of the republic,' said the guard, attempting to curry favour with his mistress.

One black gauntlet lashed out at the guard, sending him reeling across the cell. 'Take him!' hissed Charlotte, 'and see that he never leaves Devil's Island.' Cava, Charlotte's bodyguard, grasped the whimpering guard about the neck and sent him stumbling up the stone steps of the prison.

Charlotte bent to kiss each of Grace's ringed nipples. The kiss was tender, the softness of a woman's lips. 'Did he hurt you, *ma cherie*?' she asked.

A leather clad finger slid beneath the chain, cool and soft as skin. It tickled her sex mound, so cruelly cut by the tight chain. Grace moaned. What did it matter if the guard hurt her if she was to die on the guillotine?

'Comprendez-vous?' Charlotte spoke so softly that the words were a caress. 'You understand?'

The leather gloves squeezed Grace's breasts until the pain brought tears to her eyes, but then the soft lips caressed the flesh and Grace felt the pleasure building within her.

'Understand what, madame?' asked Grace.

'Why you must go to the guillotine?' Even as these terrible words were spoken Charlotte caressed her prisoner. Grace moved upon the probing fingers, unable to help herself.

'Your musk is strong, ma cherie,' noted Charlotte, sniffing the air. 'I wonder if this was because the guard excited you or because of my little attentions…'

The black lashes fluttered down over eyes shimmering with tears. They squeezed from under the lashes and fell like liquid crystals down Grace's pale cheeks.

'Tears?' asked Charlotte as she bent over the cup of Grace's sex, brushing her lips over the shadowy mound, tickling the freshly grown hair. Her tongue sipped at the gathered sap within the pouting sex folds. 'Pleasure from me, and pleasure from the guard,' crowed Charlotte. 'What more could a girl ask?'

The leather fingers parted the swollen folds and nipped the very root of Grace's nubbin. They stroked it and the girl felt fresh swirls of excitement soar through her. Her urge was to buck against the seductive touch, but she was determined not to give Charlotte that satisfaction. Two black fingers plunged into her, driving in to the hilt, leaving a thumb to play with her inflamed bud. Grace could not help but murmur her pleasure.

'You see, ma cherie? I make wonderful feelings in you, do I not? So why do you weep?'

'I weep because I am to lose my life on the guillotine,' said Grace, 'and I am innocent of any crime.'

'Non!' cried Charlotte. 'You were a plaything of the aristos! That is why you are to be punished in the ultimate way.'

'It was not my choice!' said Grace.

Charlotte shrugged and the flickering light of the sconces reflected upon her burnished breastplate, highlighting the pert shapes of her breasts beneath the metal. She began to release the chain that kept Grace so tightly trussed.

'I was homeless,' continued Grace, 'hungry, grateful for any shelter.' She stretched her cramped limbs as the chain fell from her body. 'Will you let me go? Please!'

'Stand up,' said Charlotte, ignoring Grace's plea.

On shaking legs, legs weak from the long period of bondage and legs trembling from the strength of the orgasm brought about by Charlotte's foraging fingers, Grace pulled herself to her feet.

Charlotte examined her with lustful eyes. 'Such a pity that a beauty like you must die on the guillotine.' With a leather finger smelling strongly of Grace's musk, she lifted her chin and kissed her passionately on the lips.

'Please let me go, if only for a little while,' pleaded Grace once more. 'There is someone, a man, I wish to see... before I die.'

'Lord Albert?' Charlotte's face became dark with anger. The grip upon Grace's arms was no longer tender, but painful. 'Oui, je comprend. I have always understood.'

Grace found herself flung from the cell.

'I hate you!' said Charlotte, shaking Grace until her hair was whipped back and forth like a blue-black curtain. 'You have taken him from me! My love, my life! This is why you are being sent to the guillotine!'

Charlotte pulled Grace across her lap as she sat down upon the guard's stool. 'I hate you! Spread your thighs!' A leather gloved hand beat down upon the upthrust hillocks of Grace's bottom.

Envy, thought Grace as her buttocks shook with the force of the many blows. Sometimes the smacks were laid across the spread cleft; sometimes they were aimed at the left cheek and sometimes the right. Grace could feel the glow brought about by each slap, could feel her flesh become swollen.

Occasionally the leather fingers slapped into the spread ravine, hitting the rear bud or slipping deeper into the silky valley of her front slit.

The smacking stopped and Grace winced as she was rolled over onto her beaten buttocks.

'Oui, it is painful,' said Charlotte, and Grace felt the tickle of the leather gloves stroking over her mound. 'But this…' Fingers opened her and Grace felt the familiar shame. 'This is pearled with your sap. And this…' her nubbin was flicked, 'is engorged with enjoyment.'

Lips closed around her bud and, to her endless humiliation, Grace felt it throbbing within the caress as she spiralled up to an inevitable climax.

With strong hands gripping her arms Grace was helped to her feet. 'It is time,' announced Charlotte.

Grace could not speak. She could hear the steady beat of a drum from above, and the rattle of the tumbrel wheels over the cobbles, and then an ominous silence.

'They are waiting,' said Charlotte.

'But must I go like this?' Grace gestured with her manacled hands to her naked breasts, with their rings and the gold chain slung from one to the other and to her shaven mound.

'Of course,' said Charlotte, with a shrug. 'The people know you were one of the Versailles whores.'

'Could you not allow me a simple shift,' pleaded Grace, 'something to cover my shame?'

Charlotte threw back her mane of red hair and laughed, her hands on the steep slopes of her hips. 'Did you think of shame when you allowed me to tickle this?' A leather finger slipped between Grace's sex lips and tapped her still swollen nubbin. 'No, you did not. We must go!'

Grace, her head high, turned to walk up the stone steps to her fate.

The Black Rose, dressed in rags like the people around him, held the folded whip beneath the hooded cloak. Head bowed, he listened to the beat of the drum and the rumble of the tumbrel wheels over the cobbles. She was drawing closer and he felt his cock thicken in the filthy breeches which were part of his disguise.

'She is naked, so they say,' said a harridan next to him.

'What do you expect from a whore like her?' said a companion.

The Black Rose eased himself closer to the platform, gritting his teeth to hear Grace spoken of in such a manner. He would take her, snatch her from the steps of the guillotine and they would disappear across the sea. He grinned under the loose hood. The Sheikh would delight in her; delight in her submissiveness, the way she wore her body jewellery with pride and took the taste of the lash gladly.

An inaudible groan whispered from his lips. In his mind's eye he could see her shapely bottom offered to the Sheikh. The buttocks would be parted, of course, for the Black Rose's customer delighted especially in a well-trained bottom hole. The moist labia, swollen and open, hopefully as smooth as silk, still shaven by John, would be lifted, the better to receive chastisement.

He frowned. How did that bitch Charlotte get her here?

That was what puzzled him. Grace was left in John's charge and he was not a man to take his duties lightly.

Beneath the cloak he fumbled with his breeches. The very thought of Grace being presented naked and shackled to the Sheikh was enough to make a man come. And the fortune he would get for her! The Black Rose chuckled. Given to the cause of the revolution? Never! The grin faded and he again moved closer to the terrible platform.

'Stop pushing!' said an angry voice beside him. 'We all want to see the whore get what is coming to her.'

The executioner was there, his black hood making him look sinister. The Black Rose could hear the beat of the drum coming closer.

He knew the reason why Charlotte de Levis was taking Grace to her death. Envy, the curse of so many women.

The tumbrel appeared at the edge of the square and he saw Grace, manacled and entirely naked. She was standing very straight and proud, the sun glinting on the rings which pierced her erect nipples and on the chain looped through them and hanging low on her ribs. This swayed with the movement of the cart, somehow making her look more vulnerable.

Charlotte rode upon a white horse, her legs splayed across the stallion's broad back. She smiled and waved to the cheering crowd.

'Quite the heroine,' he murmured to himself.

His eyes were drawn to her black boots and the short leather skirt. It took little imagination to know that she wore nothing to hide her sex and the horse was not saddled. He grinned. The horse's pelt would tickle her spread sex lips. No wonder she smiled!

He was at the very front of the crowd, and the tumbrel stopped beside the platform.

Charlotte held up her hands to the cheering crowd, asking for silence. 'This,' she announced, 'is the palace whore!'

The crowd booed and catcalled. He saw the shimmer of tears in Grace's eyes.

'She allowed all manner of debauchery, every perversion to be played upon her body,' shrieked Charlotte.

The Black Rose gripped the whip under his cloak, wishing it was Charlotte's neck.

'She deserves to die!'

The crowd cheered as Grace was lifted from the tumbrel, her thighs spread by the executioner's henchmen and held high above the crowd so that all could see her bruised bottom.

Suddenly the crowd fell back as a long whip lashed out, cracking convenient heads. There were cries of pain and anger. Grace was dropped in a heap as the whip lashed out at the executioner's men. She found herself dragged from the platform and in sudden darkness under a foul smelling cloak. Unable to struggle in the heavy manacles and the iron grip in which she was held, Grace remained silent.

All around her she could hear the sound of people crying out angrily. They were furious that their afternoon's entertainment had been ruined. Soon the sounds died away and the grip about her waist became less cruel.

She blinked as the cloak was swirled away from her. They were in a cool, shady courtyard. 'Lord Albert!' she squealed, and felt tears of joy fill her eyes.

The whip lashed down on her shoulders and again on her buttocks, making the punished flesh burn. 'You little fool!' he cried, and pulled her towards him by the chain which joined the manacles. 'You put yourself and me in danger by coming to Paris!' He grasped her chin and gave her a cruel and ravishing kiss upon the lips.

'I'm sorry,' she murmured, bowing her head. 'What can I do to make it up to you?'

The Black Rose grinned. 'Come with me to Morocco.'

Other titles available from Chimera (all £6.99)

All **Chimera** titles are available from your local bookshop or newsagent, or direct from our mail order department. Please send your order with your credit card details, a cheque or postal order (made payable to *Chimera Publishing Ltd*) to: **Chimera Publishing Ltd., Readers' Services, PO Box 152, Waterlooville, Hants, PO8 9FS**. Or call our **24 hour telephone/fax credit card hotline: +44 (0)23 92 598131** (Visa, Mastercard, Switch, JCB and Solo only).

UK & BFPO - Aimed delivery within three working days.
- A delivery charge of £3.00.
- An item charge of £0.20 per item, up to a maximum of five items.

For example, a customer ordering two items for delivery within the UK will be charged £3.00 delivery + £0.40 items charge, totalling a delivery charge of £3.40. The maximum delivery cost for a UK customer is £4.00. Therefore if you order more than five items for delivery within the UK you will not be charged more than a total of £4.00 for delivery.

Western Europe - Aimed delivery within five to ten working days.
- A delivery charge of £3.00.
- An item charge of £1.25 per item.

For example, a customer ordering two items for delivery to W. Europe, will be charged £3.00 delivery + £2.50 items charge, totalling a delivery charge of £5.50.

USA - Aimed delivery within twelve to fifteen working days.
- A delivery charge of £3.00.
- An item charge of £2.00 per item.

For example, a customer ordering two items for delivery to the USA, will be charged £3.00 delivery + £4.00 item charge, totalling a delivery charge of £7.00.

Rest of the World - Aimed delivery within fifteen to twenty-two working days.
- A delivery charge of £3.00.
- An item charge of £2.75 per item.

For example, a customer ordering two items for delivery to the ROW, will be charged £3.00 delivery + £5.50 item charge, totalling a delivery charge of £8.50.

For a copy of our free catalogue please write to

Chimera Publishing Ltd
Readers' Services
PO Box 152
Waterlooville
Hants
PO8 9FS

or email us at
info@chimera-online.co.uk

or purchase from our range of superbly erotic titles at
www.chimera-online.co.uk

The full range of our titles are also available as
downloadable ebooks at our website

www.chimera-online.co.uk

Chimera Publishing Ltd

PO Box 152
Waterlooville
Hants
PO8 9FS

www.chimera-online.co.uk
www.chimerabooks.co.uk
www.chimerasextoys.co.uk
www.chimeralingerie.co.uk

***

Sales and Distribution in the USA and Canada

Client Distribution Services, Inc
193 Edwards Drive
Jackson
TN 38301
USA

***

Sales and Distribution in Australia

Dennis Jones & Associates Pty Ltd
19a Michellan Ct
Bayswater
Victoria
Australia 3153

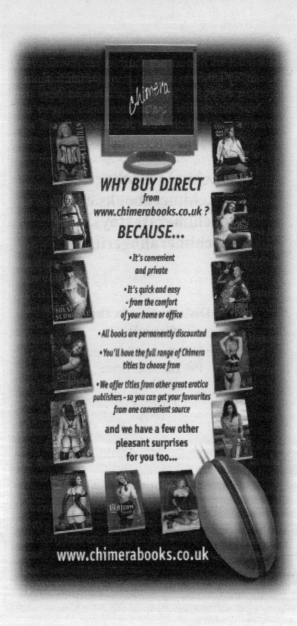